ASSASSINS
TARGET MARA
RECOMMENDED
Sharron L. Ensign

WORKBOOK PRESS LLC
187 E Warm Springs Rd,
Suite B285, Las Vegas, NV 89119, USA

Website: https://workbookpress.com/
Hotline: 1-888-818-4856
Email: admin@workbookpress.com

Ordering Information:
Quantity sales. Special discounts are available on quantity purchases by corporations, associations, and others.
For details, contact the publisher at the address above.

Library of Congress Control Number:

ISBN-13:   000-0-000000-00-0 (Paperback Version)
                000-0-000000-00-0 (Digital Version)

REV. DATE: 31/05/2022

Sharron L Ensign P.O. Box 583 Helena, MT 59624
Assassins Target Mara Bk 3
406-458-7091

Chapter 1

Finishing old business

The women had duties awaiting them, and everyone was busy for a while. The littles needed supervision in getting ready for bed, school-age told to get into PJs, and each child given love before the parent departed for the evening meeting.

"Meeting comes to order," said Mara as she looked around the group. Good start she had everyone's attention.

"Tonight, was something I had planned for some time. I want to thank you all for your kind words. Now we need to look at tomorrow and give you the game plan. Tutors, you will have the usual group under the regular schedule. For the new people that will mean we are up at five and then go to the stables where riding lessons come first with the duration of one hour. After the training, we feed the animals. You then return to your rooms and take a shower. The music lessons are in the main assembly room as soon as you can get there after cleaned up. Breakfast is at seven. Then rooms are straightened up and beds made. Everyone will clean their rooms and make beds. If we are eating in, the meals are prepared by Merry our Chef. They are at regular times, so please don't be late as it upsets her schedule as well as mine. After everyone helps with cleanup, they depart for classes with their instructors. Kids know where to go. New people, you have exams to take at the University. You will choose horses from the stables unless someone already claims them. The foreman Mark, or Gwen and Dan, can help you find ones not claimed. Only, the lead group rides the studs. Then you will ride to the U for the exams and return home which means someone will be your escort as this is all new territory for you. Often the horses chose their riders so be prepared for that as well. You will be there most of the day so plan on eating at least one meal there. Currently, don't have any plans to change the schedule for tomorrow yet you know how things go. Thank you, teachers, for bringing us the bus as you can see it was needed. Tutors and all kids who have been here all along are dismissed to go to your areas and prepare for the day," Mara said. Those designated moved while the new ones remained in place.

"Next on the agenda, new folks I need to know each of your full names, ages, date of birth, and so forth. Doctor Randy, raise your hand, will you? Thank you. Randy will see that you have any necessary shots for the trip. I will have your passports by the time we are ready to depart. Now we can finish the discussion we started at the restaurant. Your names need put on the door of the living quarters you have chosen. When everyone is told to go to bed, it is a good idea to follow suit for you may not know of something I am aware of and planning. I see you are trying on your new clothes. Good, that is after all why you have them. Everyone goes to their suite at nine. You need to be awake and alert at five. In the beginning, you might want to go to bed at nine after a shower for you will be learning and doing a lot of tasks you are not used to which causes you to wear out sooner. Once you adapt, you can work at getting up at five regardless of when you go to bed. Keep in mind that just because you go to your suite at that hour does not mean everyone does. I suggest that you remain in your quarters until the morning except in an emergency. Some still have duties and others may have injuries that require additional rest, though many of us get four hours of sleep a night. When time allows, I will enter your training. On Merry's day off, I am the Chef. There are many children in my care now. We always have room for those who are prompted to join us. I want you to know Granda. She is my Grandmother and related to all you see here, as am I. Now, I would like to hear from each of you as to what you wish to do or have me do. Have you a family; do you want to remain here always; is it your desire to be related to me or would you prefer to be workers with us? Who leads?" Mara asked.

"I'm Regina or Gene the Seeker since I started all this it put me in charge. I'm from Minnesota, my age turned twenty-one as of two weeks past. The first person I spoke with was Barbara from California though it took a while to meet with her. The guys joined us to watch our backs. However, we have become friends in the time we have been together. Mitch is our token adult, and he is twenty-five from Texas. The rest of us are in the sixteen to twenty-one age range. Few of us finished school as we were kicked out before then for various reasons. Mine was the parents who claimed lack of space when another child came along. I always wanted to finish what I started. We come from all over. Pepper is from Canada, Pedro from Peru, Nassa is a native American, George is Kentuckian, Sarge is a military kid, Sherena called Shi is from Iraq, Preston claims Germany as his country, Marsh is Italian, Pete and Repeat are Kenny and Gary the twins from NY, which gives you an idea. All of us feel we were disowned and booted as worthless. We want to count and to be people that we are proud of as well as have someone else who is proud of us and our accomplishments. Only two of us have heard of you until I found out how many were in need. Got them together and we headed out to see if we could locate you. Gypsy is the youngest at sixteen, and I found her in Cleveland. She is my second due to her street smarts and fighting abilities. Some of us pack weapons and those who do know how to use them. We would have gotten permits. However, unless you are twenty-one in some states, you can't get a permit. I have one though not all of us do. Now I must speak for myself. I left home at fourteen though did manage to make it through high school by working as a waitress. By then I knew that if life was ever to be worthwhile for me, it was time to find someplace else to live other than St. Paul. That is where my journey began. Some of these folks I met in my travels while they had met others. There are many on the roads I traveled that are not motivated, have no desires, and no direction in their lives and we wanted to be different. Each of us will need to prove to you that we are worth being part of your group and I'm not sure how to do that. It would be great to be adopted and go to work learning, however, doubt that is the way life works," she told Mara and her family.

"You can all be adopted now if you wish it. It would make me your mom. This time you will have learning to do, exams to take, horses to ride, arms to learn, as well as a place to live, an entire family to love you, and no one will be booting you out. Your nationality does not matter for once adopted you are from here. Your past becomes just that, past. What is your desire regarding adoption?" began Mara.

"Would it work if those of us who want it just to stand up?" asked Regina.

"Yes."

All the new ones stood.

"Learning begins now and welcome to my family. Pat, you will find a guest in the rear-basement section of the bus. Would you bring him to the corral please," directed Mira and Pat departed with one of the C-Quad.

"I am Shandra, Mara's guard. Tonight, you learn a sword drill, meet the horses who guard here and attend a court. Listen and learn for next time it could be you in charge," directed Shandra for Mara seemed preoccupied which usually meant she was checking with Thunder Press or someone was contacting her electronically.

The group moved outside and followed behind Pat and the prisoner who was now walking. Things changed when they reached the area where the corral was. It was full of people which only Mara was expecting.

"New ones stand here and watch. Do not move beyond this spot and don't speak unless directed to," advised Randy who was not watching the new members, she was looking at the felons ahead of them and would then move into a spot left open for her by Shandra.

Mara picked a place to stand, and the rest centered on her. Pat, Mara, and Kennet took the central positions. Jo and her group of three took the side by Pat while Shandra and her team took the other end by Mara leaving a spot for Randy standing next to Shandra. Jimmy and his group of four waited at the back of the formation with the new people.

Each of the women watched those before them waiting for something to give. The horses had moved behind the leaders as well though to the sides of the group. Then it began for a shot was fired and Lightning came out. Once all were down, the leaders remained in place with swords pointed upward while the guards removed all weapons after identifying the owner and the weapon for law enforcement. Then they were put in buckets the horses brought from the barn.

"This court is now in session. Who leads your group?" Thunder Press asked.

"I do," said the one in front of the pack.

"Who are you, why are you here, and what was your plan to accomplish?"

"I am Prizerly Portly. We heard you were recruiting and thought we would see if there were slots open." The man responded.

Mara stopped and thought a moment then continued.

"Again, I ask: Who are you?" asked Thunder.

"I am Jefferson Pazone. We came to join your force," he responded.

"As Thunder, I order all minds cleared. Now tell me in truth, who are you?"

There was some hesitation then another came from the back of the pack and spoke.

"Didn't take you long to figure out that one, which surprises me. Knew we would have to meet sooner or later. In truth, I am Ransom Perigrin.

"Okay is it Ran or Peri?" asked Thunder.

"Whichever, I answer to both."

"Why are you here?"

"My orders are to see you removed. They didn't tell us how well guarded this place is. No wonder they pay so well to have folks try to reach you."

"They are sneaky too, they hit a guy when he isn't even looking," said the man who had carried a rifle.

"Who are they?" she asked Peri.

"A big shot name of Bull Edwards, says you are a menace and need put out of business."

As he spoke, the called man was suddenly standing before Thunder.

"Okay Bull, you are in a court of law. I am the Judge, and

this is the attorney who will ask the questions. T II go ahead," directed Thunder.

"We know who you are, now what is your profession?"

"I handle legalities you could say," the man responded.

"Answer the question or be found in contempt," T1 directed.

"You have no control over me."

"Mom, freeze everyone except me," said Kennet.

At his request, all swords were aimed upward for directions from Kennet would affect all except the lead group.

She did as he requested, keeping only her, the guards with swords, and her son active. He moved to the man and reached inside the man's jacket where he pulled out a lot of wire. He removed the man's hat and the small satellite hidden within.

"Please have two guards mount and lift him up so his shoes and pants can be taken off," requested Kennet.

Jo and Shandra handed their swords to their sisters to allow free hands and moved to do as directed, for the swords remained in the open until the end of the court. The studs walked to the women, and they mounted. Each of the two women took one of the little man's arms and lifted him.

Kennet checked inside the shoes and found a lot of interesting items including an ID under another name and a pistol, another of each item was found concealed in his belt. When the man was again on his feet, the coat was removed, and his shirt. Pockets were located and emptied as well as hidden ones. He appeared to be much shorter without the shoes, and his clothing had carried pads in all the right places. It left a small man shivering in the evening air. Kennet removed the man's glasses and found a radio transceiver in the frame. A ring Bull wore had a sharp object in it, and another had a container with poison inside for Randy to test it. All jewelry was removed and put in evidence packs before awakening him.

"Mr. Edwards, you have told this court some untruths. We find you guilty of hiring people to kill us, endangering this family, giving false testimony at a trial, threatening animals as well as people with your jewelry, and trying to record the proceedings here. As a direct result, you are guilty on all counts. Give me a list of all you own no matter where it is. Now rest awhile," she told him when she had the required information, and he went to sleep standing. Next, she called forth the man who gave her Edward's name.

"You have heard this court and our judgment on your boss. Now you will give the same information he did," directed Thunder, and all were placed in the AI's database as each of the groups gave the desired information.

The copy appeared, and each of the men signed their confessions as to why they were there, who their informant and boss were, what they intended toward the family, and if there were any more like them headed their way.

"Granda?" Thunder said.

"They are on their way," she replied for her duty was not just backup it was watching over the young ones to see they were into bed and asleep when Mara wasn't available.

Pat then departed to meet the incoming law enforcement vehicles, taking the Jimmy group with her. The law enforcement officers followed Pat to the corral where they began putting restraints on all the felons. One officer was in charge, and he took the sealed container with the recordings and signed confessions while another took the evidence bags. The AI had taken pictures of everything at Mara's request. The law left with the prisoners and time resumed on the ranch.

Since they were already in the stable area, Mara asked if any of the full-sized horses would be willing to serve as partners and rides for the new group. Soon everyone had been partnered, and the new ones showed where the saddles were for those they chose. Dan said he would get them to the U when breakfast was over the next day. Shandra, Mara, and Pat mounted to give a demonstration as to what was meant by proper riding. The new group stood with their eyes large and smiles on their faces. Next was the sword drill.

While the Quads took care of that, Mara was checking on some other things she had to take care of and now was as good a time as any. She slipped into the basement of the stable and removed Swiss money for their upcoming trip abroad as well as any other currency the trip might require, like Canadian, German, or British. The Swiss money was mainly to open an account there. She had gotten the necessary amounts from Rae and put them in the vault. The money came from the various vaults that had that denomination stored there though Mara directed Rea to process all funds to keep an accurate accounting. Now she would take it to her room and put the funds in her clothing for the trip.

The group returned to the dining room where Mara asked for any questions from the new folks.

"Will you train us to do what you do?" asked Regina with a beaming smile.

"That will depend on you and the situation. Seeing something done and doing it yourself is not the same thing. It will take quite a bit of practice to be ready to fill in if one of us is injured. Right now, you must take some exams at the U. After that, we will be packing up to leave. The day after tomorrow we will be in flight at six a.m. Ask any of the adults that are here before you, and they will advise what you are to pack. Now I must check on my kids. See you all tomorrow," said Mara as she departed for her quarters with Shandra at her side.

"Thank you, Granda, for filling in. I told Joy and Kari to leave their charges with me since they will be asleep anyhow. Dan will take the new ones for testing. Tomorrow morning, we will be making a run to the bank. Must discuss some things with Rae and see where she is in getting things in order there. Then we will make a trip to pick up a plane. Everyone will be responsible for their gear. Are you ready for another trip so soon?" asked Mara.

"Most definitely," she replied with a smile.

"See you tomorrow then between runs to get things in place," said Mara who gave Granda a big hug before she departed.

"How about me?" asked Shandra of Granda.

"Hugs are always welcome though the first one you have to ask for to be sure you don't mind," replied Granda as she gave her one as well.

"Granda we are each feeling our way to see what is allowed. I never had a Grandmother that I got to know and honor you as such to my younger me. You are family to me and many others. We won't exclude you now that we are aware hugs are accepted," replied Shandra.

When Granda departed, Mara removed the electronics from her head and turned off the communication device she wore, though the AI could reach her anytime needed within her chosen suite.

"I appreciate that little gadget, also thankful when I can take it off for a while," she told her guard as she entered the area.

"I know what you mean. However, it is a great safety net. Do you feel like answering a few questions for me?" asked Shandra for they were in Mara's private conference room next to her bedroom and the kids were asleep.

"We are taking one of the Jetliners for we have no stops in the states except for fuel. We have an Alpha three-two-one which holds one hundred eighty-five passengers which might work for now or there is the Alpha three-eight-zero which has a four-class configuration and will accommodate five-hundred-forty-four people on two levels. They have developed fuels that keep costs down. Solar is part of the power base as well as various jet fuels depending on the age of the model and the upgrades in place. It seems to me we need to update them all so that we can grab any unit on short notice and not worry about the fuel issue. I need a person familiar with jet fuels and the current transition to more economical means of powering the various kinds. Want a new type of fuel found that will allow us to fly cheaper," Mara began.

"While the three-eighty would be the most comfortable I think that the countries we will be going to might think it an invasion. We need to design a new plane that works for us. Needs to carry five hundred fifty on two levels with the first level for luggage we might pick up where we are going and our four-foots. The second tier will be for the regular passengers while the top level will be first class at the front and the training area at the back. The pilots will stay centered at the front of the top section," commented Shandra as she understood what her mom was saying.

"Oh, if only. That sounds ideal, can see it in my mind's eye. The regular class would not have access to the pilots, and the pilots would have a backup if needed. Not ready for the kind of notoriety that might result in arriving with five hundred fifty people aboard, however, think that is the one we must use. That way everyone would be on the same plane," they both chuckled at the picture that recalled. If only they could do that without causing an uprising.

"We need hot meals at least once though sandwiches will work for another. Breakfast can be continental. I haven't ordered them yet as we need to look at our inventory to be sure before I stock up and fuel," advised Shandra.

"I keep thinking about the plane. The designers don't count the luggage compartment as a level. There would have to be overhead space over each seat so that whatever that person brings will be where they can keep an eye on it plus it limits how much to take. Only use the basement luggage space for the return trip. Therefore, if we took one of our larger planes and put two floors inside it would still look like it does, only a little taller to accommodate two decks plus the stock level and storage for the seat panels. The main floor would hold regular passengers while the upper front would be for the pilots and first-class with a training area behind first class and allow for the sleep configuration. There are too many people to do the same with the five hundred passengers. That would allow for all of us in one place. If some of the leaders became the trainers, like your group with the sword drill, it would be easy to move to that location. I don't want everyone in the force to know what is going on and that would be a way to keep the knowledge that only those who need it would have. What would you think of setting it up to accommodate about fifty people in first-class and five hundred on the main deck? Have the kind of seats we do now where someone can lay down or have privacy if needed which means we would have to have space where the walls remain until needed. If they were stored flat, it would mean less space used. Then have the sections automatically lock together when fully upright. Having the lead group in first-class would allow us to have meetings on the flight without everyone getting involved. No doubt some will be sleeping for the flight over since we leave rather early," suggested Mara who was getting more excited as she thought about what she wanted to see for it would accommodate everyone in comfort, security, and privacy.

"I like that idea. My mind shows a stack system for the walls of the seats. You push a button, and each wall raises in three sections and then becomes locked in place. With first-class directly under the pilot's sleeping area, you would have easy access if for some reason the flight had to be changed. Are you going to hire stewardesses, male or female, to take care of the different levels?" Shandra wanted to know.

"I have never been on a commercial flight, so I have no idea what they do, however, read about some from time to time. That might be an idea, though need ones who already have the security check. Not sure how to find them though and would need them by flight time at least on the family ship. That means we must eat out at least once," laughed Mara.

"I think I can cover that one. Have one officer that started out as a stewardess. She most likely knows of any others with the group. Consider that one done. Will the plane be full?"

"No, the plane will not be full, at least not in the beginning. The new group has been adopted as you know for you gave them the sword drill this evening. They will need some practice to become proficient. The men need training as well. Once we choose a type of aircraft, we must check runways to see where we are going to land without trouble. We could land in England which has an international airport. Might even get a hangar there and see some of that area. The quick trip we made didn't allow us to see much. We could fly commercial to Berne even if on separate flights to play at being tourists," commented Mara.

"Not a good idea. Cost is one factor. We need the plane where we are, for it will have Pi and Shira aboard plus the guard dogs that our people have for some of the military travel with them as well. Also, there is the Capital making it best to have your plane there as well in case of problems elsewhere. I saw on the news that the Jets now take off immediately in an upward thrust. The seats move to accommodate the direction of flight. The newest design has also gone to the round type of craft with a slight 'nose' to provide recording equipment for the area around the aircraft."

"I agree though wanted a second opinion. You know here is another thought. We could put a logo on the plane like the N-sign Family Band or some such. Could we have a logo we could change per what we were doing at the time? Things like Corporation or band because then they would expect a couple hundred or more for the show. We would have to see if there is a venue available, should catch Josephine on that one. That, on the other hand, might not be a good idea for it would mean traveling even with the little ones, and right now that might not be wise."

"Got it covered. Jo says it will be taken care of whether you need it this time or at some future date," for Shandra had a connection to those she oversaw like both sets of Quads and a line to the ranch and Peter.

"Now on to lodging, we have a space to park the plane for a week or two with the option to purchase in the Capital. The first order of business is to find lodging so did some checking and found several viable options. Due to our numbers, I ordered buses and drivers to get us to that location. I asked to meet with the realtor and see what real estate is available. Once all are settled, you and I will be going out on our own. The rest will remain at the lodging. When we return, we will be taking some tours to see the area and all it should offer. No one travels alone. There should be plenty of room if you want to bring your leaders along and need at least twenty trained martial artists to serve as guards for the new ones. Also, it will leave seats for those who may join us for the return trip. Not everyone wants to go out of the country. Therefore they can each decide if they stay and work or wander along with us as guards," explained Mara.

"Does a family band use guards?" asked Shandra with a chuckle.

"Ours does," replied Mara.

"That covers my questions," laughed Shandra.

"Thought it might," replied Mara with a smile.

"What is our ultimate reason for going to this nation?" asked Shandra as another thought came to mind.

"Banking."

"Banking? We can do that at home. Don't you trust Rae?" Shandra asked in surprise.

Mara laughed.

"Of course, I do, it is the government that I have trouble with from time to time. We need to have a few different points of reference for our funds. Don't want it all kept in the warehouse. Ways must be found to invest so it can grow with around twenty thousand on the payroll. We have a lot now. However, it needs to be working and not all in the same place. Every ranch and home I own conceals a vault. That stuff needs to be liquidated and put to work. I'm working with Rae to get the antiques either used or sold. She is opening a store here like the one she has in the East to begin a network of our own. That way we will have access to a larger customer base. In fact, she has added a few stores where the owners are very knowledgeable with a good customer base. She feels they might be willing to list some of our excess in areas where it is more likely to sell if we, in turn, list some of theirs. To do that we all use web pages to show our products. The items will stay where they are. However, the store that sells them gets the commission, and the purchaser pays the freight. No sense in keeping stuff in storage. Get it out where it can be put to use, enjoyed, or just sold."

"Interesting point of view never looked at it that way. Maybe I should open an account in this Swiss bank too," said Shandra.

"That would not be a bad idea at all. Ask for a number, not a named account though for you don't want anyone tracking you by your bank. In fact, I will have savings, housing, spending, and investment ones of my own," commented Mara.

"I don't know if I have enough funds for all that," laughed Shandra.

"You must have. You get retirement from the HB, and are paid by me for each type of duty you do such as guard, leader, director, Commander of the military, and adviser. Oh, plus our unique qualifications. Your actual age may also generate a retirement for you, if by number. Surely you must have a few dollars to move," Mara advised.

"Why would I have that kind of income? In honesty, I have not checked my accounts since we opened them as there has been no need. Who has time to spend money? You said you would deduct our personal purchases from our accounts and that was the only time it came to mind," responded Shandra in surprise.

"You might want to check them out while we are with Rae tomorrow," Mara told her daughter for she knew what those accounts held as she was the accountant for the lead group for Rae had plenty going on in finance without that. She began to wonder if her entire lead group was unaware of funds on record for them. It was time to bring everyone up to date in that area.

Shandra made a mental note to take care of it the next time she was where she could. She could not believe that there was money in her account all this time and she knew nothing about it.

Chapter 2

Getting it all covered

"Have some concerns about the kids. It is either they go along, and we use guards, or leave them home with the tutors. I'm open to suggestions on that one. It seems that the same warnings might apply there as in the South. We have heard of so many kidnappings that I hesitate for don't want anything to happen to anyone. It worked well for the trip to Europe. However, we managed to keep anyone from knowing we were even on the move. If the passengers drop under a hundred, then we could use one of the big planes though that wouldn't allow for any additional passengers coming home. It will be a fourteen-hour flight with a fuel stop in Canada and one in England."

"I agree, though I thought you picked up fuel on the east coast," responded Shandra.

"That was my intent, only if we use the same stops all the time it makes us predictable, and that is not a wise idea unless we qualify as a commercial flight. If we use different routes all the time, it will seem like we are just regular traffic. We need to look at a faster more cost-effective means of travel. I heard that there is a new breakthrough where sand becomes the fuel source. They said it works for automobiles and trucks, not sure about planes, though. As you have noted in the last few court cases, there are a lot of people out there looking for our heads. That is a concern because the entire family needs guarded. Never mind we will leave the kids under sixteen at home and take everyone else. At this rate, the tutors must be paid more for filling in for me. Still, should try out some of the new planes to see if they are worth keeping. Are you up for it?" asked Mara though she knew the tutors had a clause in their contracts for this exact event. When she offered to raise their pay because of the young ones, they declined. They felt they were receiving a good salary and after all, that was part of the contract.

"Never even been on one and now you're the pilot? Boy, have you come up in the world?"

"That's true. Never been on a plane until the day you put me behind the yoke. Plus, your backup will be with us too."

"You should have seen the looks on their faces when they found out that they would be flying helicopters and other ships. It was a hoot," laughed Shandra who was so enjoying her new life. She knew that she was spearheading something that no one ever heard of before, yet it felt right. Shandra knew this was what her life would be from here on and was at peace. Those from her old life would never recognize her now, and she knew it was as it should be. As the Commander of her area, she was the one in charge and could bark orders with the best of them, though she tried to delegate when she could. Now it was nice just to do as directed.

Mara looked at her daughter and chuckled.

"At least we won't be on call for capture and court."

"Are you sure? With as many courts as you have had to hold here, what will happen the week we are gone? Do you have enough guards on staff to watch over the horses and all while we are gone?" asked Shandra for she had been directed by Mara to question and make sure all bases got covered.

"Mark is not going if his kids are ill. Mary said the same. They will remain here. Mary will be on Communications and Mark as foreman. Both have direct communication with Randy and us via our AI. That reminds me, we need a guard furnished for both of those folks and prefer that said guards be knowledgeable in the positions those two currently hold. The Rangers are still working the property and rounding up anyone that should not be here. They weren't very happy that that last group blindsided them and tied them up. When we offered to release them from working for us for their safety, they said the workforce didn't need them and asked to stay. Since they have full clearance, named them the Rangers and they remain though under Clarence. Once notified, perhaps, we can hold court from where we are then the Rangers turn them over to the local law. We have tutors that have martial arts skills to watch over the kids. Since there are six teachers as I recall, they can surely watch over what we have. In fact, Pat asked them, and I believe they agreed to take on all the kids while we are gone, regardless, to include the under-five group," Mara advised.

"Then it looks like everything has someone in charge. Martial Arts experts serve as guards for Mary and Mark. With the AI to monitor the stables and house, the tutors with the children, Mark taking care of horses, and the Rangers on watch, I think it will all be okay. The inventory is complete, and all products are accounted for and put away. Both banks are in operation. If we take forty guards with us that will still leave plenty of room for the leaders, I think. Now I must think. Can I do that tomorrow?" asked Shandra with a smile.

"I'm for that. Goodnight daughter of mine. It is bedtime for me," said Mara who gave her daughter a hug and then headed for bed after checking on all the kids. She had to get the funds put away before she went to bed.

"Mom?"

"Yes, Rae," replied Mara for there was an AI contact in every room of her suite that wasn't used by kids. She always had to be in communication with the leaders.

"I contacted the Swiss bank and asked what kind of funds they accept as a deposit to open an account. You said that is where we were going. Was advised of the name of the president, the location of the bank, and what would be required. You can do the impossible, as your alternate. Why not shrink what you take to make it easier to hide? Otherwise, one of the inspections required to be in the various countries could bring to light what you carry. They accept any funds you wish to use. A hidden vault on the plane we use might be a plus as well. I'm not sure you want to use your gold, even if we have an abundance. Perhaps use some of the secondary metals or even foreign currency. The bank president will meet with you when you get there. If you need me as your banker, I am available. Good night mom," said Rae, and the connection ended.

Mara sat and thought for a time then smiled. She could not

do it all herself and those who were trusted needed a chance to use their talents. Yes, Rae would go with them. She would open accounts for: operating, housing, backup, and investment then she decided that one for savings might not be amiss as well plus her personal accounts. If they worked out more funds would be added for it was time to begin investing in other ways besides real estate.

No sooner did her head hit the pillow than she was asleep.

The following morning Mara was up at four. She put out clean clothes for the kids then ran to the stable where she mounted to ride and was not surprised to see Shandra at her side. They ran their mounts through the pasture then did the riding drill before brushing down their mounts, putting feed in the bins, and putting the saddles away. A quick run to the house and a shower had her ready to start dressing kids to prepare them for the day. Shandra helped her get the under-fives ready while those over headed to the stables for their lessons. The littles went to the assembly room, and there took music lessons, if old enough to handle an instrument. The smallest ones clapped their hands and tried to sing. When the older group of kids showed up with wet heads for their music lessons, Mara departed with the littles for their breakfast, while Pat oversaw music training. Once the littles were taken care of, she put them playing in a large room in her suite. They seemed content to play while she met with Granda after seeing if Pat needed any help.

Granda and Mara discussed the day and who was where. Granda would take over the small ones after breakfast as they had breakfast. Next was a visit with Randy to find out the status of the kids at the hospital.

"They seem to be doing okay. Some specialists are now on-site, and there is a consultation that Mary and I will attend. Mark will be working, and if she isn't going alone, he doesn't mind. That was a good piece of business to pick up that bunch with Regina. We will be gaining fluency in a lot of languages they speak. Did you notice that Regina speaks them all? That is how she got their aid. That kid that works as her second, Gypsy is it, needs to be taken aside and properly trained with weapons. She has developed some bad habits, and they need to be corrected now. She reminds me of an assassin I knew once. He carried about a million bucks in his clothing always, along with both guns and knives. Pleasant young man though he was always watching his back and the areas around him. The only problem was he refused to practice with the weapons he carried, seemed to feel it was like riding once you know how you never forget. Also, ran into a mercenary in my travels and you only got to meet him if you had the right contacts. At the time, I did. You could put out a contract on anyone in any city for about five dollars per person," Randy told her mom.

"You surprise me more every time I get to chat with you. What a different past you had," Mara laughed.

"Yes, well, I worked my way through college by being a security guard and found myself as the owner of the company when the boss went to prison. The only thing was he had collected funds for a year in advance on contract then got sent up. Since my name was on the company logo, though I wasn't in any way connected to his problems which happened long before he met me, it meant I worked for a year with no income while balancing school requirements. Most of the work was at night so would sleep a couple of hours then do a check and if all were quiet would sleep a couple more then catch up on my studies and go to school. Lived in a van in those days, had a bed, and a dog; that was about all. Glad that is behind me," Randy said with a smile.

"No wonder you fit in here so well. Want to thank you for helping with the new ones. Want them to feel like a part of us yet am not sure how to do that."

"When we first came, what did you do?" asked Randy for she knew that Mara was asking for her aid even if she was not aware of it.

"Let me see, when we got Pat she was older and knew how to ride. She had lost her family and was invited to join ours. Made her my twin and here we are. With the first set of Quads, I met Shandra at the restaurant and invited her to join us with three more. We needed pilots at that time. When they showed up at the ranch, they ran up the stairs and listened to the first-ever concert by my family. Then joined in," Mara responded.

"And then?"

"Next was the third Quad for the kids of B Quad were all stuck with me," smiled Mara for that group came from the book world.

"I didn't hear any of them complain," commented Randy.

"I was closer to being one of them than being an adult," Mara laughed.

"How did you relate to C Quad?"

"Shandra said she knew some folks nearby that would be an excellent addition to my group. She made a call and even went to get them. All of them were in their thirty to fifty age range. That is what my Mom was so no problem there."

"Now look around you, what do you have?" Randy asked.

"I have forty-some kids under me of which the oldest is ten since I have graduated and moved up all teenagers. Don't see any problem there. There are six teachers, not a problem. All leaders under me are in their early twenties with me a year older. I know them all and love them all. That works for me. Some of Regina's group needs to finish their education plus they all need college testing."

"Then it is time you started seeing the new young adults as needing you and you needing them, for they are trusting you, as all the rest have. They need you to train them, love them, and make them feel welcome. Don't shy clear of them for they will feel it. They have been hurt too many times not to. Make it apparent that you care and will do what you can for them. Leave no doubt as to their welcome," advised Randy.

"Thank you, daughter, mine, now I know what I have to do," she gave Randy a hug and left on the run only to run into Shandra who was looking for her.

"What is our agenda now?"

"We are going to breakfast then we are mounting up to take this new group for testing at the U. Both of us will be doing the equestrian drill with them. Then the music training, though the tester won't see us. Only the kids will know we are there, once they are registered. When the testing is over, we will bring them back here, so they can clean up. I'm sure that Jo can put them to work. We will take another shower and meet with Rae. Then back here to start loading the plane. Once you and I decide what we are using for transportation we will know better who we can or cannot take. I thought about using the new ones. However, the number each of the planes holds might not work. With just this family we have around fifty plus fourteen guards for the new additions. Hopefully, you have chosen those who will be going with us," responded Mara.

"No, I have not chosen, though I will. First, we need to know what size of aircraft we are taking. The criteria for going on my list said they had to be martial arts qualified and never been to Switzerland, except for ten percent who would serve as guides to see the area. Needed male and female, current passports and their spending money. You have about fifty going on the military side if I turn them loose. Add in the fifty that are family and the new ones make for a fair-sized group," commented Shandra.

"Are you telling me that if we take military with us, we need to use two ships and even that won't do it?" asked Mara though she was thinking of the one hundred passenger ships, not the five hundred passenger ones.

"Remember the military are travelers. They love to travel, and a free trip anyplace is a bonus to them. It might be best to leave them all here, except for the guards for the new people, until they get up to speed. We have seven women and seven guys in the new group. Can we match them up with guards? You are making a business trip to try out new aircraft, look at the property, and take care of a few things. Do you need everyone to go? Could we leave the new ones here to get training from some of the military trainers and take just the leaders and close family now? The fact that they have no training makes them not ready for the trip," Shandra chose her words carefully for she had steered Mara into an empty suite to talk.

"Not everyone goes every trip. I need to see if Melissa and Merry want to go for their assigned duties will be less if the lead group is on the road or flying. Then there are the two from Tennessee. No idea if they even know we are going. We might need to drop them off on the way back, so they can catch up on all that has taken place there while we had them here. Jo is working with them, and Jero should go because she is looking for contacts to sign up for shows. Also, if we use the leadership team as guards, we wouldn't need to take any extra. Maybe that is the way to go. We could still use the five hundred passenger plane, and everyone would have room plus there would be room for extra if needed. Looking at it that way we could take the new people plus those who are already family, that want to go. I still must check with the housekeeper and cook. It does mean the military won't be going except if part of the family, though," said Mara with a frown.

"See why I don't pick anyone or even notify them of the possibility until all the facts are known? Let's eat then take it a step at a time. It will all work out," said Shandra.

Mara laughed, and mother and daughter went to the dining room. The schedule worked as set up. Ride, music, home, Rae, then? Well then, they went to look at some aircraft.

They went to the airport in town first to look at what they had there. The guards let them through, and they parked by the walk-in door to the hangar. Once inside both began to laugh.

Sitting before the pair was the plane that Mara had described. The difference was you could not tell there were windows on the upper level, which was where they began their inspection. The nose of the craft had a device called a baffler that would cause all birds to be pushed away from the pilot's area so that no flocks would break a window and cause death to those in their planes. An inside computer gave them a full view of the area around them. Even hailstones would slide off instead of creating damage to the craft, due to a repelling force. That same computer system would alert the pilots of another aircraft in their vicinity. It even had a backup system in case something caused the operating equipment to malfunction.

The first-class section had large seats which could be beds or walls could be raised for private conversations or sleeping. Between the pilot's cabin and above First-class was one room on each side of a short hall. Inside were twin beds where the pilots could sleep in their off-duty shift without their sleep patterns being interrupted. Due to her dual positions, Shandra would remain with Mara for sleeping unless she was flying. With A and C Quad on the flight, only those to fly next would use the private bedrooms. Everyone else had seats in first class.

Behind that was a conference room where the leadership team could have meetings. It held the same number of places as first-class though it was with chairs locked into the floor framework around a conference table. Last on that level was a training room with stairs leading down to the middle main level of the craft although the stairway was secured and would open only for one of the leaders or pilots. As with all aircraft, soundproofing kept the passengers from hearing the engines outside. This time the same thing was used to keep each private area from hearing those around them.

Moving to the second tier, via the circular stairway, they found the same type of seating as above in first class. The seats were as requested in each section. There were fifty in first-class while the main had five hundred seats.

"I wonder why that number of seats? Let me ask," Mara reached for her sword and stood for quite some time.

Shandra also had questions and did the same.

"We will be bringing out more military. The exact number is subject to change as you know. These are some of ours who were left stranded in Europe and must reach us. You need to house all we will be gaining when we get home. That means you must screen them before I employ them. Prefer to keep with you holding that position for you have the knowledge and do it well. Also, a few of our ships will be going empty. They follow the same pattern as this one. Do we have pilots in our Military inventory? I do not want the family lead group split," commented Mara.

"Yes, we have pilots. I will call one of C Quad and ask that those who are already pilots go to the U for pilot testing only. Not because they can't fly, but just aren't familiar with this unit. Then a test flight must be passed today for them to pick up the planes and preflight them for tomorrow morning," responded Shandra.

"Do it please," replied Mara with a thankful heart for Shandra and her willingness to aid any way she could.

The orders went forward, and five teams of four people each arrived immediately already tested and having flown the new ships. The new pilots went to the conference room on the ship that Shandra would be flying and the orders passed as to what was going on.

"Your flight leader is Shandra who is over all the pilots in my employ. Your Mission Commander is me, Mara, and the order of flight is Shandra leads. Your ships will be empty for the flight going, however, full coming back. If trouble happens, you need to stay out of the line of fire, because we need you to get everyone back that will be on your planes. Are you all arms qualified? Who of you is in charge?" asked Mara.

"I am Sherry and understand that I will be Lead. Only for this mission is my understanding. Yes, we are all arms qualified. Concealed weapons permits were validated locally. It is a pleasure to be working with you ladies."

"Welcome and glad you have the training. You are to be ready to depart at zero six tomorrow which means zero four is when we will be here. Have personal gear for seven days only and pack lightly for you may want to bring an item or two back with you. Each ship will have two sets of pilots aboard due to the distance we will be going. One pair can rest while the other flies for there are beds above first class for that purpose. Our flight out is at zero six. Are there any questions?" Mara asked.

"No Ma'am," said the lead pilot as she saluted the Commander. Sherry was very relieved that she would still be allowed to fly though she had other talents as well.

Mara was pleased that three of the teams would be female and three males of those going. She had her orders as to how to watch over that many in both directions. The newest pilots were released, and Mara closed the hangar because they had other ships to check out.

When they reached their airport, they found five ships sitting on the tarmac, and they were all the design of the one in the hangar at the main airport in town. Touching a door unlocked it, and the two women went in to check out each one to know what to do the following morning when the full teams would be there. They also checked the baggage level to see if only the lead ship had space for their mounts or if they all did. There was room on all the ships. The twelve teams would cover all six ships and of that Shandra would control the family ship with her copilot and backup from both A and C Quad would be available.

They sat in the conference room of the last ship and had another discussion.

"Mom, everything is ready. The fuel is taken care of, meals are aboard for what is needed, and the tower personnel will be here for our takeoff then again staffed for our return. The ship from the town airport will be here in time to depart. Since the clock tends to change on us, this way we know we can land," laughed Shandra.

"Now that's a novel idea," replied Mara with matching laughter.

The new pilots were at the airport when the women got there the following morning. Each was inside the assigned planes putting away their gear and getting more familiar with the interior of the ships. Mara had advised the home AI as to who would be pilots for each of the ships, and they were given immediate access when requested. All the planes had a flight crew from the military which included two mechanics, stewards, pilots, and luggage handlers. At five a.m. the buses arrived, and everyone loaded onto the plane that Shandra would pilot. It was a silent boarding for half of them were still asleep it seemed. Only assigned pilots remained on the other ships.

"Shan how are we going to keep six planeloads entertained on the return flight?" asked Mara.

"You don't, they often take long trips, and they will sleep, read, look out the window or chat quietly with friends nearby. Some will play games on their game boards or with cards now that the two seats can face one another to do that. Also, there are movies they can watch using headphones. My concern is with six ships we might have followers."

"Won't happen, for no one can see the extras. It will be the same returning. Therefore, no one will be looking for us. T has it covered," Mara advised on her private line with her pilot.

She had asked Shandra once how many conversations she could handle at the same time, and the response was impressive.

"If it is just you then you have my full concentration. If it is military business, I hold at three. If I'm flying, I have the plane and tower control in one ear while your connection is in the other ear. All you must do, if I am busy with someone else, is hit that little button on your transceiver and you have an override. Why?"

"Didn't want to interrupt your flying yet prefer to be able to contact you if something comes to mind. I've grown so accustomed to having you in my pocket that it gets lonesome if you aren't there," laughed Mara for she had once told Shandra that she was better than any mouse in her pocket. They both had a good chuckle at that.

"Which is where I prefer to be, thank you," replied Shandra with a smile though it was not a comment she ever expected to make, let alone to mean it as she did, fully. She was thankful and amazed that Mara had the same training as Shandra.

The flight was smooth and beautiful. The fuel used in flight was another surprise. Remove one little coin and put in another one. Therefore the airplanes didn't have to land at all on the flight to Switzerland and Bern its capital.

When the flight landed, they were given directions to a hangar that had a for-sale sign on it, and that is where they parked the ship now known as Tango One. The number on the airplane garage came to Mara from the realtor she contacted. The five ships were placed inside before the main ship was placed there as well. The other pilots moved to the Mother Ship for the inspection of who they were and to be sure they had passports and such. The security detail inspected the main ship, and they were ready to depart when a call came from the airport terminal that people were waiting to meet with a representative of the group.

Mara agreed, and while the rest of the team filed into the private aircraft terminal, Shandra and Mara met inside the building in a private meeting room where they found a woman waiting.

"Hello, would one of you be Mara N-Sign?" a woman asked.

"Yes, may I help you?"

"That is my line. I am here because you contacted me to meet you here to look at a hangar for your planes and a place to stay while in the country. There are buses outside to pick up your group. Therefore, I returned the ones with me. If you direct your drivers to follow me we will look at the house since you have already seen the hangar though that was the only way I could think of to know who you were," replied the realtor who had used binoculars to identify the people departing that unit.

"It worked, didn't it?" said Mara with a smile.

"What did you think of the hangar?" the woman asked.

"Depends on the price, what is it going for?" asked Mara for she learned early on not to like or dislike a property until she knew the asking price.

"Same price as the house actually and you are the only one currently qualified to purchase either of them," she replied.

Her driver was told to follow them, so she could ride with the new people. The questions would be answered, however only when it was just Mara and her chosen people. The realtor had lost sales by speaking in front of the wrong people.

It turned out to be a short drive, by Montana standards, to the home that was for sale. The outward appearance was that of a Swiss Chalet, which Mara knew would not hold their group, especially with the ones they were picking up.

"This is a country estate that was listed just before your call. As your call was the first one to request such a place, you have first rights of refusal. Please go in and check it out," they were advised.

Mara frowned until she realized that it was not the Chalet. The nearest house looked like a motel or mansion. The building on the property was sitting back from the road. The vehicles would not move inside the garage. Since the driveway was two lanes and paved, the buses were parked on the blacktop of the circular drive until Mara decided if she wanted to purchase or not. In that manner, the place would remain clean for whoever did buy it. It sat back from the road and from what she saw outside it had a large, enclosed parking lot which was like a four-story garage matching the four-story building.

"Would everyone, except the lead group, please remain on the buses until we check out something? Will get this handled as quickly as we can. Quad A and Twin team to go inside with Granda and Kennet. Everyone else is to wait," directed Mara for she realized that the new people might not know who was considered a lead.

Once inside, the group was told to check out the place while Mara and Shandra spoke with the realtor.

"Now, please explain to me, what is the deal? What does it cost; can I own it as a US citizen or will I need dual citizenship for here; who will maintain the property while we are elsewhere; what are the taxes; and how soon can we take possession?" asked Mara.

Within an hour, the building was theirs, along with the hangar at the airport that would hold six planes the size of the one Shandra flew. The paperwork was signed, and she received the keys. Cost? A dollar is what she was told for each of the properties and for that the taxes, closing costs, warranty contract, and people to do outside maintenance were in place for five years. She never commented just made sure the paperwork was legal then told her group to unload.

Merry found the cupboards stocked with foods that had good dates on them. The units inside were not motel rooms; they were suites like at home. Since it gave no outside sign, that it had been for commercial use, this would give them additional privacy for Pat would have an AI in place the first hour most likely.

Once the papers were signed, the buses were put inside the garage, where no one was apt to notice they were there. A car representative arrived due to a call from Mara. She chose vehicles for the group. The contract showed she had purchased four vehicles of which one was a car and three were large vans. Mara paid a week in advance for the lease of the buses which they would need for any group activities.

Once everyone had chosen their new suites, Rae and Shandra departed with Mara. Since it was a long flight most just wanted to get settled in and enjoy the scenery for it was not the time for bed in Switzerland and most slept on the plane over. The views around them were spectacular.

For the trio, it was time to visit the bank and speak with the president. When they got to the location Rae told Shandra and Mara to have a seat; she would locate the person they needed. She saw a desk with a large sign on it, and that was where she headed.

"May I speak with the bank president please?" she asked politely.

"If you wait just a moment I will locate her," was the equally polite response.

When Rae returned to the two, right behind her was a woman who had learned that Rae wished to speak with her.

"Hello, I am the bank president. What language do you prefer?"

"I am Rae N-Sign and spoke with you on the phone. We speak your language as well as several others. At that time, I told you that I was the head banker for a group of corporations and that the owner of said businesses wished to speak with you when we were in your country. That time has come. We ask for some private time with you at a secure location," advised Rae.

"Very well, follow me please," replied the well-dressed woman.

They entered a room that had huge glass windows all the way around three sides of it. The president needed to have others aware, not of what was said, but that she had protection if the need came up. The door was part of the back wall, and it was closed, though not locked before the President sat at her desk.

"Thank you for meeting with us. We wish to open a few bank accounts here, and it needs to be done by number, not name," advised Mara though both she and Shandra had moved their chairs to give each of them a view of not only the woman also the room around them.

Chapter 3

Don't speak too quickly unless necessary

The door burst open, and the women noted that people in masks were taking over the area. Rae moved to the President and advised her to go beneath the desk, please. Then Mara and Shandra went to work while Rae watched their backs. They took down all in the president's office, froze them, and moved to the main foyer where they used the weapons that were still in their hands and began taking on those who were armed. Once the robbers were secured, Rae was directed to bring the bank president to the court.

"You are now in a Thunder court which is called to order."

The felons were on one side of the entry foyer and the Thunder trio on the other side. The full Thunder lead group strode into the area, and all had drawn weapons. With them was Shira.

"I stand as a prosecutor on behalf of the bank that you tried to rob. Who oversees those who broke the law?" asked Pat who filled the slot now for that duty was rotated as was a prosecutor.

"I am Your Honor, you can't prosecute us because you are not a native of this nation," said a man who stepped forward.

"In your tongue, I direct, my license says I am to enforce the law wherever I find it broken regardless of the nationality or people like you. I am Thunder Press, though you won't know that for long. Doctor, will you see if any of the people who work here, or their patrons, were injured?" directed Mara.

Randy moved to do as directed and the only one who kept their sword aimed at the felons was Shandra, and she did not need to tell anyone she was adept in its use. While the others had their points upward, they still held the handle of their weapons. All understood the message after seeing her and Mara in action. The wolf circling them added to everyone's caution.

"Two are injured, Your Honor. They will be okay until the court is over then we can take care of them," replied Randy.

"Thank you, that puts attempted murder as one charge. Please ask the injured to wait for us," said Thunder.

The Judge called the person in charge of the felons. From there on it was following the trail. As each came before the Judge, they were required to give names they used, their home of record, their nationality, race, and everything they owned. Who gave them the information on when and how to attack the bank? When all reports were in, additional people had been brought to the court and judged as well. The paperwork was signed, and the recording and weapons went to those that the President was asked to call.

The Swiss Police were advised to bring a bus, which they did. The men who had attacked the bank president faced murder charges for every one of the felons had received bullet wounds. Everyone had been tried and found guilty by their signed confessions. One of the officers asked to speak with Thunder. The bank president directed that her office was available for these were private people who did not need their names and pictures all over the media. The woman agreed.

Mara gave a small smile then nodded at her team who cleaned and shielded their swords. While Mara and Shandra met with the officer, Randy was taking care of the injured, and the rest remained on watch.

"Ma'am we apologize for meeting you this way. It was not our intent. If you wish to see my information, it will be given, however, prefer, as you said, that we not be known to any of your media people. Officer, what do you wish of me?" asked Thunder and all noted the change.

"We were advised that if the personage known as Thunder Press were to visit our country to give them due courtesy as a free agent and officer of the law with her family. Are you that person?"

"I am."

"You are welcome and will be worked with any time you call for us. Thank you for allowing me to know you. You will be identified by no other unless it is the bank president. I am the leading law enforcement officer in this nation and can verify that you are who you say you are. Wish I had been here for the capture though it is because I am curious as to how you managed with three people to take down forty for my understanding from the record was that your backup only came after you completed what you did," Officer Sedric told Mara.

"That can be arranged if that is your desire. Here is the address where we live when in your country. Please come there, and we will fulfill your request. Give us a couple of hours to finish business here, and we will return home," Mara advised.

"May I wait here until you complete your business? I get the feeling that this day is not over yet," said the woman.

"You are correct. However the next party will be at home," responded Mara.

The officer moved to the foyer to wait while the three women met with the president of the bank who thanked them profusely for her timely rescue. From what she had seen it appeared that part of the action was to be her demise. She had remained behind her desk yet watched what was going on for the women with swords were directly in front of her desk. When the action was over, she followed them to the main foyer, again keeping them in front of her. She would have to give testimony as to what she saw and heard. That report would go to the head of the board for the bank and possibly the owner as well, with her report to the Law Enforcement Officer already done.

"We need several bank accounts that cannot be in consecutive numbers. The numbers will show issued to this corporation, and we will divide them as necessary from our end. The accounts will be both personal and business. I hold the title of Fiscal Head. I will control how the numbers get used. The ones that only the corporation uses will remain separate if required for your accountability," Rae advised.

"No, it won't be done that way totally," said a woman who entered the door after a quick knock in time to hear Rae's last comment. She was well dressed and probably in her late seventies.

"I happen to own this bank and have a different offer. Gretchen, would you excuse us for a few minutes. I need to speak with these folks," directed the latest arrival.

"I think you need my full name for what you have in mind. However that requires an oath," said Mara with a smile.

"It would help if you don't mind," replied the woman who then took the oath.

"I am Mara Thunder Press N-Sign. My home state is Montana. With me are other members of my family. Meet my personal bodyguard and daughter Shandra Thunder N-Sign. The banker with me is Rachael Thunder N-Sign, another of my children. My name and theirs vary due to the duties we are required to fulfill. What can we do for you?" asked Mara though her Thunder side was the one most evident.

"This bank is in my name through a corporation which I own.

Some pressing personal concerns make it necessary for me to step down and dreams said you should be the one given control. Since you just saved the bank and thus my future, would you be willing to take over as me due to needing to be a citizen to own it? You can handle the problems that may continue to happen while I try to cover other bases. If you are not willing this bank must be closed," the woman advised.

"First I need to know what to expect. What are the issues you are facing, why did that bunch hit the bank today? Yes, I know the testimony as my twin was the judge. However, your point of view would be of interest."

"My Ex-husband just found out I own the bank, thanks to a loose-mouthed former friend. The bank needs protection, and since he can't get it through our divorce, he is trying every way he can to empty it of funds."

"In that case, your corporation is now mine, and your name will no longer be on it. Please know that I will charge a fee to do that. However, it will remain yours if that is what you want. Another option is, to purchase it outright for I am a citizen of this nation. Here is my passport," she handed over the document for Thunder.

"It is yours. My concern is those who work here. The employees are in danger due to those Mash sends to try to get the contents of the bank. My funds are hidden, and he will not get access to them. By the way, I am Alina Heisenkend with the last being my maiden name."

"Your Ex is in prison and will not be getting out. He fired on the Thunder team and thus will not see daylight in his lifetime, which could be rather short depending on the laws in this nation. Those he brought with him to hold up the bank each received the same judgment due to their agreeing to the directive given. How responsible is your current bank president?" inquired Mara.

"The president has been with me for years and is ready to retire. She is very reliable. The divorce judgment required that I sell one property and give him half the proceeds. That property is on the market."

"Was it by any chance an estate that looks like a motel?" asked Mara with a smile.

"Yes, and with it went a hangar at the airport," she responded in surprise.

"Thank you. The papers were signed this morning."

"Good that is one more arrow in my quiver. In truth, I'm glad that it went to you. The X will get half of what I got when it sold," laughed Alina.

"Where did you learn that trick?" asked Mara.

"I have a dear friend that had the same problem. Her husband purchased a home with his money though her name was also on the title. Once he had it fixed up the way his Mistress wanted it to be, my friend submitted that property to the divorce court as the one to sell; only it would be sold by her. She charged one dollar for it and paid him with two fifty-cent pieces. One for him and one for his mistress." The woman laughed.

"Never a good idea to underestimate a woman, it was our fortune to be the ones to purchase that property as well. At present, we have need of a place to house a few thousand people for a few days. Have you any ideas?"

The woman laughed and laughed.

"If you would purchase it for one year then return it, yes, I have such a place. On second thought knowing how divorces drag on, make it two years. It needs a clause that if something should happen to me, you retain the property."

"Here is the paperwork if you will give me the location. It shows it will be mine until two years from today. My enterprise director will keep this document on file though no one else will have access. You can prove it is not yours if necessary, yet neither of us must pay transfer fees," responded Mara with a smile for her AI had just notified her of a change of name and complete history for her to work in Switzerland as a native. The information for Thunder in that area was a copy of Alina's changing only Thunder's age.

"Thank you, you know it might work to just sign everything I own to you. The court papers will not catch up with me until I allow it to happen."

"Since I happen to know the man in question and he will not be doing anything except through others, go ahead. I will see that whatever you put in my name is taken care of until you are ready to have it returned. Once it is all settled we will meet and find out what you wish to do then," said Mara for she had asked to see the woman's ID when she gave an oath, which the AI recorded. She knew who she was speaking with and how large the estate offered was. It was not her intent to keep it, only use it for her needs for the two years then return it to the woman with hopefully an increase in value.

The bank accounts were set up for Mara's group by Rae, and

they departed. Alina received an invitation to go to their home and meet some of the family. She was thrilled and immediately agreed.

When they left the bank, it was a small convoy, a bus, a car, an unmarked patrol car, and a luxury vehicle – which Josephine drove. Joy knew that they were on their way.

The vehicles were put in the covered garage since no one could see inside the building. Mara gave the access codes, and the group moved inside both the garage and the house.

"Joy, these are some guests that are just here for a short time."

"I told Merry they were coming. Are you ready for a meal?" asked Joy.

"That would be a good idea. We have one hour then it all begins again," said Mara.

"Sounds about right, the rest are getting ready for a meal as well," advised Joy.

"Joy is another daughter. Granda, we have some guests. May I introduce Officer Brea Sedric and Alina Hesenkend Brieson? Alina and Brea meet Shelly N-Sign, my grandmother. Granda would you mind holding down the fort for a few minutes?" said Mara and led the ladies to the dining room where they could visit.

Shandra departed for her new quarters where she could change, wash her face, or whatever she wished until the meal. Mara did the same since they had been in an all-out battle it was time for another shower and clean clothes.

As usual, mealtime was a time of laughter and family. They chatted with the new ones and made everyone feel comfortable. As they were finishing dessert, Kennet got Mara's attention by nodding at Shira who suddenly stood up.

"You are now going to get your wish. Some things to keep in mind: do not pass those in Thunder formation. Stay behind them always to not be injured. Do not participate in what is going on for you are not trained to do so. Thunder!"

Those who would be participating rose from the table and moved outside the front door where they noted men were getting out of vehicles.

"Granda, may I ask a favor?" asked the Heiress who remained inside with Granda who never moved into the formation as she was their backup to call for help if needed.

Sharron L Ensign P.O. Box 583 Helena, MT 59624
Assassins Target Mara Bk 3
406-458-7091

"What may I do for you?"

"I have a feeling I will not leave here alive. I need my will changed and a copy sent to this location. Is there a way to get that done immediately?" Alina asked.

"Yes, it can be done."

The people outside were frozen, and the woman requested her lawyer. She made the changes she wanted, and he thought he was in his office. Her entire estate plus all private funds, vehicles, property, and all she owned was left to Mara N-Sign dated the hour she landed on Swiss soil, and it listed Mara as her mother. The Corporations Alina controlled were also turned to Mara using another document. Once the lawyer finished his work, Alina signed it, and he retained a copy with the original remaining with Granda.

"Thank you for your assistance. You have an amazing grand-daughter, and it seems her family is equally amazing. I wish all of you the very best in all things," said the woman who moved to the front window of the home to see what was happening outside.

Neither of the women in the house heard the shot that killed her and instantly the people, not part of the Thunder group, could no longer move. Thunder and Shandra followed the line of the shot and captured a man with a rifle. When they reached the assassin, the man was loading a weapon. He was killed soon after the bullet left his gun, and it was by the very shell he had just loaded.

Officer Brea Sedric had her wish to see the N-sign group in action. Yes, she wanted to see Thunder in action, and that she had done. At the same time, she was sorry to see the end of a valuable citizen one well-known within social circles in her country for as requested she remained active to see what happened. The news release gave the location as someplace else. Nothing mentioned the gunman except to say he was deceased. It was months later when a small clip in the news said that a memorial took place for Alina and that her family was in attendance. The family mentioned was Mara's for Alina asked for adoption under Mara just before being killed. She said she had no family, and her Ex would get it by default unless she did something like that though the action got backdated to when Mara began gathering up her group.

The window was removed, and Thunder repaired, to keep anyone from knowing what happened. Even the title to Alina's car turned out to be in Mara's name. Mara wished she had been able to get to know the woman before her death.

Since the tasks were complete that Mara needed to do, except for gathering up the military folks, who had been directed to go to the place Alina gave her to use, it was time to see some of the areas. Now Mara owned the location where the military personnel hid.

Mara moved outside the house and sat on the lawn looking at the magnificent views around her. It was a gift to Mara for she seldom had time just to sit. Shandra was nearby and on watch, yet not interfering with her mom. A young woman was noted walking down the street looking at the various houses. When she reached where Mara was, she looked carefully to identify the number written on a piece of paper, then asked if she might ask Mara a question.

"Certainly, though can't guarantee an answer," replied Mara with a smile.

"I received directions from someone unknown, to go to someplace never seen, to meet someone that is unknown and yet feel such a compulsion that I came immediately. My name is Alina, and I'm an orphan. Why did you wish to meet me?" asked the young woman with astonishment for she was usually very cautious with strangers.

"What is your age?"

"I am eighteen and just released from state control due to being in the orphanage."

"Shandra, please join us," directed Mara.

"Hello, this is my mother you are speaking with, and I was asked to join you," said Shandra by way of explanation though she had her Mom's signature smile.

"I have always believed that there is something wonderful ahead in my life yet no idea what it might be due to the start I got. Have no family or even friends at this point in my life."

"You are wrong there. You have a family with about forty siblings younger than you or more. There are also a few older, and I am your new mom if you wish it," replied Mara for she knew she was meeting Alina as she had once been. Due to adopting the first Alina, who had died, those memories were now Mara's to help her control what had belonged to the woman. They were a part of her mind that she didn't share. One woman ran the estate previously, and it continued to be run by one woman, though others worked for her. Those funds were kept separate from the ones under her as N-Sign for in due time they would be turned over to this Alina.

"But I'm a stranger to you," stammered the woman.

"Not really, you are someone we need, and we love you as you are. We will love you, train you, and put you to work if you are willing."

"I'm more than willing, and it is the best option I have ever heard," replied the youngster in shocked surprise.

"What are your interests? Do you ride horses, have you ridden in a plane, do you know how to use a sword? How good are you at caring for children on occasion? Do you have a strong faith and if so in what?"

"I've never done any of those things, except watch kids, does that mean you changed your mind?" she asked with some anxiety.

"No, you are my daughter as if born to me. The young man coming from the house is your brother Kennet. A wolf is moving toward us called Shira, and she is welcoming you as well. Join us and meet the rest for we prefer not to be known to just anyone," directed Mara.

They moved inside, and Joy was at the door.

"Hello Alina, I am Joy, Kennet's sister, and have a one-year-old son though he stayed home. You are now my sister, welcome."

"I'm Granda, or grandmother to Mara. We are glad to have you with us. Shandra why don't you show Alina her new quarters here then we need to take her shopping. We have other business, and for it to be taken care of, we need to be out and about."

"Meet you in the garage in thirty minutes if that works for everyone," replied Shandra as the young person she had become.

"Alina, we are only here for a little while then must go home. You will be going with us if you don't mind. Here is your new suite for when in this country. No one except mom, her guard - which is Doctor Randy or me, will ever enter here without permission. She wants instant access to all her kids in case of illness or injury. You have three bedrooms in case you later marry. That is your choice. Why don't you look over the suite? Don't rush. However, you need to realize this is now your space. Do you have belongings anyplace that you want in your new living quarters?" asked Shandra.

"We are given one set of clothing, plus what we are wearing, and a copy of our school records. That is all. Please tell me how to earn money to buy what I need."

"Not necessary, as one of Mara's kids what you need will be furnished the first time around. This suite comes fully furnished with furniture, linens, food, and security. You will receive an income once an account is in your name at home. There is a computer that monitors the whole building to keep us safe. If you hear someone speaking to you, yet there isn't anyone in the room, just answer as you would normally," Shandra suggested.

"You truly mean it? I am part of your family and welcome? You even give me this beautiful place to live? I don't understand," the shaking girl said.

"Remember your new mom asked you how strong your faith is? You must trust that what I am telling you is the truth. We will not lie to you; however, your faith will determine whether what you want will happen or not. Now it is time to meet everyone in the garage," said Shandra.

They ran to the garage with Shan leading the way. Everyone was waiting in the larger vans, and they were soon on the move. A stop at a store allowed everyone to pick up a few items to take home with them, that way the new girl would not feel she was the only reason they were there plus they needed to set up the new home with essentials anyhow.

"Get what you want or need, and mom will pay for it when we leave. Only mom carries funds for any of us. You will do the same at each of our homes," directed Shandra though she was also keeping an eye on Mara while suggesting what Alina would need.

"Shandra you have duties, let me take over here," advised Joy with a smile for she was now fully trained to serve as a guard if required.

"Thank you; I will do that. Welcome, Alina, this is Joy in case you forgot," then Shandra departed to Mara's location.

"So, what do you think?" asked Mara.

"She seems like someone we knew for a short time. She needs us, and in time I believe we will need her."

"We already need her. Her spirit is that of the one who gave us the property we own in this nation and even made it legal for us to own all that is here. It is important that Alina wears the same kind of clothing, and is trained, tested, and accepted. Didn't ask her about music though I am betting she plays something or can learn. Again, she is starting at the very bottom and will hopefully have a long and productive life with our family."

Mara did not add that the first Alina had been adopted as well only by a couple who owned a great deal and taught her how to take care of it. A plane crash over the ocean left her as the sole beneficiary two years later. Now the cycle was being repeated for it was when she was eighteen that she lost her adopted parents and the rest of the empire she built on her own.

"I agree and will help every way I can," replied Shandra with tears in her eyes, for now, she saw it the way Mara did.

Though the young woman saw this as an opportunity for her, others saw it as the spirit of the woman who was their benefactor. Both sides benefited from the meshing.

As they were finishing their shopping and moved to the mall boardwalk, Jo stood speaking with a man and woman.

"General call: everyone finds a place nearby without being noted as being all together," directed Mara as she moved to Jo with Shandra.

The family group walked into stores nearby to keep an eye out without being noticed by the pair talking with Jo.

"Hello Commander, understand you are looking for us," said the woman.

"Could be, are you looking for a ride home?" commented Mara.

"Commander?" asked the woman with a puzzled look at Jo.

"We have a home here, who is Commander?" asked Mara though she was picking up clues from her team for Jo appeared a bit concerned, though only by lifting an eyebrow.

"If you don't recognize us then we must have the wrong group," replied the woman.

"This is your new Commander above me. She is a BG and directs our lives to the saving of all of us. She is my mom, and her name is Mara. Would you like to go someplace a bit more private to talk?" asked Shandra for she wanted this over and done.

"My apologies Commander Mara, we have had others looking for us, and we know two of those with you by sight. It was the only way to make sure all was well, and we were not in danger," advised the woman who had seen Jo in a dream and was advised when and where to meet her.

"I cannot guarantee you are not at risk. However, you do need to follow us if you will. More of your group is waiting for us I understand, therefore if you are using commercial transportation then ride in the van with us. Is the rest of your group nearby?" asked Mara.

"Yes, give us an address, and they will meet us there," replied the woman.

Shandra did so, and the pair moved off and soon returned.

"They are on their way. Go ahead with your business for it will take them a little while to get there without being followed," the woman told Mara.

"LTC Sheson, this is MG Mara. We know we all have the same name, therefore, please use Mara as directed. Rank can get one killed here very soon," directed Shandra sternly after asking Mara to give them silence.

Mara had her hand in the air immediately. A slight shaking of her head and the woman was taken underarms as was her partner. They checked and found the woman was carrying and wired. Though Jo and Shandra seemed not to trust the female, Mara too realized that the woman obviously was not who she said she was. The entire group departed for their bus with the pair under guard.

"We must make a detour," said Mara with a smile then added, "Good catch."

"She said she knew me, none in the military would do that for we have changed a great deal. Caution in the brief of everyone was not to use anyone's rank. Yes, she had your name. However, I asked Thunder to remove it and scramble the address. There are eight of us she should have recognized if that were true. Now we need Thunder aid to find out what they were after," explained Shandra.

"It is possible the right people have identified us. Let's find a park nearby and see what this pair can tell us," directed Mara.

A bubble of silence formed over them as soon as the lead group was off the bus with their captives.

"LTC Sheson, front and center!" ordered Mara.

The woman moved forward and snapped to attention giving a brisk salute.

"What is your full name and why do you seek a group of the military?" asked Mara.

The woman stuttered a bit as she tried to tell the story that was false.

"I am Danson Sheson, and this is my husband, Fredrick Sheson. We are looking for the lost Brigade. No one leaves the military with intent to do harm and gets away with it," the woman advised though with some stuttering.

"What makes you think they are going to do harm?" Mara asked.

"The way they did it. Someone designed this defection well, and our task is to find them. At first, we thought that some of the top female Commanders were involved. That has since proven untrue for they were discharged to several different places and had had no contact with one another. Many now work in private industry. Those have also been ruled out. Nothing gave us a starting point to find them. Someone I know sent me a message that the Lost Brigade was assembling. That is the first and only clue we have been able to find. The letter said to find those we sought at the location where we met. You are too young to be a BG."

"Looks can be deceiving you know. I am also a Swiss citizen. We are here to take care of the death of my daughter. Where do you live?"

"The Sheridan Arms," promptly replied the woman for she was trying to keep the subject discussed in a format she could answer to in truth without giving anything away.

"Who do you have contact with?"

"The 1SG of the Battalion, him and his wife, took discharge due to the illness of their twins, or so the report says. We speak with him from time to time," she replied though they knew from her thoughts that she had never met or spoken with Mike or his wife.

"Interesting, who else do you have contact with?" asked Mara for she knew that was a false answer.

"Thought we had located the former person in charge, one Brigadier General MB Tridine, though we discovered it wasn't her when we checked the records."

"What did you check if this is a lost Brigade?" Mara wanted to know.

"To be an MG she would have to be at least in her fifties, though we had one who was younger than that."

"What is your age?"

"I am forty-seven."

"Who do you work for?" Mara asked.

"Military security," all felt her caution in the response.

"Answer truthfully," advised Mara.

"Military security," she again replied more firmly.

"Of what nation?"

She answered in another tongue.

Mara replied in the same language.

"Now that we know who you work for, why are you seeking the Lost Brigade?" Mara asked again.

"They are people already trained, and we need their expertise. They know the American military and can teach our people to take over that nation."

"That makes you a traitor. Where is Danson Sheson and does she even have a husband?" Mara wanted to know.

"She is a prisoner. No one can find her," responded the woman though she didn't mention a husband.

Shandra shook her head slightly.

Before Mara stood another woman, who looked not at all like the one they were speaking with, and she was in raggedy clothing with no shoes.

"Hello Dani, you are with friends," said Shandra.

"Hello, watch the tongue of this one," Dani warned in quick response.

"We know, however, thank you. Will you move behind us please?" advised Shandra while keeping her eyes on the one they were interrogating.

Chapter 4

Going my way

Dani moved to Kennet and asked a question.

"Who are these folks?"

"I am oath sworn and cannot answer. Friends are all I can give without the express permission of our leaders," he replied.

"That is good enough for me. Do not turn to me; I identify your voice. Would you ask permission for me to enter this interrogation?" said Dani.

"Do not step in front of us, give your information where you are," Mara advised as soon as she heard.

"Hello Shee, about time to equalize accounts. Name Shee Shenova lately of the Russian Guard. Age fifty-two. Profession: hatchet woman for the leader; Specialty: impersonating people of high rank. Identity: Assassin for Hire; Current Duty: capture as many militaries as possible and force them to serve the President of Russia. The US Military received a warning, and I was the bait. Currently, she has none of us, thanks to you. The young man and this woman both tell me you are friends. I believe you both. Please give me that oath only make sure this woman you are holding does not hear it."

"Thank you, Dani. May we have your actual name?" asked Mara who called for the bubble of silence.

"Certainly, I am Dannielle or Dani Copra Sherson. I can get a message to those you seek. However, it would be best if I went in person due to this woman and her infiltration of my group."

"We are in Bren looking for those who wish a ride to the states," explained Shandra.

"Your voice would give you away. However, no one would know you by your looks. Now let's have that oath," said the woman.

It was given by Shandra who swore her to Mara and her lead group.

"There is one other tool you will require. Do you want a name change?" asked Mara.

"Yes, being captured once is quite enough for me," she quickly replied.

"T let her see Shandra as she should be," directed Mara.

"What a relief, it is you. I know you have a story to tell only not now, we have some folks to get to safety," Dani told them.

"Your last name is now N-Sign, and Dani or Dannielle is your first unless you prefer another. I am now your mother," said Mara.

"Give me the name of Deranga with call name Dani since I never used the abbreviated version until now."

"Remain here, we have work to finish," Mara ordered, and the team knew Thunder was in control.

"Shee Shenova, you are on US soil and have been found guilty of plotting to overthrow the government here. None of your electronics are working for they do not operate in my vicinity. The previous message you sent never reached its destination. Your so-called team will face the same charges you do. Interrogators are waiting for both of you and those you had in reserve. These are the directors of the CIA/CID and FBI. Enjoy your stay. We have both recorded and written confessions with your signature on the latter. She needs to be strip-searched for she is an assassin as well as other things," advised Thunder.

"Thank you Thunder, she will be taken care of," said the woman in charge.

She then signaled and armed guards quickly put chains and cuffs on the woman. With a push of a button, she was in electronic restraints, which Thunder allowed. She was strip-searched in a cell where they had better control though Thunder caused her weapons and wires to be laying on the floor by her.

The group was again in the park.

"Dani, we need to free some captives, would you care to join us?" asked Mara.

"Most definitely and might even have an idea on where they are," replied the new woman.

"From this point on we are civilians. Your name is Dani N-Sign, and Mara is your mom, even as she is mine," directed Shandra.

"They took my passport so that could be a problem."

"Not really," responded Mara as she handed her the new document.

"Mind if I drive your vehicle? I refused to memorize the address where everyone is. However, I have been there, and therefore it is easy to find," responded D with a smile.

"You took your training well," Shandra replied.

"You taught well," she replied.

She climbed into the van, and they were on their way. Mara suggested that a quick stop for some clothing for Dani was in order. The stop was made, and Dani soon looked much like the rest of the family.

When they reached the location, Mara could not help it, she laughed, and soon the two sets of Quads and her twin joined her. It was the building loaned to her by Alina, her deceased daughter. No wonder she had laughed when asked if she had such a building Mara thought.

When they entered the building with the codes that Mara had in her head, there wasn't anyone inside. It had the hollow sound of being empty. Mara thought a moment then moved to a different area and asked her group to remain where they were. Shandra joined her and with permission so did Dani. They took a passageway that Mara opened and moved downward.

Before they departed the stairwell, Mara asked if there was an AI in place.

"Yes."

"Shena, please advise those below that we are friends seeking them," directed Mara.

The door opened on people standing in columns for formation. The lead person in each unit ordered "Present Arms," and Mara returned the salute for that was part of the training given by Shandra.

"MB, we are going to take you home where others are already waiting to welcome you. We know why you are here. However, it is only for a short time so that we can get you aboard private jets to take you out of here. Trust that what I say will happen. Now follow Shandra in the oath if you will," directed Mara.

"Attention!" commanded Shandra.

"Everyone here is to follow me in an oath, where it calls for a name put in your new name ending in Maybourgh. Some of us have a different name for Mara adopted us as the first level. You folks are as a military family taken under Mara. Giving a name change will protect you from those who are trying to find you."

When the oaths were over, she continued.

"All names are now on record. You are to walk through this doorway with your gear. Trust it is so. What you will be doing is loading on planes that are waiting for you. Tonight, that is where you will remain. We will join you in the morning for the flight out. Speak to no one and keep the noise down in the hangar," directed Mara.

"Mom, you were expecting a certain number, however many thousands additional answered the oath. They are stranded in this part of the world and need to go home," Shandra advised.

"The ones here will load on our planes that are waiting until they are full. The others will file through here and to the pod yard. My understanding is they are not getting on the planes. Due to the numbers, we are processing; it must happen that way. Many of you received discharges in foreign countries and then were abandoned with no way home. This time you are going to Montana where homes are ready. The families will meet them there. Their names will be a variety. However, all will show them as enrolled in my training base. From there they will work for me in some form. Thank you for your aid in doing this," Mara advised her daughters.

Each company came to attention and repeated the oath as if Mara was leading them in the words, then they moved to follow their fellows.

Mara had advised Sherry to take over counting so that no ship would end up with more than it could hold. The people were quickly assigned for it was nothing new to the woman. Then Sherry departed with the first group to keep control, of the planes, and her backup went with her, for all planes under her direction.

Within the hour, the house was empty of all except the N-Sign leaders. The entire building had been cleaned and was ready for the next influx. Thorough checking of the building was done by Shandra and Mara for they felt that there must be a vault on the premises, which there was. Also, they needed to be sure there was no evidence left of those who had passed through the area. Some items of interest ended up in the vault in Montana, and the rest remained where it was.

"Shandra, it is time to take our family shopping. We have some tours to catch up on and this time we see the area while we are here," directed Mara.

With a smile, Shandra got in the driver's seat, and they returned to the place known as their Swiss Home.

"Meeting time," said Mara, and the word passed to everyone to meet in the dining room to find out what was going on.

"Mom wants you to see some of the attractions in the nations we are visiting," began Shandra.

"We have tours arriving at the door and will be going on as many tours as we can handle. It is best that we remain together yet not appear to be together. Everyone goes. Dani and Alina travel with my guard and I. Jo, raise a hand please, will take the new group we picked up at home. If she tells you to do something, don't ask questions. We are now in a danger zone and all questions asked of any of you will be passed to me. If possible, we will return here for sleeping. Do not ask any questions of anyone that could compromise our security although you can ask questions about the location and area or event you see happening. Once we return here, there will be a time for questions, if you have any by then. The first tour is waiting outside. We will see the city, and if you see something you would like to look at better make a note, and it will come to pass if we aren't holding up others to do that."

They walked outside, and a woman was waiting for them.

"Hello, I am your tour guide. The company said you have a large family and your bus. Rather than have us use our buses you asked that we send someone to show you our city although the price will be changed to reflect that," the woman told them.

Shandra immediately moved her hand to the sword then gave the nod, and Jo ran to get the bus. Once everyone claimed seats, Pat advised the guide that if she would like to speak inside the bus, they would hear her. Pat then took the driver's seat, and they were on their way.

When they returned, they had been, by the clock, gone one hour, yet Shandra knew it had been three days of nonstop sightseeing. It was time for some sleep. They were soon settled in and sound asleep. Pi and Shira remained inside due to the location, and they too got some rest.

The clock said it was four a.m. when they awakened although Mara chuckled. If that were the truth, they wouldn't feel as relaxed as all of them did. Everyone was told to wash all bedding and clothing. Everything was packed; then they were ready for breakfast.

"Mom, could we eat out? We have been here a week, and not once have we eaten a meal out. I don't mind cooking at all though would sure like to taste some of the Swiss foods before we leave," commented Joy.

"Merry? Can we skip breakfast for now? It seems the one thing we haven't done is eat out. Are you willing or have you something fixed that we need to eat?" asked Mara.

Merry had a full breakfast ready and then watched it disappear. Later they found out it fed the troops while the family went out to eat. When they reached the hangar, they found everyone rested and full. The military had not eaten well during their captivity to avoid the agent trying to find them. They didn't want to give away who or where they were and kept a quiet low profile.

Mara asked Alina for the name of a good restaurant that would meet the requirements of the large group. Alina complied and even directed them in finding the location.

The building was of Swiss manufacture and large. Upon entering, the family heard the native music coming over the loudspeakers. The view was beautiful with the Swiss Alps in the distance as they sat overlooking a lake and ate their meal.

Kennet immediately asked for pie or its equivalent.

They had a fabulous meal, and nearly everyone tried one of the local dishes. There was a gift shop next to the dining room. As different ones finished their meal, they moved in pairs to the store. Many gifts were tagged and wrapped for the trip home.

Mara told the cashier there that she would pay for all purchases when her group finished.

Rae stood at the register to record each person's number to buy with so that the proper accounts were accountable when they reached home. What she did was give each person a number, and their expenditures went to that account. The AI they all were connected to would keep track of what everyone bought.

When Mara had paid the bill, they loaded up and departed for the airport and their personal hangar. It was time to fly home. The bus returned to the leasing location, and the purchased vehicles remained parked in the hanger for future use.

Shandra and Cherry had a visit with the military folks on the planes to keep the noise down. They advised what the plan was, and the pilots had a briefing. When all were ready, the lead plane moved out of the hangar with a tug, and like chicks in a row, the other five followed, though only Shandra, Jo, and Mara knew they were there, other than the pilots onboard each of the units. They were amazed at the numbers they had seen pass by them as they moved to safe areas.

Mara put up the walls of her personal area and sat staring at the wall. Something was bothering her, and she wasn't sure what. She ran through her thoughts of the last week and tried to figure out what she had missed. The military was secure;

the new girl would replace her daughter who died, they had met some new people and even kept some. Pi and Shira were aboard, yet something was missing.

She moved to the cockpit and spoke with Shandra.

"Shan?"

"Yes."

"Private line?"

"Yes."

"Why am I so unsettled? I can't find what it is. Please help me," said Mara.

"Cherry, take over the flight please," said Shandra, and she put the plane on autopilot for the transfer.

"Pat, need a copilot please," directed Mara.

Immediately the replacement was there, and Mara departed for the conference room in the back of the plane on the pilot level. With airplane soundproofing, the silence was complete once the doors shut.

"I'm sorry to bother you. However, I must get me settled before we land at home. I'm sorry, but something got missed, and it could cost us if it isn't figured out," Mara advised.

"Okay, I know you have been back in your memories so allow me a moment to do the same please then we will discuss it," responded Shandra.

Mara nodded and sat to wait.

"Did you speak with the Military Pilot Sherry? She asked for your time when we loaded in Switzerland," Shandra said.

"I show no reference to such a conversation. Please contact Sherry and ask if it is still necessary to speak with me," Mara replied for Shandra oversaw the fleet and unless asked to, Mara would not take her place.

"Seeking Master designer to meet with the builder, how is your time?" asked Shandra after plugging her headphone into an outlet hidden in the wall.

"Wait one," was the immediate response as Sherry turned her seat to her second and called for another pilot before preparing to move.

"Location?"

"Top, back, right panel."

Then Shandra said something else to the speaker. There was a pause allowing the woman time to reach the location given and to the plugin as well.

"Go ahead," said the Pilot as soon as she secured the doors.

"Did you request to speak with the Family head?" asked Shandra.

"Yes, I did. Had to be private and saw no opportunity," Sherry replied.

"I am here, in fact, we are both online with you. Go ahead for Shandra has full clearance to me," replied Mara.

"We have a Trojan. There wasn't a Company K in any of our units. One of those we are rescuing has identified as CO K," the woman reported.

"Which flight are they on?" asked Shandra.

"Mine for I made sure they were together as this puts all trouble on one unit not scattered throughout," Sherry replied.

"Okay, I am going to activate your ship, though you will be the only one who knows that. You are about to have two pilots appear on your ship. We will take over the flight as your ship must be used to put these also into the hands of those we have already turned some people over to. Are you war rated?" asked Mara.

"Yes, I am and standing by."

"Shandra, do what has to be done to secure this ship," Mara directed then raised her hand as her pilot left for the cockpit.

"Pat put a new team here. You cannot be the one for we are

traveling. Advise whoever you select to circle and keep everyone else with you except for number four. We are leaving you, however, remain where you are until we rejoin you," directed Mara.

"Yes, Ma'am, and good luck," replied Pat.

"Keep flying in a wide circle; you will not be picked up on radar. We will rejoin you when we can. Hope Marsh remembers to hide her coin," Shandra said to the air. However, Mara heard her and relayed it to Sherry.

The leader and guard entered via the conference room on Sherry's ship. The passengers on that ship were frozen while the pilots remained active. Shandra and Mara took over the flight while Sherry guarded their backs.

They landed at the location of the first bunch turned in, and after Thunder had identified, those on the flight designated as CO K fell into formation and unloaded. A Thunder court was activated, and all testimonies were received. The group was found to be part of the former problem, as expected. They were taken away by the law enforcement of the Nation though when asked they reported that there was only one drop off by Thunder.

"Mom, leave the door open," said Shandra as another company marched onto the field and headed for the plane they were on.

"Sherry, identify incoming," directed Mara who then took over as a pilot and sent Shandra to join Sherry so that if one of them didn't know the incoming group the other one of the women might.

"Ma'am, we are special Ops and directed to make ourselves available now and at this place," said the Captain in charge.

"Hello Robin, how did we miss you in the roundup?" asked Shandra.

"Commander? Have looked all over for you, have a dollar to return," she told her, which meant her company was ready to be given to the missing Brigade.

"We accept. Get your group loaded and hurry; we need to be in the air as soon as possible. Explanations can come later."

No one counted they just kept them coming and told them to take any vacant seat they could find. None of the soldiers knew that some would be put on different planes to accommodate all they needed to, yet seats were available for all they received. Since the lead pilots were watching those joining the flight, they directed the incoming as quickly as they could check and authorize them to enter the craft.

The new unit loaded as fast as they could, by running aboard. Everyone found a seat, and Mara called for a place in line for departure. Thunder held all flights until she was in the air then the tower again took over the airport and never knew Thunder had even been there or that a separate company departed on the plane.

"Sherry, assemble all your passengers in the main cabin. We will join you," directed Shandra at Mara's request.

Thunder continued to fly the plane while Mara took over the meeting for everyone had to attend the brief.

"Hello, one and all. We need some oaths, Shandra if you will please," directed Mara to use as little energy as possible while splitting. She was now the aircraft's pilot, still aboard her family ship, and now giving a brief.

When all had taken the oath, Mara continued.

"I am Mara and ranking officer though we now work with civilian names and don't use grades, except on special occasions. There are jobs available for all of you and your families. Housing will be available as soon as possible. Remember your oaths, for to not do so could cost lives, including yours. You will be under persons that you know. I am the one overall. When we land, there will be officers in place to direct you to your new homes. We have two more pickups I understand then you will all be in place. Thank you for trusting me to do the duties per my orders. Keep watch for we just found out that an entire company had slipped in with those we picked up in Switzerland. Be aware of those around you and make sure they are who they say they are. Sherry and Robin, will you join us for a meeting please?" directed Mara and the meeting ended as the officers departed.

Another meeting was held once in the conference room on

Sherry's ship,.

"When we tell you that something will happen, believe it. When told to do something, do it without question. There may be a time for questions later, however, at that moment, it is necessary that you do as I have directed. You two ladies will be meeting with the leadership team when we reach base. Please be available once those under you are loaded and on their way to the base. You are very welcome, and everyone will be given a name change to make it harder to find you. Hopefully, it will make you impossible to find. Now we turn your ship back to you and see you at home," said Mara.

Sherry ran for the pilot's cabin and took over as a pilot for her second was already in place. When she looked back, Mara and Shandra were no longer there.

"Well Guard mine, it is time for some rest. Find a place to relax for we will need to sleep until rested," said Mara who then lay down and was instantly asleep.

Shandra thought for a moment then smiled and did the same. Jo and Rae could handle the ship, for now, was her fleeting thought.

Randy checked on the pilots and noted that Jo and a member of her group had taken on flying duties. She saw Mara and Shandra were asleep when she softly opened the door to their area, therefore, it was time to make some changes including which was for her to take over while the pair slept. Randy reviewed what the brief attended said had to happen and recalled that there were to be two stops on the way home. That could be covered at other times and in other ways. Therefore she directed that the flight be direct with the stops showing as completed, which they were, for the two women dropped off in Tennessee, they believed.

When the fleet landed at their private airport in Montana, it was dark out. Therefore, the passengers were told by Randy to get comfortable they would not be going anyplace until morning. Soon the ships were quiet and all lights were off. Once all was quiet, she made sure all ships were secure and went to sleep.

When Mara awakened, it took her a while to figure out where

she was. In a plane, yes, however in a plane that was not moving. She looked at the seat next to her, with walls on all sides of the two seats, where she saw Shandra beginning to awaken as well.

"How did we end up here and where is here?" asked Shandra when she saw her mom sitting up looking puzzled.

"On a guess, I would say we are home and that no one was prepared to receive us. Therefore, everyone is still on the planes until we awaken. My guess would be that we timed it, and that is why we were so tired. In fact, everyone must have been exhausted, I know I was," commented Mara.

"Oh yes, now I remember. You did your split act, though that one involved three personalities and we went to another ship because Sherry had caught some infiltrators. When they were turned over to the authorities, we picked up another two hundred and didn't have that many seats. Moved some of them to this ship and that meant everyone was timing it. We needed to sleep for, however long we did," responded her guard.

"Wonder who the pilots were?" asked Mara.

"Guess we better go find out and get everyone moving," laughed Shandra softly.

They hit the button on the seat they slept on, and the walls dropped. Moving quietly, they headed for the pilot's cabin where they found Jo and Rae sleeping in one of the bedrooms and Cherry in the other one. In the space, next to where Mara had been they found the two newest members Dani and Alina. The women slipped down to the main floor and found all asleep there as well.

"Well, Daughter mine looks like you better alert the teams to get everyone moving. Don't rush though for they must need the sleep, or they too would be awake. Someplace is breakfast and a shower, not necessarily in that order," laughed Mara in a whisper.

"Let's move outside and use the comm line. Let everyone remain asleep until the buses get here, and we can begin getting things moving. Would you ask T to move Shira and Pi?" asked Shandra.

The two requested were with them immediately.

"How did you like your trip?" asked Mara then she laughed.

"Yes, it was a good nap. Run and enjoy while we get everyone awake and moving," commented Shandra.

"Let me call for the guard dogs and give them some time as well," Mara reentered the plane and whistled softly. All the guard dogs moved immediately to where she was.

"Out you go, this bunch has a little more time to sleep," she laughed.

"Shandra, do you realize this is a first? Other than when we are in a secure area, we have never had time to ourselves. Want to go for a run?" asked Mara.

Like, two truant children, they took off running. By the time, they returned, people were beginning to awaken. The guard dogs had joined them on the run while Shi and Pi were with them as well.

"They are making sure we have guards," laughed Shandra as they ran.

The two were laughing as they entered the area where the planes sat on the tarmac. Then they noticed the buses and sobered, to become respected leaders, though both were still smiling.

"Sherry and Robin, front and center," ordered Mara in a voice that carried throughout the area.

The women came on the run.

"Reporting as directed," said the women with sharp salutes returned by Mara.

"I have some options open for you. Come with us," directed Mara and they entered the empty hangar.

"Due to your diligence, we made it home safely. Now you have some choices. We said you could be adopted if that is your desire. Is it?" asked Mara still smiling.

"Ma'am, I am almost forty, no one wants to adopt an old woman," replied Sherry.

"Sherry, what were you told in the brief you received?"

"To answer all questions and not ask any unless told to," she replied then thought a moment and replied. "I have outlived my mom and was the last of my line. Yes, I would like adoption if offered."

"Now Robin, what is your decision?"

"I am forty-three. My family is not willing to accept me back, that is why I was traveling still. Yes, I would welcome adoption."

"You have just become my daughters. Shandra is one of your sisters. You will meet the others as we go. How firm is your faith?"

"Yes, I have faith, I'm here after all," Sherry laughed for they had been ordered to run at a blank wall and it put them on the ships with her leading.

"I watched my company disappear like smoke as they entered the flight. Yes, I have faith for they are all here for accountability. Adoption, yes, in a heartbeat," said Robin with a small smile and sparkling eyes.

"You are now twenty-one years of age. Do you have any problem with that?" asked Mara.

"I have... oops sorry, questions are for later. Thank you, Ma'am, I am dumbfounded and honored," replied Robin.

"What is your retired rank? What is your preferred profession?" asked Shandra for she knew what Mara needed.

"I retired as LTC over the Bowler Company. Despite all odds, we made it thank you for the rescue," Robin replied. The Bowler Company gave reference to those who served all over the world and would never be higher than LTC until they retired.

"You are to aid in getting everyone on the buses. However, you will not be going with them. Once all is secure the lead group will depart," said Mara with a smile at her newest daughter.

The buses were loaded and departed. Shandra checked out all the planes with Sherry to be sure they were secure. Mara met with Dani and Alina. A tug was waiting to put the ships inside the hangar. When they were secure, it was time to utilize the vehicles that they removed to make room for the ships.

"Okay, gals you remain with us. We must secure the area before we depart. I am not allowed out without guards. Therefore, you two have just taken on that duty until my pilots get the aircraft in place," Mara directed.

The younger of the two, looked shocked, while the older was looking around at the area and who was where. Mountains were fully around the area, yet one could see for miles in any direction.

"Don't worry about it, you will learn in time. For now, one guard is enough, yet you need to learn by watching those around you as well as by training, which you will get. Have faith, it will all get done," said Mara with a smile.

"You had me worried, I wouldn't want to rely on me now," replied the young woman though she relaxed a bit. She liked Mara and was comfortable in her presence. In fact, she felt as if Mara was her birth mother, and it was a very comforting feeling. Little by little, she forgot her orphanage days.

Chapter 5

Making it all work

"Remember everyone was new once. We won't abandon you, and you will receive training as a member of my family. I have many kids, and there are about fifty in the lead group. My grandmother is Granda who works for us; my mother is training a young woman in sewing and design of garments. From there down I am the eldest and the one in charge. I have a twin sister, and we both have people under us. You will figure it all out as time goes on. We don't want to overwhelm you. Presently, we are going to run to our home and shower plus get clean clothes then we will go into town and have breakfast. Typically we would be taking care of horses and giving riding lessons. Then there are music lessons followed by a morning meal. We are close to our regular schedule and will be at breakfast at about seven-thirty. Follow Shandra and me around until you get your bearings. Pat is my twin and Randy, the doc, is one of my daughters. We will get you set up with a suite then you can have a private place of your own. I am allowed in any room in the compound in the case of illness or injury. However, I don't abuse the privilege," Mara explained for she knew that both women would need the information.

"Can we ask questions here?" asked Alina.

"Come with me," directed Mara and the two women followed her to the hangar where the ships were in place and being locked up.

"What is it you wish to know?" asked Mara.

"Are you my mom now? We learned to speak American in school which is good because I can understand everyone. When does my training start? What comes first? Above all thank you for adopting me. I had about given up on anyone caring that much," the girl replied.

"It took a while for me to get there though have known for a couple of years now that as soon as I could, that was a place I needed to go. Now you are an American with a new name, new family, brothers and sisters, a ranch home, and more surprises on the way," Mara advised.

"Mom, gee that sounds good, may I have a hug?" asked the youngster.

"Anytime you like," replied Mara with a face-splitting grin.

Each gave the other a hug, and when Mara looked over at Dani, she saw a look of longing and gave her one as well, much to the woman's surprise.

"Be not surprised daughter mine. Hugs are free, and next time it could be me asking you for one," laughed Mara.

"How old are you that you term me daughter?" asked Dani in surprise for she had not realized who had adopted her.

"I have yet to see my eighteenth year though my age is twenty-two and will be for the rest of my life even as the two of you are twenty-one going on nineteen and oh forty-some."

"Whoa, I'm twenty-one," replied both women in unison.

"Yes. I will always be older than you, however not by much," laughed Mara.

"You have got to be kidding," said Dani in amazement.

"I assure you she is not. I am twenty-one going on fifty-some," Shandra told the woman for she had heard the conversation via Mara's communicator.

"That is why I had trouble identifying you. You are a lot younger than I remember you as being," responded Dani.

"The lead group is all that age, and you two are part of that group. Now we have buses waiting, and it is time to go home for a few minutes then we go out to eat. Must see what adventures are waiting for us to resolve due to our trip," Shandra advised for she knew her mom was ready for breakfast.

The trip home was a short one of about ten miles. The newest members chose suites then it was showers and out to the vans and a trip to town.

Mara and Shandra were speaking in low tones.

"We gained a lot this time," said Mara.

"Oh, not so many, you had twelve thousand on-site at home, brought out about a hundred thousand, rescued Dani, turned in an entire company of terrorists and their leader, a spy, and undercover agent. Add in Sherry, Robin, and Alina which gives you adoption of four. The rest were for my command. However I have already turned them over to others," commented Shandra.

Mara began to laugh and the more she thought about it, the funnier it became. Soon everyone on the bus was laughing though no one, other than the two women, had any idea what caused their laughter.

"Let's not explain," said Shandra.

"Oh, I don't intend to," replied Mara with a smile.

"Pat, where do you plan on eating?" asked Mara as she changed her communication device setting.

"Thought you might like a change of pace, how about the truck stop?"

"Works for me, did you happen to notice we now own four restaurants in this town? Which reminds me speaking of owning, why don't you move your ranch here with all the rest? That way you can stop in from time to time," advised Mara on her private line with Pat.

"I had a feeling that was coming. I will see if the caregivers agree. Thank you."

When they reached the parking lot, there were a lot of vehicles in place. Mara directed that all personnel remain on the bus until she checked on seating for everyone. Shira was at her heels and Shandra at her side as she entered the restaurant while Randy stood at the open door of the bus.

"I said give me the cash, or you and those in this place are dead," said a man at the cash register with a gun.

"Hello Sir, we do not work for you, why should we give you the money in our register?" asked the waitress.

"You get one more chance then you are dead," he replied.

As he raised the weapon, Shandra hit his hand, and not only did she knock the gun out of his hand she shattered his wrist. He screamed, and everyone was immediately alert.

"Sorry folks, just a bit of a stumble. It is under control," said Shandra who directed the waitress to call the police.

As soon as Randy heard the yell, she was on the move.

"What have you got?" asked the Doctor and Mara immediately requested a silence bubble.

"A guy was holding up the restaurant, and I objected," replied Shandra.

"In that case, what do you want me to do, if anything?" asked Randy.

"They will take care of him once the officers pick him up," advised Mara.

They moved outside to the parking lot and the Thunder team formed up.

"You want all of them, don't you?" asked the waitress.

"Yes, court time," replied Mara and she watched as about sixty people moved outside. Then she froze time for all except her, Shandra, and Randy.

"Okay let's get some answers. It does not take sixty people to hold up a restaurant. Not cost-effective. Someone expected us for it tastes like someone is recording what is going on. Our seating area is empty for I called in a reservation. What is your take on this?" asked Mara of Shandra.

"I agree. Also, why would a man with a gun repeat his request? Usually, they use surprise as a weapon, and this time it was not plus the waitress was in on whatever it was because her response to the gun holder was strange, to say the least," replied Shandra.

"First you might want to disable all electronics, except your own and that means any place in sight of us. Next, maybe interview each of those you have in court starting with the gunman and waitress," suggested Randy.

"Just a moment, someone else wants in this conversation, though this is a new one," Thunder offered.

"Yes Alina, what can we do for you?" asked Mara as the girl departed their transportation and joined her mom.

"This is not resonating right. It was a setup like when someone planned on making me the fall person for something they did. Pull all your people and depart without leaving even a memory. Let them figure out what they did wrong and find a different place to eat. You are becoming predictable, and that must stop. Sorry, mom, I should not have entered a private conversation, however, thought I saw something you didn't. I apologize," Alina told them.

"Never apologize for doing what you believe is right. Thank you. Load up while we get some memories removed," directed Thunder.

Randy told everyone to get back on the bus. The weapon of the gunman was secured, and Mara's people were advised to get on the bus. They moved to a different restaurant that they had not tried, yet Mara said they owned. It was on the other side of town where they had a relaxing breakfast in a room like the one at the former restaurant. Kennet was watching for any vehicles following them yet didn't see any.

When they finished eating, they took a back-road home. When they reached home, the horses were lined up on both sides of the driveway, and everyone had to say hello before going inside although the buses were put away as soon as the passengers departed.

"Alina come with me, please. Pat, would you take care of Dani, Robin, and Sherry for me please?" asked Mara.

Mara entered her suite and then led her new daughter through it and out into a second hall although her suite and Granda's were the same size, large.

"This is to be your new home if you don't mind. We have similar housing in several locations due to travel requirements. You will own the same place in each of those homes. Since you have become part of my team, pending training, and are a birth daughter to me, you need to be closer to where I am while we get to know one another. Shandra will be in my suite as we have new people though she too has a suite of her own. She is my personal guard. There is an AI in this house, so you can sleep soundly I assure you. My grandmother, and now yours, lives in the suite on the backside of my suite. I have many children that live in this wing, and most of them live with me. Knock on my door when you get up, and you can cut through to the dining room plus I can fill you in on whatever you need to know to begin the day, that is not knowledge for everyone," said Mara with a smile.

"Am I the only one on this side?"

"Hello Alina, do you mind if Sherry, Robin, and Dani are your neighbors? We are filling up this area next. The other half is full," said Pat for Mara asked when she heard the hesitation in the girl's voice and asked Pat to move the three to a new hallway for they could fill the last couple rooms at another time.

"My suite is larger than normal due to having so many kids. You four will be next to my quarters in the second corridor. We fill as people come though try not to isolate anyone," explained Mara.

"Pat, how many do we have that need tested now? I lost track," said Mara with a smile, though Pat knew she didn't have to ask. The list was up for testing the following day. Mara would make it a point to be the escort for this group. They had saved the day more than once.

"I think you said that the instructor would not be available tomorrow. That means we do the other training that day. Can we have a day of catching up?" asked Pat.

"Sounds reasonable to me, I have some kids to catch up with as well," laughed Mara.

"Mom, you said we would be getting music training. Will we get instruments too?" asked Alina.

"Yes, what instrument would you like to start with?" asked Mara with excitement.

"I love music and always wanted to play trombone," responded the girl.

Now there was a new one. The band had none of those. Mara raised her hand, and that instrument fell into her hand. She gave it to the girl.

"If you like you can have your first lesson now," offered Mara.

"Oh yes, please," the youngster responded with a grin.

Those in the hall immediately departed behind Mara as she made her way to the music room.

"Dani, Sherry, and Robin what are your instruments of choice?" asked Mara.

Pat sat down with a saxophone. Each of the new ones picked up whatever instrument they were interested in which was in a bin labeled new. Soon the jam began. Mara was aiding them in getting started. As soon as the first note sounded, Granda was there to play the piano. Kennet drifted in and located his trumpet. Bins on Wheels were behind a wall in a hallway full of containers. They had rollers on them, and each belonged to one of the band members. Soon a full jam was going and as the music was heard others joined in.

"Oh, I love this," whispered Alina.

Mara smiled and asked her if she was ready for her next instrument. When the new folks, each had a chance to use the other devices, the lessons stopped. The teacher sat down with a twelve-string guitar and as she played Granda, and Pat joined her. Then Randy picked up the tune though that was all that played then.

"Thank you, Sis, that is what we needed," said Pat for she was now relaxed and ready to go.

The next stop was the stables where everyone was matched

to their mount before the ride began. When the leaders were seen moving through the compound others joined them until the entire group was in place.

"We will be in a riding show soon. Some will be in drill style while each of you will also have a chance to display your personal skills. On another day, the family band has a performance at the stadium. For the new ones, here is Twin style riding," said Mara as she saddled then mounted one of the studs that came to her, and Pat did the same for they tried to match the horses when it was a Twin style mount.

"And this is Quad style," said Shandra as her group mounted then Jo and her bunch were doing the same though each did a different drill.

The five and under team rode on their small horses, and they did their style. Then it was age groups followed by precision as a family. Mara felt they had good enough form to do the show.

Pi had offered to be the mount for Alina until another one agreed to take her place.

Mara chuckled as she heard her family's comments.

"I've never done this before."

"Gee they are good."

"We are going to do a show. What fun."

Mara was looking forward to their first public appearance. She also noted some performers that were headed their way and recalled her promise to Jimmy that she would see he had a free ticket if he came.

With the music and riding drill finished everyone was lined up and either watched or did the Lightning training. Each had a sword though only the leaders had Lightning. The swords used for the exercise were similar in look and felt the same yet were not Lightning of the leading team.

"I just received a call that the tester at the U is ready for our next group," Mara said, and she asked who had yet to take the exam.

She saw very few hands raised yet told those to get their mounts that she was taking them for a ride. Shandra would be with Mara though she called for Granda and Randy to join the group. When they reached the U, they placed their horses in a pasture behind the main hall. Shira would watch over them while the rest went inside to take the tests.

"Hello, Mara. A few more for testing I see. Don't know how you find such talented people," said the man in charge.

"These are my children. Give him your names; he has the list," Mara advised.

Alina would have the full list minus the talents of leader and medic. Sherry was well educated as was Dani and Robin. That meant new skills for the lead group. Therefore, the Twins made sure that Randy, Shandra, and Granda went along for a new list to be submitted. When all exams were over, they declined lunch and headed home. By the house clock, they had been away the amount of time it took to ride to and from the University. Everybody passed.

"Thank you for the new education, whoever you got that from was very well educated and a Professor no less. Your little Swiss gal didn't do too bad either. You will be busy if you put all you have in your mind to use," said Granda as they sat in her suite for a moment of catching up.

"It is already in use. There is now an airport to run, new planes which we designed and thus carry the patent. Then we will be doing a horse show, and the family band is also on the schedule. That restaurant we visited that had the bogus hold-up is no longer open. We own four operating restaurants in the city. Nice variety in fact so we need to spread out our visits to different ones while not becoming predictable. Add in the gold mines that are now in operation; the leather business is doing a booming business with Gary teaching many of the new hires to aid him in keeping up. Rae has the banks in operation, Becky oversees Restaurants, and Heidi does the Motels although they, in turn, are being supervised by Jo until she is sure they know their jobs. The events schedule is full for the next year. I understand that some well-known performers are coming. Having an auditorium that holds ten thousand might have some bearing. Peter Valeshan has passed his training and is now a professor at the U and is training people in managing a ranch the right way. We have helicopters and smaller ships to check out. Everyone has music training and can ride. Sword drills are complete, at this time. Kids graduate when they are ready. Joey is talking, can you imagine that? Merry is planning a huge BBQ to go with the riding show, and if we don't get others to take on that event, we may have to do it at least once a month. Doing a show once a month allows us time to do other business and still see any of the shows we wish to. Only when the family is scheduled will there be two shows in one month, until we see how good a draw we will have. Merry says she doesn't mind cooking if she can vary the menu. The hospital and clinic are in the black as are all businesses we own. Everyone gets their vehicle changed every two years, and they come from the dealerships that Jo oversees. There are thirty ranches and farms on the property we own which covers food requirements for our restaurants and our tables. Every property has a certified well that won't go dry for it has artesian as the source. We have a reliable chef, housekeeper, and enterprise director. You are alive and with me. I'm so humbled and honored by those who have asked for adoption as the lead group. Just love them all. The Regina group of kids are learning all we send their way and much quicker than I expected. Right now, all new members are doing a weapons drill with the adult Quads. Therefore I must stay home and visit with you and the kids," laughed Mara.

"Well, you could always go for a refresher course I guess," laughed Granda for she well knew her granddaughter's schedule.

"Oh, I do that daily, and she puts me through the paces. She has selected people in the new branch that are weapons experts, and all our people are receiving training. Those who once had concealed weapons permits have them again though they must pass an exam periodically to show their proficiency. Then Merry gives me a cooking lesson, Kennet is learning to make pies, and as you know, the list goes on."

"Yes, I do know and can't think of anyone better equipped to do the duties you have taken on," Granda told her granddaughter and meant it with all her heart.

"I intended to let you know, that the first ranch we picked up, the one with the two sets of twins; is now part of the local horse farm scene. Pat's horse ranch moved over last night, and that means her horses are here as well. You did another good piece of business in the land you scooped up, so we can put our properties nearby. That has another plus because if we are busy yet scheduled for a horse show, we can call on the ranches we own to put on the show. I find it interesting that we now own the property space the ranches were moved from. We can hold them, which I'm currently doing, sell them, or build another enterprise in that space. Due to so many felons visiting us here I've asked for underground stables at every ranch we own. That way our managers can sleep nights which means we can sleep nights as well without anyone stealing stock."

"Sounds like you have a good handle on everything. I think you have a couple of kids or more that are ready to graduate. They are under graduation age, yet they have mastered all anyone required. It's B Quad. Are you going to graduate them and move their age or are you going to let them grow some and maybe lose interest in what knowledge they have?" Granda asked with a smile.

"They have been graduated as far as lessons go. Not going to push them faster than they are ready to go. Think we will do as was done with Gwen and Dan. They will continue to study and look for ways to help. I'll know when they need to be tested to become adults. Think they should be at least sixteen, however, if that were done then the ones from the book world would not be there yet. They seem to learn so quickly and be eager to progress in life. They could take over the duties that Dan and Gwen normally do which will allow them to make a trip or two with us," replied Mara.

"I agree that is the best way to go. Those two have good defensive skills and should be allowed to spread their wings as well. Another that needs moved up is Joy. She is always into something to take the stress off us. Bless her heart, how she loves you," Granda advised.

"I know, the thing is she has a young son that will slow her progression unless she wants to turn him to me to allow her also to spread her wings. Will talk to each of them and see what they desire," Mara told her grandmother.

Since things that were put off never got done she moved to

her suite and sent for Joy first. Then the Quad reported one at a time. When done, the next flight showed that Joy would be on it with Gwen and Dan while B Quad would begin being the trainers in riding and music. They would see how it worked out.

Joy had already proved her metal as had Gwen and Dan. How quickly they were growing. Then Mara looked at her life and signed off for the three to be advanced in ages and responsibilities. While she was doing that, she checked on Kennet who was taking over bakery duty. He too was shooting up. All of them were now in the six-foot range. They were stable young people to be proud of and how very proud she was. B Quad was young when added to her family, and now they would take over duties that Gwen and Dan had done so well. With weddings on the horizon, there might be a rash of new additions by birth in a year or so.

The entire family was directed to have a riding drill, shower, then a music drill. They needed to be ready for the shows ahead. Mara was so very proud of every one of them. No one could identify even the newest in the group; they did so well.

- - - - - -

"When do you plan on having your first craft show in the East?" Granda asked at her next meeting with Mara.

"Usually October, we are full-on requirements until then. It will allow us to enjoy the fall colors there and hopefully avoid any adverse weather. We need to do something different, yet I'm not sure what. Since the kids are in school on Friday, would you like to take an outing with Shandra, Alina, and me?"

"What do you have in mind?" asked Granda with a smile of acceptance.

"Wait and see. Must be up at our usual time and from then on, the day is just for us. I will ask Joy to watch the kids under five for that day," replied Mara who immediately asked, and Joy agreed.

When the day arrived, it was beautiful. A few fluffy white clouds in the sky yet it was mostly a bright blue. Not too hot or too chilly. Two vans were sitting ready to go when they reached the outside of their home. Granda and Alina were in one with Mara and Shandra in the other until Kennet called, and he was told to climb in.

"I would ask why so many vehicles with few people yet will see what you have in store," chuckled Granda for she loved the surprises gifted to her by her granddaughter.

They stopped at a local grocery store and picked up newspapers, bottles of water, and some packaged snacks. There happened to be some backpacks and small coolers on sale closing out the season, so Mara grabbed those as well. She put a newspaper in each of the vehicles, water, and some snacks in each of the backpacks for the five and threw the rest inside the vehicles in case of later need.

"We are looking for estate sales and if a garage sale is on the way we stop," directed Mara with a smile and Shandra was suddenly grinning broadly.

Shandra said not a word though she now knew they would also have to look for a large empty building to use as a 'you name it' store so that people could name their price. Granda drove one van and Mara the other as both were familiar with the city. Laughing like the twenty-some kids they were they began their first garage sale for some of them. Shandra was the only seasoned buyer.

While Mara followed Granda, she was also having a conversation with Shandra. Mara learned about garage sales and how they worked.

"If we do this the way I see, it means we will need people to cover the most areas," commented Mara.

"Have just the persons. In fact, you and I could go with them next weekend and see what you think of some ideas they have. Not expecting this to be a money-making event. However, it will aid any in the area who are short on funds, and you might even run a few things that are overstock from the stores. That means we need a not-for-profit corporation. It is school time, and I keep thinking of Kari and her situation. We know there must be others like her," said Shandra on the monitor.

Kari had funds, in fact, the eight properties she sold gave her over half a million in income. However, after being short most of her life, she left that money in savings for her daughter to have a college fund. Little did she know it would not be needed.

"Set it up because if we put it off it will never get done. Need to know when everyone wants to start. The money will be furnished if this seems workable. However, this is a fact-finding mission. I wanted to have Granda, and Alina goes as well though I think that having no more than three in any of the vehicles would work best to allow space for whatever gets purchased. Also, this serves a dual purpose as both Alina and Sherry need to know the area," replied Mara though in time she would use sixteen passenger vans leaving the driver's row and the one behind it in place while all other seats were removed. Those vehicles were shown as owned by the Garage Sale/Estate Corporation.

"If you allow us to use vans we can put what we purchase inside, especially if the weather changes on us. The vans are the favorite ones for this endeavor. Those and pickups, depending on the weather," replied Shandra who was smiling to herself and wondering if her boss had any idea the can of worms she had opened.

"No, however I will, and you will keep me out of trouble along the way, won't you?" replied Mara with a matching grin as she answered her daughter's thought.

"Start by giving everyone going ten twenties. Then you carry about a grand per person going, in your pocket, without letting anyone other than you and I know that. Give them the task of seeing how far they can stretch the money given. Have a couple of the guys, like maybe Jimmy and Dan, follow us around with a truck of some kind that has protection in case of bad weather, and see what everyone finds. Later, if he needs a larger truck, we can do that too though not sure how good an idea that would be, except to pick up furniture. Seriously, if you are going to do this, it must be done cost-efficiently and well. avHDon't take away the income folks derive from selling, however, do take away the stress, cost, and difficulty of a sale. Anything sold in your store must be clean and repairs done as well as tested for use. No one is to pick up junk. It must be something used in daily living. It is my belief that you will have people who volunteer to help with the duty. If you decide to go ahead with this tell anyone who wants to participate to pick a partner and make it a day, though they are to give us this weekend to try it out," said Shandra.

They laughed when Rae asked if she could choose a partner and go the next week. Mara agreed for her expertise was much needed.

They left early on Friday and Joy was the only one who knew what they planned on doing. Mara wanted to try out this new game before having others join her. It was not long before the message lines were busy. The women were laughing and having fun. Granda was concentrating on toys for the under-five group as well as clothing for them.

At the end of their first day, they picked up some beautiful furniture from estates and acquired collectibles that went to Rae. They also found places where people were moving and wanted to sell all they could to save on the expense of moving.

Toward the end of the afternoon, the two teams came to a large warehouse that was only open one weekend a month. A woman they met at one sale suggested the location.

The proprietor told them that she was indeed only open one weekend a month as she could no longer do the four a month due to health.

"Would you allow us an appointment to visit your store and get familiar with what is here? It is my belief we will purchase enough to make it worth your time. I have some families in need, and there are items here that would benefit them," Mara advised.

"Yes, I can do that. In fact, would be willing to sell you the warehouses and full contents for a given sum. My health is not the best anymore, and my doctor recommended that I move to a warmer climate. The buildings have served me well. However they could use some updating, paint, roofing, perhaps some insulation, and the like," the woman responded with a smile.

"What is your price and how many buildings are involved?" asked Mara.

"There are seven buildings, and some of them have that many connected buildings making them a single unit. If you have someone knowledgeable in internet sales, they can sell a few of the items and make back what you pay inside of a week or two. I never had that expertise and wasn't good at hiring people to do it for me," the woman responded.

"Teams, join me at this location. We have a decision to make," sent Mara.

Soon eleven additional people were inside the warehouse for it would require the leadership team in its entirety.

The owner said her name was Jennie and she asked Mara to step into a small office to speak for she had no idea what must remain between the two of them and what would be known by them all.

"I must have my guard. Meet my daughter Shandra, who watches over me," Mara advised. Every time that Mara introduced Shandra that way a grin appeared on her face.

"No problem, if that is your guard also you can bring them in," said Jennie, and Mara looked outside to see Shira standing by her van. At a signal, the wolf entered the store for a door was left open and she moved to Mara.

Chapter 6

Another estate turned to Mara

Shira lay in the open doorway of the woman's office yet faced out and watched the interior of the warehouse.

"Another has joined our team, Shira is here," Mara sent for she knew it would mean something to her team.

Everyone came in alert and ready for trouble. A quick look around and each found a place out of sight within the warehouse property with some inside and some out.

"Mom, there is stuff here from when this nation began," commented Rae who then explained that while it might not have a draw in their location, it probably would in areas to the East and West of the state. Some could also be donated to historical societies within the area.

The logistics team was a block away waiting to see what their boss required, and Rae was keeping them posted on what she found.

"You have incoming," said Jo as vehicles in convoy headed toward where the Mara group was. She had remained as a backup and was where she could see what was going on without being inside with the rest and her second was there as well for Mara directed that none would move in less than pairs when in public. Fortunately, there was only one road into the area where the warehouse sat.

The vans were moved out of sight when Shira joined them. In fact, Jennie opened a hidden garage door, and they drove the units inside. Throwing a few blankets over one outside made it appear to be part of the junk in the yard. Which left one available if needed. Watching from inside were some of Mara's group.

"I cannot take this with me, need to sell it where is and as is. It has been my income for years, however, now need to pass it to younger minds. It is yours and here is the title for all that I own in this area."

"My goodness, you can't afford to do that!" replied Mara in shock yet she noted that it carried her full legal name.

"Yes, I can. The bank will send me an income each month, and it will last until I am long dead. Please, make use of it, and it is yours."

"I am advised that there is a convoy of people headed here. Not sure if it is business or not, however, wanted you to know. That is also why my team is hidden. Were you expecting company?" asked Mara.

"No, however that is why any income is dropped immediately into a vault below ground. Whoever is coming won't find anything here worth having I would guess," the woman told Mara.

A man cleared the doorway looking for Jennie.

"Hello Jennie, we are here to clean out this place since you don't need it anymore," said the man.

"There is only one way you would have that information and that is if my lawyer gave out the info. Have felt for years he was not as honest as he should have been. Now you can be charged along with your boss and his employees," replied Jennie with a frown.

"Jennie, may I take over here?" asked Mara with a small smile.

"Are you sure? This could get messy," replied Jennie in surprise.

"Cleanup time," said Mara to the lead team connected to her communicator.

"You aren't going to be doing anything about us taking over because if you get excited it will kill you and if it doesn't we will," responded the man with an evil grin for he had not heard their conversation.

"You see, this property does not belong to her. I happen to own it and have the paperwork to prove it," said Mara who had put the original title away in a safe place, by sending it home via Thunder, though she kept a copy with her.

"No woman is going to take from us anything we have had set up for years," the man replied for there were several valuable items hidden within the warehouse that even Jennie didn't know about for the man had gotten a duplicate key for the store to allow them unlimited access. Now that Thunder was aware of the duplicate all locks were immediately changed.

"Team, round them up," said Mara though she remained relaxed before the man who noted as the wolf stood up to allow Mara through the doorway.

The man pulled a weapon from a shoulder holster. However, he never got a chance to fire it for Mara hit him head-on and laid him out flat. A weapon firing in that old warehouse could start a fire that they didn't need. Neither was she going to allow him to shoot Shira, which seemed his intent, though it might have been Jennie.

Mara put the weapon back in the holster. Since she wore gloves, her prints would not be on it though she thought twice about whether to remove the shells or not. Finally, she did so for the fire threat would still be an issue. The bag with the shells was labeled with the serial number of the weapon they had been in.

"Where do you want us to put them?" asked Randy over the communicator for the parking area outside the warehouse was getting full.

"In that open area in front of the building. Am bringing some out from here as well and have someone that I want you to meet," replied Mara.

Shandra stood up the prisoners inside, as soon as they were awake for she got her share as well. They were pushed outside to join the rest of their group.

"Thank you, Jennie. I have a suggestion; you might want to watch and listen. Then you will leave when we do to be sure you are safe. Can you dress as we are?" asked Mara.

"Yes, for that is how I looked when in public," replied the woman and went to change.

Doors to the building were locked, and the keys were given to Mara, once she knew how to access the vault built into a wall in the basement although the woman advised that the contents of the secure room would now belong to Mara. She would need the funds until an income began to build.

When Randy, Shandra, and Mara exited the building with Jennie, they found over one hundred people waiting for them. The felons heard the rules, and the court began after a protective bubble was placed over the area, for homes were too close if this became a shooting match.

While everyone was getting in place, Mara was looking through her memories for a place that might work better for the business she had acquired. Since she now had a full company of carpenters, it would be quickly brought up to code. At the same time, Mara didn't like the location, and the places would need to be emptied to allow the carpenters to remodel any buildings that were salvageable. Mara didn't like the dead-end road that led to the facility, for she felt that any business needed more than one way out. Her decision was that the buildings would require moving, though she wasn't sure to where. By stripping everything, they could make sure electric, insulation, AI, plumbing, windows, doors, and inventory were all addressed.

By the following morning, the snakelike buildings were at a different location with the buildings' contents in a new warehouse nearby for sorting.

"Mom," came a warning from Shandra that she needed to get her mind on the men before her.

She gave a small nod of acceptance and waited for that first shot.

When it came, Shandra was the first to react. She smiled as she returned the shell. Now they could legally call for the court to begin. The lawyer appeared as soon as his name was brought up. That also resulted in a few additions.

Finally, Mara called a halt and Thunder moved the entire proceedings to an empty book. When court ended, they had over a thousand prisoners all with signed confessions, testimony recorded, and all weapons removed for some forensics checks.

"Sis," said Mara.

"When we are home," replied Pat for something told her not to call the Police at that time.

The area around them changed to the warehouse district again though only through Thunder was there enough space to contain them until law enforcement could move them.

"You know we need a football field-sized area where we can place groups for court. It needs to be close to the police station or holding area where they put the ones we contribute. It would save both us and the Officers time and fuel," commented Mara to her guard.

Shandra chuckled for she knew it was already in place. She again thanked the one God for her new mom, the dual personality of Thunder, and that she was part of such an impressive group.

The team looked around and found themselves in a large flat field and to one side sat the police station.

Pat called the station and told the duty officer that they had around a thousand prisoners to be picked up.

"They are in the field behind the station. Where you send them, is up to you. However, the testimonies and confessions are ready as well as many weapons requiring a forensic check. If they are free of criminal activity, we get them back. Otherwise, you do what you must," Pat advised.

The weapons would be turned over to Mara's weapons section where every weapon would be gone over thoroughly once released by the forensic lab at the station. Each weapon was checked, cleaned, and repaired if needed. After they had passed inspection, the arms were secured. Mara did not want weapons hitting the market all at once. Her thought was that time might come when weapons would not be available to the citizens. Therefore, a bunker was in a secret place, and the arms remained stored in a climate-controlled series of rooms sorted by type. Another area carried whatever type of ammunition was needed, solar, arrows, or whatever the requirement was to make the weapons useable.

The weapons were picked up by a man in a van so that Jennie

or anyone else watching would have no idea either what was in the van or where it was going. They also had weapons given to Mara because of the courts they held previously. It would be a busy week getting it all properly inventoried and put away.

One thing that Mara noted was something Jennie did not mention. There was a hidden vault under the warehouse she now owned, and it wasn't the one that Jennie told her was there. This one had a concealed door, difficult to open. The hidden area would be looked at by Mara and Shandra once they had a few minutes. It would take them a while to get it done. She was betting there would be a bit of value in that area. That proved to be the case. In fact, their search also led to where the felons had stored valuable items they didn't want Jennie to find. Rae was flabbergasted when she saw what the men had hidden. It brought in more than Mara paid as income to the entire employed base.

When they returned home at the end of the day, they had a list of purchases that the men had picked up. Four estates became theirs as they had available an extensive collection of antiques. Those were turned over to Rae for her store chain. Mara had a consignment deal with her and received a percentage of what they sold the products for, after expenses. The rest paid for the building and the two clerks who worked there plus additional income for Rae, which she put into improvements for the locations or opening another branch in a different part of the nation.

Jennie was directed to choose a suite for now, and they would see what would need to happen next. Mara didn't want to send the woman home where so many seemed to know that her health was an issue. Randy was advised and asked to see that Jennie had a full physical at the clinic. A report would be needed to determine how to aid this woman who had gifted them with much. They learned from the court that the lawyer and doctor were in cahoots, so the diagnosis was suspect.

Once the first garage sale day ended Mara felt that it was indeed worth doing and she gave the go-ahead to have another outing. Just to have something fun and different to do from time to time made it worth any price.

Mara and Shandra located a business and warehouse for sale.

Rae got it to store items she would liquidate online with help from those she would hire. She also hired an accountant for all enterprises that had to be kept separate as corporations at tax time. Mara learned that many people needed a qualified person to deal with the online liquidation of items they had. A split of the income gained helped both the person requesting and the corporation.

"I want to go garage sale hunting next weekend. Maybe we can come up with something to make our store a little more user-friendly. Spacious, clean, out of the weather and have it open every weekend, or perhaps it would be better to have it open during the week and closed on weekends so that by then we would know what the needs are. I'm sure we can find someone with that kind of expertise," Mara told her guard who would never admit to having the knowledge without a direct order from her.

"Why not set up a revolving duty roster? That way those who want to be buyers can convert to sellers and be part of all phases of what is happening."

Now that Mara had folks thinking, she could allow that to generate new ideas while she dealt with the day-to-day requirements for her growing family. There was always training to keep proficiency. New people to break in and emergency calls from someplace.

Finally, she scheduled a meeting for Thursday morning at seven in the conference room in her suite. A man that none of them knew, except Mara, was sitting quietly by Jimmy, at Mara's request.

"Okay folks, here is what is going on: we are going to try something. Each pair will be in a vehicle. Jimmy and Dan will have one vehicle, a delivery truck. I have Shandra and Kennet with me. Alina is going with Granda and would prefer that Randy goes with them too. That means Russel goes there also. Now let's stop here. Are any of you against the idea so far?" Mara advised the teams to take the big vans, cargo vans, with seats removed to allow more people to travel together and still have room for what they bought.

"What is going on Boss lady?" asked Jimmy with a smile.

"We are sending you all out to work estate and garage sales. You will have an expense account of two hundred dollars. We are taking the sixteen passenger vans, so we have room for those of us going and still have room to carry what we purchase, except for big stuff. You, sir, will be out in a truck so that if we purchase something of size, you can pick it up for us, would that work? At the same time, there is a list of items we would like you to watch for in your travels. They relate to tools that are new, next to new, or have a lifetime guarantee. The section covering those items can get them replaced if they have a guarantee and are damaged. There will be a lot of sales not listed for people to ride free on the ads of others due to cost. What that means is one person advertises in the news that they are having a sale, and individuals in the neighborhood have sales at the same time without putting an ad in the sales area. If you see a sale that is not on the list, stop, for it might have some good buys or what you are looking for."

"Not a problem, I like those things. Where is that electronics person? We need wires so that we can let one another know what we find because one house may have all Christmas stuff, and another might have nothing but Halloween while one of your seekers will be looking for children's clothing in various sizes. You have no idea what fun you will have at Christmas doing it this way," replied Jimmy with enthusiasm for he had worked the sales that way to have products on hand at Christmas for those who had little to nothing.

"If you find a bargain of some kind, like a garage full of collectibles which would work well in an antique shop, new books, etc., then let central know, and if it is needed someone with knowledge of that requirement will go get it. We discovered that if a family is downsizing, you can probably buy out the whole thing for a set price if you feel it is worth whatever they are asking. Don't buy out a sale unless you need everything they are selling. Keep in mind that there are others who also need what we will be looking for unless we need most of what is on sale. I went to one sale where a family was shivering in the cold and were worried for the husband had to be at a new job out of state in two days, and he wanted to take his family with him due to having only one vehicle. In that case, see if we can pay for our time to pick it up and help them. If it seems like something we can make a profit or pay expenses on, then it needs to be purchased. Be sure to call in the address as well, or it will cost you your expense account. Another idea is if you get a full load, any of you, call for someone to bring you a vehicle like you have and that vehicle will be taken to the GS location and unloaded for the next requirement," said Shandra with a grin.

"Who is central?" asked Mara.

"We have a woman who broke her leg. It is now working, however, due to the way it broke, she wears a supporting cast, and isn't supposed to be walking around on it for at least a year. Sit her in front of a communication device with a computer, and she will give you information about what is happening and who is spending what where. In fact, your computer system might be willing to do the task though I think it is best to keep your various enterprises separate. Pat can have one of her computer techs build a computer just for this purpose. Each of you needs a copy of the Classified section of every paper for the week with a map, for not all addresses are given on the map of sales for it costs more. Also, if you see someone who needs to liquidate everything due to moving, household needs, and the like, ask them for the leftovers when their sale is over, or depending on their needs you might just purchase outright. Keep in mind the leftovers might not be something we want, however, if, for instance, it is clothing and that is what we need, then take the leftovers. We can repurpose them to be useable. We don't want to wipe out anyone unless they need to be doing something else," Shandra advised.

"Would each of you please keep an eye out for young couples that are looking for something specific and the price exceeds what they can afford? Now I am talking about others who are buying at the garage sales too. Get an address for them, and the item can be delivered at no cost if they will allow it," advised Mara.

They had their marching orders, and each called out what they would cover such as a building to sort things in, and who would get the printouts from the computers. Everyone needed to have water and a snack with them so who would purchase cases of water and snacks? In no time, the teams departed the house if they had duties waiting. For some reason, about a dozen estate sales were going on, and they started on that day. Therefore, they were on their way.

"Now see what you did. You gave us something fun to do, and the rest of the work will get ignored," Mara laughed.

"No, it won't they will get it done quickly to go on another treasure hunt. You need to look at who needs what you find. There are areas where none of the kids have school clothes and supplies. How about large families whose income is not meeting their needs? Some could be left there. Put some away in emergency kits for families who are burned out or in some other disaster. Make it all useable items, not junk, and to do that suggest some folks take the duty of cleanup, fixup, and repair. In fact, you can pick up a lot of school supplies in the late summer for those who will need them once school starts. How about for a family with a medical situation and their entire family shows up the day before Thanksgiving from the South and has no coats, hats, gloves, or boots let alone money, food, or even transportation? Those kinds of things need setup. We have done this for years where I used to live. It seems like I forget something since we don't do it anymore. Please, will you try it until the end of this year? Keep track of who was helped just between us. See if it is worth doing. It isn't always about the money; it is about making folks and kids feel they have value. Have you thought about Christmas and Birthdays for this bunch you have adopted?"

"No, I try to spend time with them and meet their needs plus let them know they are loved and welcomed. Timewise that is often all I can do. Don't want my kids to be so much into material things, yet they need to know how to use things like technological gadgets: computers, book readers, and the like. Pat, come in please," directed Mara.

"Here," came an immediate response.

"Just had a thought and am not sure how valid it is. I don't want a lot of items we will never use. At the same time how about setting up a technological center and if those who work there want to have computers they can teach others how to tear them down and make them work for kids who are just learning within our workforce, whether to repair or program. Would you be willing, or have the time to, take over such a task? I don't want you to do it yourself, just get it started and find those with the talent to keep it going," asked Mara.

"No problem. Okay, it will soon be ready for the rebuilding crew. Remember that old school that is vacant at Pinehurst and Century? It is made of brick and has a lot of space inside. I just purchased it. The carpenters could revamp the inside to be sure it has the power that will be needed for our people to be trained and make it self-supporting. There needs to be solar and satellite connections to keep down energy costs as well as security overall. It covers a lot of acres and has many buildings on the property. We will need to have a way to liquidate what is not useable, though a lot will be broken down to use the parts and I have someone who would jump at that chance just to know what is available. Then we can put out a list of possible training available to our groups. You have horse shows why not have those who can train in riding or riding equipment maintenance? We will participate when we can. However, we also will need backup in case of other requirements. Then there are the planes. Some need to learn to fly similar ones, especially the helicopters and small jets. Training would be required though it might be best to do that at the private airfield. The leather man is training those who want to make things as he does, and we could have this school utilized just for the training of various kinds of requirements. Allow a certain percentage of students that are not part of our group and offer them scholarships if they can't afford the classes. The rest would have to be part of our employee base to be allowed to attend as the startup group," began Pat.

"Sis, you don't have that kind of money," said Mara in surprise for this sounded like a massive undertaking to her.

"Ah, you are wrong. Remember I own a ranch, received an inheritance before joining you and it too needs put to work since the ranch is self-supporting. Have you looked at my income of late? I have tried to get involved in whatever you start. Now there is a high demand for the horses raised on the ranch that used to be mine. The base group that works on AI installation and security has been allowed to spread their wings some plus it will allow us to keep our technology up to date at a better price, and the list goes on. It is all bringing in income for you and me both."

"Pat, you must know that what I own, so do you. Why do you feel you must pay your way? You bless me just by being who you are," said Mara with a frown though she had placed a security bubble over the conversation.

"Sis, I have always earned my way, and in this case, it is for love not for a paycheck. My life got an entirely new start because of you. Let me contribute to what you are doing because it is something that needs to be done and benefits not only ourselves but others. Please let me do my part when I can that adds to and doesn't take from our base. You have no idea how much this gal loves getting up in the morning just to see what will happen that day. This property will be the same as any other property under you. My guess is you will make a corporation of the school and training offered there though this time it will be purchased from my account. Now another issue to discuss."

"I spoke with a person met over by the stadium. She wanted to know who owned the place. When I asked why she said she wanted to work for whoever that was. Now, she is here with me though far enough away to not hear our conversation and asleep courtesy of T. From what I understand about her she wants to learn and is alone. She has a high school education though that is all she was allowed. When her schooling ended, in fact, that day, her parents packed up and left while she was at school. A note wished her well and left her a one-hundred-dollar bill. Would you be willing to speak with her in person?" asked Pat.

"You know I will. Where are you?" asked Mara.

"At the new school, we are discussing, and signing some papers, could you meet us there?" Pat wanted to know for her preference was that Mara signs for everything though they would share throughout their lifetimes.

"We will be there as soon as the meeting I'm in is over for there are a couple of requests for you as well," responded Mara then leaving her comm line to Pat open she finished the garage sale meeting.

"Okay, I have another call. Shandra and I are needed elsewhere. Work with what you have. The technology aids will be in place by next time. For now, we have run out of time," Mara advised.

The teams departed to begin this new task and started with estate sales for those events would be only on the dates advertised most likely.

They went to the address that Pat had given Mara and found her waiting. By her side was a young girl of maybe seventeen, thought Mara.

"Hello Sis, what are you up to?" asked Mara.

"Ran into a young woman would like you to meet. Shaniah, this is my twin, Mara. Please tell her what you said to me. Oh, the second woman is her daughter and guard, Shandra. I am Pat."

"I had a feeling that my life was about to change yet not in the way it did. I went to school to pick up my diploma for I finished all classes in the middle of the last school year, yet the principal would not give me my recognition until this school year due to my age. When I showed up as directed, he shoved a piece of paper at me and said good luck. Went home to show the folks I had graduated and found a note lying on the table. Here it is," she handed Mara the note to which was attached a one-hundred-dollar bill.

[You have passed, per the principal, and will receive your diploma today. Now you are on your own. The house rent is up today, so you have until midnight to move elsewhere. This money should help you get started someplace. Good luck, the Gigamores.]

"What a strange way to sign. Is that your parent's name?"

"They had a different slant on life and used that as a way of closing out a contact. Now I have hours in which to locate a place to live. It is my desire to learn, and a voice in my head said to come here and speak with whoever I saw. Pat was who came," the girl told them.

"A home and further education is not a problem," said Mara upon receiving a nod from Pat who had her hand in the air to check out the girl.

"Really? You mean I heard, right?"

"Yes, we will even adopt you since these folks gave up their rights by what they did. Have you any belongings to pick up where you were living?" asked Mara.

"Not much, I have a few clothes though all are second-hand. Have a guitar that I like to play and a few books. That is about it. They took everything else, and I can leave that behind. Would like to keep my diploma to prove I graduated and that is all. Did you say adopt? Oh yes, I was never chosen to start with, and it would have made life so much better," Shaniah said.

"Pat, you wanted me to sign some papers as I recall. Shandra would you keep an eye on Shaniah while we handle business?" asked Mara in private sending to her twin and guard.

"No problem," replied Shandra with a smile for she knew that meant that they needed more information than the girl had given.

A realtor departed her vehicle when the woman finished speaking.

"Okay, Jake says the property is clear of all encumbrances. Taxes are current, all repairs are completed, and you can take possession today if you like. Here is the paperwork for you to look at," she advised the twins.

Mara read the document and with eyes sparkling she signed where required. They had just added two hundred acres of land, and the property had one residence plus a dozen or more outbuildings that would become training centers for various requirements. She was not concerned about the price for it had been on the market for quite some time and she knew what its value was. The asking price was about half of the market value.

- - - - - -

Shandra was watching around the area in case of problems while at the same time she was visiting with the newest addition.

"Did the twins mean that, that they would really and truly adopt me? Why would they do that?" the girl asked.

"Because they can, because you asked, and you are by no means the first to do so. Pat said you want to learn. What do you have in mind?" asked Shandra.

"I always wanted to learn languages, as many as possible. Want to know how to ride a horse properly, train a guard dog, ride a train, fly in an airplane, be wanted someplace, and have folks that love me for me, not for what they can get out of me in some way," replied the youngster.

"I don't see any problem with any of that. Do you currently know any foreign languages, or how to do those things you have in mind?" asked Shan.

"Well... I can read, write, and speak Spanish, French, German, and English. No one knew I could do that though as I took the courses online using the money I earned. Even sent for some of those special training aids and had them sent by General Delivery so that no one knew when I got them. Had to do it at the library so that no one knew what I did. Been on a horse a couple of times yet can't say I know how to ride. Trains and planes are things I have read about yet never been on either. Training dogs, horses, and kids would be fun I think. Only want them to know that my goal is to help them learn not hurt them," explained the young woman who had been hurt far too often in her life.

Shandra changed the language used each time she asked another question of the girl.

"Do you have any desire to see a foreign country?" German.

"It would be great. However that kind of money was never available," the girl replied in kind.

"Do you have a passport?" French.

"No, however, I don't have a criminal record so that shouldn't be a problem," French.

"Do you know folks who speak any of the languages you say you know?" Spanish.

"Only you," she replied with a smile.

"You have been adopted by my mom, Mara. All three of us speak those languages, and we also speak many others for we need them in taking care of those who work for us," responded

Shandra.

"Pat said you were a guard for Mara. Why does she need a guard?"

"All of us need to be defended because it is our duty to enforce the law wherever we see it broken. Thus, many people wish to eliminate any of us they can find," Shandra told her.

"Then teach me to guard as well. Of all the things, I have dreamed of, being part of a loving family has been first on my list. I graduated top of my class, yet no one cared. They wouldn't even allow me to get the diploma with the rest of those in my class. I'm surprised that the principal even gave me an award, was afraid he might not. Wasn't even allowed at my graduation," though it was said in a matter-of-fact tone, not as one looking for any sympathy. She even showed Shandra the document to prove she spoke the truth.

"There will be some changes in your life due to your trusting us to do what we say we will. Mom told me you are adopted, and you are. Learning will follow and knowing her you will see your dreams realized over time. Wait here a moment," said Shandra who moved off to speak with Mara.

Chapter 7

When theory becomes the truth

"Mom, I have a feeling that it is important to not go to this girl's home. Would you be willing to send for her stuff and have it delivered to our home immediately or would it be best to leave it all where it is, with fingerprints removed, and replace what is left behind? Otherwise, we might be bringing a Trojan home. She said she could leave everything behind. She would like to get a newer guitar when she can afford one. I have no problem with it being put in my suite until we get home yet feel a disquiet in my spirit for some reason," commented Shandra.

"We will leave it all behind. Yes, I agree. We need to get this waif to the ranch and as one of us before they come looking for her. It may not be those who raised her for a time, however, whoever seeks her will not be allowed to find her," replied Mara.

As soon as the realtor finished the paperwork, Mara and Pat departed in different directions. Each had guards, and each of them headed home. The new girl was told to lie down in the back seat, which she did immediately. When they reached home, they found her sound asleep which seemed to be the sleep of pure exhaustion. They found her dressed as they were and a new guitar laying on the floor by where she slept. On top of it was her graduation certificate.

When Shaniah awakened, it was to become Lynn for she said it was a name she always liked. She admitted that she had not been sleeping well lately and was exhausted. The clothing she wore was new, and she noticed that though it was as if it had become hers just before falling asleep.

Since everyone had completed University testing, except for her, she was given a cosmetic makeover and taken to the University for testing. Mara loved watching her as she passed each exam. When it was all done, they returned home on their mounts. Shandra rode with Mara as always, and they chuckled at how well the youngster now rode. Her eyes sparkled, and she was heard to chuckle from time to time. Just for fun, they spoke with her in the various languages each of them knew. The youngster could not seem to learn fast enough, and she was so thrilled with all she now knew.

- - - - - -

Everything the garage sales furnished, that was not personal, was taken to the new GS warehouse and broken down as to types of products. Mara had called this their test day, and from there she would decide if the adventure would continue or not. New, almost new, then by use: kitchen, bedroom, tools, dishes, clothing for everyone in the family, then holiday items. They hadn't been there long when Rae showed up with her Logisticians who had been left at the newly owned warehouses to note what was there, not to do the work, which would happen later. Soon that day's purchases were sorted, and a meeting was called for the following day. It was getting late in the day and supper would be ready. There were two more days to get all sales covered, so folks had two options. They could sort, fix, or go out and find.

"Since you have the bank and warehouse done, thought we would work on some other requirements. We now have a lot of folks in our employ. They need access to cost-effective products from the area. Thought we would open a company store at the new location. The only way we sell new is if we get a deal like a store closing, surplus in stores, or things from a boxed lot store. Want a variety, however, don't want to spend a lot of money for that savings needs passed on to our customers, once we pay expenses. Need to see if this is doable. Would you be willing to test drive it for me if I do the shopping?" asked Mara though she knew they had ended up with four vacant business buildings with warehouses on the property for she knew they would be needed.

"Most definitely, also I know of a dozen people who love to buy this way and are sharp at finding deals. Give them a list of what you are looking for, and they will be in heaven. Set a budget for them and have a bundle of papers dropped here every Thursday and Friday. Map where the sales are and send them out. They can return here with what they don't wish to keep, and we will sort it and put it away as directed," said an excited Rae who loved sales.

"A few changes there for I understand that the sales are now online, and maps are available the same way. Pat will have them placed on the garage sales computer system. We can each have the info posted to our wristbands and not have something else to carry. At least one person in each vehicle should have a connection to one of us. Can also put notes on those that were a bad experience. It means that whoever is recorder will carry a second contact for Pat is setting up a GS computer that will keep track of just the sales, whether an estate or regular. Okay, that means we three teams will be out shopping the weekends we don't have a show. Sunday is Church and Fellowship, which means taking folks home to get acquainted. Try to help some of those in the community that needs help. Prefer that it be done quietly so that no one is offended or greedy," Mara advised then she stopped to look at something in her memory.

"Speaking of help, we now own a training center. It will have a computer training section for sure, which brought up pilot training, horseback riding, hand-to-hand, etc. Therefore we need to look at Peter also having a place there for ranch running unless he is covered best by teaching at the U. We already have the leather business." Mara stopped to think.

"Don't think about weapons for that has to be in a very secure location and is. If anyone comes across weapons, and it does happen, you let central know and some of your weapon masters can go check it out. Also, training of your personnel should happen there," advised Shandra.

"Mom?" said Cherry.

"Yes."

"Please, can we maybe do the nearby towns? They must have sales as well and need the added income. We will leave the in-town ones here to the teams you already have and concentrate on the small towns nearby which will help them in sales as well as give us an idea of those who live around us. All the adult Quads want to join the fun. Pat says her too plus she will have the base set by next weekend," Cherry added.

"In town, teams are Shandra, Kennet, and Mara; Granda, Randy, Russel, and Alina; Rae must remain in town unless something special comes up and can pick her partner. Cherry, would you mind adding a new one named Lynn and overseeing the out-of-town teams in each area? Also, there will be six unnamed ones that Rae will assign to do different parts of town using directions like North, South, East, and West as areas. The rest of the lead group will hold down the fort so that if something happens at home, we can get there quickly. The rest of you chose your partners and have fun, though keep your travel within a reasonable distance of maybe forty miles and make sure you have competent guards for whoever is on your team."

She paused to gather her thoughts. After all, she wanted a diversion, and one had come along.

"Mara, the new computer will have sections for auctions, estates, and Garage sales by category to make stuff easier to keep track of. Have teams working on it now. We will put them on an AI so that we all have the information immediately whether right or wrong also it will allow our pickup teams to know where we are all the time. All you must do is push a receive button, and it will note where each of us is. That way we have our database to keep track of who has regular sales, where the best deals are etc. Also, if we come across one that we don't want to ever return to, that will be noted as well. Keep in mind that people often have sales because they are moving, and the next homeowner might have them get rid of excess when moving in, which will be in the notes. If someone is advertising and we find it is a home business, be cautious. We do not want to challenge those who had that kind of business. Maybe purchase just an item or two to find out what is going on. One I just learned about is people who purchase storage lockers then have sales where they live. Those need to be noted also for they usually have sales two or three weekends a month. Some of their purchase sites are out of town so they close for those times. Don't rule out store sales too. At the end of a season, there can be some good buys there as well if we have an idea of what the average price would be for the items advertised as being on sale. Then if someone hits a sale that is sold out or had nothing we are interested in, everyone will know and bypass that one. It will show estate sales versus garage sales too," Pat offered for she wanted to participate as well.

Pat didn't recall ever having been to one before. Besides, she had people, trained in setting up a computer, and they seemed ready for this new challenge. A few of her team went to sales with the others to watch for things that would work for the training of her group in repairing, replacing, and recycling what was found relating to technology.

"Mara, play dumb, it will get you a better price, and always haggle for a lower price. It is part of the game," advised Shandra though all the leading team heard the message.

"No problem there, only know what you have told me about them. I want some fun and think we have reached a time where we can do that. Kid's clothing is always needed so pick up what is in useable condition. We may have to assign people to wash what we get plus do a bit of mending here and there. It seems many who sell things can't afford soap and don't know how to sew," Mara advised for she had done a little research and asked a few questions of her family. She was amazed at how many of them were garage sale addicts.

"Family, please, remember that we only have September to work the garage sales for we have a horse show the first weekend in October and it will require the full day most likely for the animals must be moved early on Saturday, maybe even during the night if we put guards on them. That, however, will be on Saturday only which means if the sales are there we can go out Thursday and Friday. The following weekend we can go out weather permitting then it will be a Saturday as a family band. It is coming close to the end of the sale season for garage sales. However, that is when the craft shows begin. After the Family Band, we will load up and take a flight to Tennessee where Becky is setting up an art show to allow us to see what is available in the eastern part of the nation. Put your thinking caps on and keep me advised," Mara told her group.

The following morning Pat received a call from the Chief of Police. He requested a meeting with Thunder. The message was recorded by the AI and sent to Mara. Pat joined the two women at Mara's request. They rode together in one van. Pat drove, and they were on the way.

When they reached the Station, a patrol car sat in front of the building. The Chief exited his vehicle once Pat was identified.

"Hello Pat, thank you for making the connection. We need to meet someplace private, however for there is some new information that you should know," he explained.

Mara knew by the look on his face that it was a bit of good and a bit of bad for he was keeping all facial expressions under control and even turned off his communicator when in her area. Since Mara shared her thoughts with her twin all were aware of what was going on.

"In that case how about taking a ride with us? Your mode of transportation is a bit obvious in this case," chuckled Pat.

"Glad you understand. Thank you," the Chief responded and climbed into the front seat by Pat.

"Remove your hat and jacket please," directed Mara.

He did as she said. They stopped before what looked like a bank building. Mara took out keys to unlock it, and Pat immediately checked it for recording devices though she knew that an AI was in control at that location. Mara spoke into the speaker on her jacket which caused the relay to open.

Once inside they moved to a conference room that had glass on three sides which allowed them to see the entire inside room.

"Now, Chief what can we do for you?" asked Pat for in any law-involved meetings she would be in control unless Mara chose to take over.

"This last batch you sent to us has caused some waves. Can you possibly take over all the inheritance immediately? Our underground tells us that some heavy hitters are involved and headed this way to claim what is now yours," he sat quietly waiting for a response.

"It has been removed. Thank you for the warning. Would you please explain?" asked Mara after Pat nodded her way.

"Thunder, it was never my intent to meet you this way. For the safety of you and your group, you might want to disappear for a while. Assassins are on their way. Some people have been asking questions at the station, about who you are and your location. Our response is we have no idea. The officers on my staff have all taken oath from you and will not disclose anything about you. That includes those who answer phones and work in our business offices. I directed it once we knew you would not use us, and that you were only protecting your own. Each time you call for pick up some of those folks were included to take the oath from you. Everyone has sworn to keep you safe, and you can feel secure about the Police Force. We have screened everyone on staff in any form to be sure that this is not an empty promise. Those weapons you turned over have been traced to several felonies including murder. Thank you for matching up the arms with the person who used them."

He paused to think and wait for questions.

"Chief, why have you taken us entirely on faith? You are correct. However, I wish to know the reason," responded Mara though Thunder was who they heard.

"Do you recall a ranch you inherited when you began business? An elderly couple owned it and left no heirs. They were friends of my family, and you sent us their killers. That was when I called everyone together and suggested that if they heard the name Thunder to make sure they took the oath with them. Since then, you have met and sworn in all of us. Now the public cannot know about that, or it would seem you control us. Those who work for me know better. Here is a list of the known assassins looking for you. Received a call from contacts in the East, and they said to relay to you some other information. That was when I found out that all Police and Sheriffs' offices in the Nation have been advised to take oath from your folks if they have occasion to work with you though only another such group knows that. A flight is scheduled to arrive here in four hours. Those aboard will tell you they are businessmen and women; however, it is a private fleet of four planes and their sole reason for coming is to find you. That translates to about a hundred agents coming," he explained.

"Silence," directed Thunder and the man sat as if asleep.

"What is your plan Mara?" asked Thunder and the Monarch spoke in response.

"We must keep the HB hidden. To remove them is to tell the whole world who they are. I'm not willing to do that. They are all gainfully employed and have name changes which should protect them. The ranches are under Corp names and those adopted there are also under different names. That will not give the adversaries a starting place in those areas. The Hospital and Clinic are also under Corp without our names entering the mix which will protect them, and they too are oath sworn. The bank we use has many branches and is another Corp. Our people utilize those facilities to make it easier and more secure to keep everyone paid without leaving a trail to anyone. That should have them covered and protected. Next Saturday we have a concert at the Stadium though it has been changed a time or two, due to other people being available suddenly. A week or so after that we will have a riding show in the arena. It will be this group, and we change our persona for whatever we do that is public. Hopefully, that will block that avenue of research. It has always been my practice to not identify with anyone unless they are oath sworn to you and thereby to me. There are managers at all our homes in other states and countries. They too are oath sworn. If you have any suggestions I am willing to learn," Mara replied.

"You have done well, just wanted you to realize what you have done. This bunch will not find you or any of those you employ or call family. The fact that none of you are the ages reported will make it even more confusing for them. None of those you have held court for could describe any of you, where you live, or anything else that might leave a trail to you. I do believe that you need to hold court for those who are coming as well if you have the opportunity. Someone sent them word as to where you are. We need to find out where that leak is and stop it."

"We will do our best," replied Mara who could easily hear Thunder's comments since both entities dwelled within her.

The Police Chief was released from silence and never realized he had a short nap.

"Thank you for the information. Will see what we can do. Have you any other information to share?" asked Mara.

"Need to let you know that I will be retiring at the end of the month. My twenty years will be up, and my mandatory retirement ordered," the Chief responded.

"No, that isn't going to happen. With those that are incoming, it is necessary that we do not give anyone a means to get to us. Having your position open would do that. Who directed the retirement?" asked Mara.

"The Mayor," he replied in surprise.

"We may have our leak," commented Mara who then called for the man to join them.

"Hello Mayor, we have an appointment as I recall," said Mara.

"I saw that and wondered what you wanted," he replied with a frown.

"Just a little matter of a group of folks you sent for and wondering why," replied Mara.

"What group? I never asked for anyone," he responded although a flash of fear went through his eyes.

"Mayor are you armed?" asked Mara though she already knew the answer.

"No one would dare injure me, why should I wear weapons?" he asked belligerently.

"You don't consider that single shot pea shooter as a weapon?" asked Mara.

"No, it is preventative maintenance," he replied.

In that instant, she knew what he was up to and what he had already done. Now it was necessary to get it as his confession, though the entire conversation was on a recording. Shandra had moved to the door where she stood guard to allow Mara to do what needed to be done, at her request.

"A weapon is a weapon regardless of size, how hidden, or its intended use. Any guns you carry will be removed and placed on the table by you," directed Thunder immediately.

Before the Mayor had figured out even what she wanted, there were three weapons in the center of the table, for two more joined the first one. Each carried two shots.

"May I see your permit to carry these items?" asked the Chief.

"Don't need one. I'm the mayor and need these things to keep my person secure," the man replied.

"Now how about removing those knives you also carry," directed Mara with an amicable resolution. This man would be put out of business if she had her way, and she would.

Those weapons joined the first three.

"Mom, jewelry might be an idea as well," sent Shandra in a whisper to her Mom.

"The silver goes as well," directed Mara with a nod of appreciation that was barely seen and only by her guard would know what it meant.

As the pile grew a protective bubble was placed over it so that the Mayor could add to the stack yet, he could not remove anything. Suddenly the Mayor jerked erect, and his mouth flew open. Mara was equally as quick and had a device in her hand that checked out his teeth. She removed three teeth that were removable caps and under each was a lethal pill.

The Mayor was shaking by that time. All his preparations had no effect on this woman and it had him scared. Finally, he had met his match.

"Time for some information, start with your name, next comes a list of everything you own, followed by every offense you have ever committed. Before we start you need to know that anything you say will be on the record," Mara said to him.

He did as he was told to though it was evident he was trying not to say anything. The list was long and would have taken a significant amount of time done the usual way, however with Thunder in the mix the report was complete in a matter of minutes. The documents were signed, and it was all placed with the Chief.

"That should put a cap on it all. Those who were to come from the East will no longer be coming. They have engine trouble in all units plus none of them can remember where they were going. You will remain as Police Chief, and a new Mayor will need to be elected. Have you any suggestions?" asked Mara.

"With your permission, would suggest Gregory Joeson. He has the expertise to do the job, is honest, and has commented to me privately that he admired whoever was cleaning up this area, which would be you. Don't take my word for it, though, check him out entirely if you will and while you are at it check me as well. You need to know who you are working with and that they have the welfare of our citizens as their top priority," replied the Chief.

"I did that when you called for us to meet you," smiled Mara.

She saw the Chief as another that could be fully trusted and it was suggested by Thunder.

"We know exactly where you stand and your entire background. You have beat all odds going from a street rat to Police Chief. We are so appreciative of your service. Keep up the good work. When you are ready to retire, give me a call. There is a way you can continue doing what you do, for any amount of time you wish, though it would have to be your wish."

"Per the city laws, which this idiot put in the legal form, whoever takes his slot must retire me," responded the Chief.

"Do you have a name you particularly like?"

"Yes, my birth name was Michael Rogers. I quit using it when I began using the string of alias used in my lifetime. In fact, let's reverse it to make it harder to find me. I'm Roger Michaels."

"Would you like to resume it? You would have to apply for the job you now hold under that name."

He looked a little puzzled followed by a face-splitting grin, and they were thankful the Mayor had no idea what was going on around him.

"Remove all wires, recording devices, satellites, and anything not a natural part of the former Mayor's body," directed Thunder with a roar.

Devices flew from the Mayor to the table. Fortunately, no electronics would work in Thunder's presence. Another man appeared before Mara. He was tall, lean, and clean-shaven. He was dressed neatly yet not overdone. His hair was gray, yet the twinkle in his eye said he had a lot of life left in him.

"I am Gregory Joeson, called Greg, and think you sent for me so that I might know you when you need my services," said the man.

"I am Thunder, you are going to be an excellent Mayor," the female Thunder told him with a laugh.

"That is my intent. It's a job I always wanted because I didn't like the way others were doing the duty yet never felt that qualified," Gregory Joeson replied.

"You have taken over that office. You will need to clean it out carefully for your predecessor was far from being anything considered honest. A few people need to have new trials for he manipulated their incarceration. If you let me know when you have the list, some sentences will be corrected. Oh, never mind I have it. Would you like to attend a court Thunder style?" asked Thunder.

"Yes."

"Then let's be about it. Thunder Team to join us," sent Thunder.

The room they were in enlarged as the lead group of Thunders answered her summons. People began dropping into the room until it had all it could hold then they felt a stretching, and the room grew to again accommodate those within.

Everyone was oath-sworn, and the AI made sure that all gave it. When Mara heard, she called for court though asked that Pat take the call for it required her expertise.

Her twin laughed and wondered why switch now since Mara was doing a good job thus far it sure didn't need her to finish it up.

"I am biased. I would like to put the former mayor in a book and leave him there, however you won't do that so, please take it from here," smiled Mara.

"Very well, the court is now in order. Is the prosecutor here?" she asked.

Randy stepped up and replied "Yes."

By the time court was over both Mayor and Chief had seen Thunder in action and this time instead of incarcerating folks they were being set free. The proof documents were in the hands of the new Chief.

"By the way, you are now twenty-one and will be for the remainder of your life. Get your application in immediately for you both to start work tomorrow. Every twenty years you must choose a new name and reapply or repeal the law the former Mayor put on the books," laughed Mara for all except her Thunder Team, the Chief, and the Mayor were no longer in the room.

"Did I misunderstand you? Are we both the same age now? Can we continue to hold these positions any amount of time we like? Who are you that you can do this with a thought?" asked the new Mayor Gregory Joeson who felt he had missed something.

"She is Thunder," replied Roger Michaels who knew the oath would protect her.

"In that case, I withdraw my comment," responded the new Mayor with a big smile.

The new Mayor Gregory Joeson returned to where he had been though Mara wished to speak with the Chief before taking him to the Station.

"Chief, here is a secure phone. It won't work for anyone except you. If you have further information for us call and we will meet as we did this time. It limits who knows of our contact. When it affects the citizens of this state, we need to know and try to take care of the problem before it grows."

"It will be my honor and thank you for cleaning up this mess before it became any bigger. We do not need the kind of trouble that bunch would have generated just by being here," he responded honestly.

"Agreed, now we need to return to duty, and you do as well," Mara told him.

The team was Thunder returned to finish their interrupted

tasks while Shandra and Mara took the Chief back to work.

They dropped the Chief at his vehicle.

Mara asked Shandra if she would mind a side trip.

"Not at all since we seldom get the time that doesn't have demands," replied Shandra.

"Well, this will have demands, however, think it needs to be taken care of before we go home," Mara advised her daughter and instantly had her interest and attention.

Mara drove to a nearby park, and the two of them went for a walk. When Thunder spoke to Shandra, she knew that whatever was nearby.

"Mom, what do you think of the new man?"

"Depends on which one you are referring to, your new father or the two new guys and by the way when do you plan on selecting? Goodness knows enough have asked," Mara chuckled.

"No one would want to marry an ole gal like me," commented Shandra without thought.

"Look again dear one, old?"

"Oops, well..."

"Randy is getting married, and we will be in the same ceremony. Make your choice and join us. Hear a rumor that Pat will also be in the mix. Even Granda will be joining us. Our Pastor will be marrying us as the lead group will be the ones getting married, unless they already are."

"Oh, what fun, let me see..." then Shandra stopped, and Thunder looked around her as they walked. She loved the seasons in Montana. It was fall, and there was a chill in the air. It felt like it might rain which was usually a preparation for winter.

"Twice at two," said Mara.

"Got them. Also, twice at eight," responded Shandra.

"I'll take my pair."

"I'll handle the other two though I'm betting we will have others join them."

"Should be within our capabilities," commented Mara.

A smile was her only answer.

Before Mara could ask she noted that her main team was appearing around the park, though they seemed to be just going for a walk, walking a dog, running, reading a paper, and such. She did chuckle a bit when she saw Randy and Russel sitting on a park bench near them. Jimmy and Kennet were playing Frisbee with Gigot within twenty feet.

Those that had already been identified by Mara and Shandra were soon out of commission. Everyone in the park was involved. Kennet took roll call and said they had three hundred twenty-two prisoners.

Mara turned the trial over to Randy and took her guard position.

"This Thunder court is now in session," called Randy.

Pat was the prosecutor.

Mara noted that the secure shell, which not only protected but blocked out the external sound around them was being hit rapidly by enemy fire. She reverted to Thunder, and though the court continued she moved to one side and asked for an opening in the shell, and as she stepped through, she felt Shandra with her. Since Pat was part of the group judging, as was Randy, the inside would be in good hands, or so they felt.

"I don't understand how they know this much about how we operate. We need to have the minds of all we have put in prison checked. Somehow something remained in their memory that should not have. Do we have a leak by new additions of any kind?" Mara asked Thunder.

Once Thunder advised them that the leak was gone, they moved on.

The two women moved in the direction the projectiles seemed to be coming from using any cover they could find. Neither stopped moving toward the area as they whispered into the mikes each carried or used hand signals to show intent. Suddenly Shandra dropped, and Mara followed her lead. They crept closer and closer to the place where the firing seemed to be originating. When they felt that they were in line with the noise, they moved behind it and came from the back. The shooting continued.

"Mom, they are doing this to trap us. Can you Thunder us gone?" asked Shandra in a soft whisper.

"Yes, however, it might affect those in the court. Let me try something else," replied Mara who directed that the gun location, to include those using the weapons, be moved to an empty book.

Chapter 8

Finding her balance

As they looked around them, it was easy to see what was going on. All that remained were the weapons set up on a rapid-fire computer aimed at any large group of people. The pair captured those who were now in the book world. Once the felons were secured, the women moved to check on the weapons. They quickly disconnected the lines and leaving the machine guns where they were the pair returned to the site of the court.

No sooner did they land than they were under fire. The two females moved to a frontal assault and once out of sight dropped to the ground **and did not move although now each had** picked places where there was some cover, and they were near one another.

"The court is done. Law enforcement should be here soon," commented Mara though she was watching all around the area.

Shandra began to move. She was like a mist before a wind.

Mara remained in place and occasionally fired though it was usually at the ground. It was imperative that she not injure her daughter. She never thought that in doing that she was allowing her adversary to locate her.

The shot caught her unaware, and she dropped like one dead.

Everyone became silent.

"Mom?" whispered Shandra.

"Hit," was all she could manage.

"Thunder call, leader down," said Shandra into her speaker and the area erupted with people and animals.

Law enforcement, helicopters, horses, plus the entire core

group were moving inward from one mile out, and they were moving quickly for the horses picked up their riders and were on the move in a trained pattern toward the center. The military made the second ring and ran behind the leading group. Anyone the first group encountered was immobilized and left to be picked up by the second group as the two teams pushed toward the court site.

Meantime Shandra moved toward where she had seen a flash. She crept up a small hill, and there was a rifle mount with a person reloading to fire again. This individual had no chance to finish the action for she had the individual in a death grip at the first lifting of their hand.

She called for Shira and asked her to watch over her captive while she called for Randy.

"Sister Randy, our mom is down. They shot her, and I'm not sure how badly she is injured," warned Shandra though she had called for Thunder to freeze Mara in place until help could aid her.

Shan was on the move immediately and met Randy who was looking for her. Shandra explained to Randy where she had last seen Mara for she still had a job to do. Randy found Mara in a hole in the ground behind some shrubs.

Randy dropped and pulled her medkit to begin work on the woman. As she worked, she shut out all sounds around her to concentrate on Mara only. The only one who could break that concentration was Shan who was keeping watch even as she moved toward the next challenge.

"We must get mom to the hospital. She has a wound that runs front to back. Whoever shot her was behind her at the time, and the only thing that saved her was the bulletproof vest. It caused the projectile to be thrown to one side and saved her life," Randy reported.

"Both of us were moving forward toward a computer-controlled set of guns, though we did not know that was the case at the time. Will you be okay while I check this out?" asked Shan.

"Find the one who would do this to our mom and make sure they are alive to tell their tale though they won't be for long afterward I am betting," said Randy with a frown.

If she had to do it herself, it would happen! was what Shan heard.

"Stand in line sister mine. We will get her out as soon as I find the one who did this," replied Mara's guard.

The Assassin moved again toward the bubble she had asked to remain to protect the prisoners they already had and those who had to control that location. Everyone else was on the move.

"Team leader?"

Shandra was surprised and knew she had to take the call.

"Team Leader."

"Charlie Three here. We have four people fleeing the area. Each is moving in a different direction. What are your orders?"

"Bring them down and keep them alive. Secure the four with immobilizers if you have them, remove all weapons and stay with them until I can reach you," Shandra directed.

Even as she watched, the helicopters dropped in unison to the ground making it appear they were shot down, yet she had no report that that was the case. As she turned to resume her run, she noted one person standing off to one side that felt out of place. Instead of running this time she walked to the person.

"Hello, any idea what is going on?" she asked the individual when she was close enough to be heard.

"Yeah, some smart asses just got what they deserve."

"Oh really, what might that be?" she asked.

"Shot," was the response and that was all he said for Shan had laid him out with a well-placed uppercut.

She threw the man over the back of a mare that appeared when she realized it was Pi. She tied the prisoner in place, mounted another horse that appeared, and began again to move. It proved to be the lead stallion, Bolt from their ranch. They continued to make progress toward the court site, yet she was watching and keeping her focus on if there were more of the Assassins in the area.

When everyone was rounded up, there were a hundred prisoners added to the checkout. Local Law was asked to take the first group with their confessions and testimonies. The next bunch was left standing inside the bubble where they were watched over by some very steely-eyed women who knew what had happened. None of the prisoners so much as moved once in place.

"Roundup," directed Shan, and the helicopters flew into the air to bring their prisoners to the head group.

The entire lead group moved to herd the rest of their prisoners to the field. When all were inside, Shan noted that an ambulance had picked up Randy and Mara. She wanted so much to be with them yet had to make sure the sorting got done.

"Sis, I have it covered. Go, just keep me posted please," said Pat with tears in her eyes.

Shan nodded then pointed at PI.

"That could be your killer," she said.

Pat ordered the prisoner taken inside and Shan mounted on the run for the hospital. When she got there, the director was waiting and took her immediately to where Mara was. Randy had left orders for her to be allowed. Pi departed quickly for the field to aid in cleanup.

When Mara began to awaken the first two she saw were Shan and Randy.

"What happened?" she asked softly.

"Someone tried to kill you. However, we believe that we have the person in Pat's care now. They will not hold court until we know your status," responded Shan with tears rolling down her face.

"The one who captured the sniper and possibly his boss was Shan with C Quad getting the rest. They are in holding at the field," added Randy as she put her arm around the shoulders of her sister who was shaking so bad she could hardly talk.

"Anyone else?" asked Mara.

"No one else injured on our side," replied Randy who had checked in with Pat as requested.

Pat was waiting for Mara's status before going on with the trial.

"Mom, you need to rest," said Randy.

"No, I will be okay. Thunder is taking over," replied Mara before rising from the bed and dressing with the aid of her two daughters. Clean clothes were waiting in a nearby locker. The clothing she wore when shot by the sniper became evidence. She was not going to stay in a public place, which the hospital was, with so many looking for her.

The administrator was standing by with the paperwork. They moved outside after signing the necessary paperwork. Sitting at the door was a vehicle that Kennet had been driving. Shira was in the back, and Mara was advised to remain in the center of the car to be better protected. Randy became the driver, and Ken moved to his mom where he asked for a full report, which she gave as it had to be AI recorded. It couldn't be what someone told her, only what she saw.

Shan said not a word, however, rode shotgun.

When they reached the location, they moved through the small door that Shan and Mara used when they left. It closed behind them and became part of the stable bubble around them.

Thunder called for a report from Pat, once the women received a greeting.

"We have been waiting for a report on Mara. If you allow we will now hold court," responded Pat though she looked carefully at the three women who just joined them for they looked identical.

"Go ahead," Thunder responded.

"Pat, it is okay, just do as you normally do. We will sort us all out when we get home, not here, however," said Mara in her soft voice which Pat quickly recognized.

"The Thunder court is now in session. Is the Prosecutor here?" she asked.

"Present!" replied Jo in her drill voice. She was going to take care of whoever would do such a thing to her mom. Took her too long to recognize Mara as her mom and to have her nearly killed shook her to her foundation.

"Who oversees the people standing before us?"

"I have that honor," said a person moving from one side of the area.

"Who hired you and what is your assigned duty?" asked Pat.

"Never mind who hired me, I am here to put you all out of business," the man replied.

"You get one charge of contempt of court. Now as I asked the first time, who hired you, and what is your name and assigned duty?"

"This is a farce. I am not answering any questions of any of you," the man roared.

When he came to he was lying on the ground with a mouth full of dirt and before him stood Shandra.

"You will answer the questions one way or the other. Cherry, strip him," directed Shandra as she stood over the man.

When he stood in only his shorts, they had a large pile of electronics, weapons, dual ID cards, as well as a lot of other miscellaneous that were not legal anyplace. The small entry door opened and inside stepped the local law enforcement. Space was enlarged to accommodate them as they moved behind the Judge and Prosecutor.

"Your Honor I believe he is now ready to speak with you," Shandra told the Judge when Cherry completed the directive.

"This is your third strike, don't muff it," said Pat in a level yet steely voice.

"My name is Pricer Shankazar. My nationality is Sprie. My duty here is to remove all of you from power. My employer is…" and before he could say more, there was weapon fire both inside and out of the bubble.

The Thunder group quickly returned fire inside and then they saw Shandra begin to grow. She stood taller than the bubble and, in her hand, was a Thunder sword known as Lightning. Shan stepped carefully outside the bubble which then resealed the exit location used. Then Shan began returning fire in all directions. When the noise ceased, she strode to the different places and picked up those she had disabled. Once they were in hand the trip back to the bubble was taken, and there Shan carefully stepped inside, dumped the captives on the ground, after disabling all electronics and weapons they carried. She remained Giant sized and waited for the court to continue.

"We need to strip search all in this area, except for the Thunder group. Lawmen, please do the honors, however, remember that Lightning is very dangerous, and you need to stay behind them, please?" warned Pat in her steely tone.

Shandra raised her sword upward and stood guard while the rest of the group sheathed their weapons and waited while law enforcement thoroughly searched the felons. Due to her size, the team knew they were secure, and it was the only time, to that point, that they had ever sheathed their swords before a court case was over. Once the necessary pictures of arms etc., and the person each related to was matched up, the court continued although Shandra shrunk once again to normal, and the Thunder Lead again pulled their weapons.

As quickly as the people gave confessions and testimony, they were immobilized until the full court finished. The paperwork and arms plus electronics were turned over to the Law group. The bubble was released, and everyone headed home. No one was speaking. Each person remained lost in their private thoughts as to what had happened and what was learned.

Everything in Mara's care under Thunder was taken home including vehicles, animals, and personnel.

Shandra walked by Mara's side and aided her up the stairs. They went to Mara's suite where she was made ready for bed by her daughter.

Randy said she would be by a bit later as she had some work to do first. In truth, she knew that Shan needed the time and would not interfere.

"Sit down Shandra; it is time to talk this out. First off, you have done nothing that requires an apology. Because of you I am trained and still alive. I love you, daughter mine, and that is not going to change," said Mara with love.

Shan began to cry and was soon sobbing as she gave up trying to talk. She had been so scared when she saw Mara drop and knew she had to keep going or they would all be dead. She did her duty as she saw it and continued until the area was secured and her mom was taken to help.

"I know how scared you were, yet you did the job, and now we are aware of who and why. Shan, we could not do without you. Do not let this create a problem for you. You did your job and did it well, both as a daughter and as a guard. I'm alive because of you. You yelled, I turned, and the missile passed through without hitting anything that could have killed me."

"Mom, I did not call. I was trying to find who shot you. Until I got them stopped, didn't dare return to you for it would have told them you might still live. I met Randy and told her where she could find you, and that was all. To me, it seemed like my duty was to find your shooter so kept going to not think about whether you were dead or alive. I've never been so scared in my life!" then she cried again.

"As you can see I'm not that easy to kill," said Mara with a smile of love.

"Thank the power above," replied Shan when she finally could talk.

"I had another bed moved in here so why don't you move over there and get some rest? No one is going to let us go anyplace until I'm ready. You will remain here if I do. In fact, if you prefer climb in on the backside," said Mara.

"No, I take the front, however, yes that is my preference. No one is going to get to you ever again," said Shandra.

"My darling, you cannot protect me to that extent. I have a job to do like you. We each knew what the odds were going in and gave our best. We cannot be smothered and still get our jobs done. Do what you hired on to do and I shall do the same. We won this one, and hopefully, we will continue to do so."

In minutes, both were sound asleep, and when Randy checked, she smiled and then closed the door to check on the kids and be sure they did not disturb the two in that room. She knew what had transpired. Randy heard them speaking for Mara had not closed her mike. Even asleep it was still on so Randy asked the AI to turn it off so that neither woman would realize their conversation went to even one person.

"Randy are they okay," asked Granda in a broken voice over her speaker.

"Coming your way," replied Randy as she walked to Granda's suite where she found the woman waiting for her.

They moved inside, and both shut off their speakers for the AI could reach them anyplace in the holding.

"Yes, they will be. Mara was shot and will need some healing time. I will keep an eye on her medically. Shandra felt she had done something wrong, or they would have accomplished what they set out to do. At a guess, I doubt you will see those two separated from the main group ever again. It was a scare for all of us, and now we look at how we take those two for granted. At the same time, they need to be allowed to do their jobs without interference. It will take them a while to see what works for them now. I would trust either or both with my life, and I plan on continuing to do so. Their balance will come back. It was an eye-opener for mom as she had never been truly under fire before. It will sharpen her skills. Shandra needed to know that even mom can be injured or killed. They both thought they were invincible. Now they will start looking at it differently. Shan called me as soon as she saw mom fall and gave me a clear picture of where she was as she tried to stop the guns. She got them stopped as I reached mom."

"It scared me half to death when I heard and felt the shot. Now I know how she felt when she found me after Star beat me so badly. This event will solidify our family as nothing else could have. The MB joining in the cleanup was a first though I think not the last time. Never do I recall the law enforcement groups meeting with us before the trial. There will indeed be some changes, and hopefully, we can make them good ones," replied Granda.

"Events like this one are needed to sharpen our wits as we learn. You know I would never wish this on anyone, yet it is what we know can happen. When it does, it focuses our training even more. I am so thankful that mom will be okay. It was a scare for everyone concerned, yet the entire family reacted favorably. They backed us in every way they could. Now we are wiser and will continue to do the best we know-how as we endeavor to control whatever situation comes up," Randy told her.

"No one could ask for more. Thank you for all you have done and continue to do. You realize you are a large part of the reason we still operate, don't you? We could not do it without you. May I have a hug?" asked Granda and Randy quickly complied.

"By the way, I spoke with Pat, and she feels the same. She is taking roll and making sure no one was injured plus putting fears to rest. When done, she will report to me, for she will need the release of fear also. I've no doubt she will do her job first. Jimmy is standing watch at the front of the house with the men. All who were not with us, yet need to be told, have been. The studs are running loose on the property, and no one will get anyplace near us. We can do what we must and get everyone settled," Randy advised.

"Randy, how did you get so well trained?" asked Granda.

"Mara knew my background and insisted that I be the next in line, for if anyone got to Mara, Pat would die as well. That is not for general knowledge, however. For your sake, do not even hint at knowing that information. Hopefully, no one will think of a Surgeon as being over this amazing family as a leader. It might be the thing that wins for us later," responded Randy.

"She sure knew how to pick each of us. Yes, you are well qualified as I did your background when you first joined us. Mine was the surface stuff and then she did the deeper check. Whatever she saw would have given her what she needed for the decision. She said the first time you met her that you were a definite plus and would remain with us for all time. I don't need to know what she found. What I would like to know is what your part is in what we do next."

"I will call a meeting and fill everyone in on what happens now, though Pat will be the one giving orders for me," Randy advised.

"We don't need anyone else in jeopardy, and she already is, being a twin."

"What should I be doing?" asked Granda.

"Joy has taken over the home direction. Shan is asleep with mom. Pat is getting everyone where they should be and settling their fears. Kari took over all kids knowing how this would affect you as well. Kennet is advising all livestock of the situation and making sure they are taken care of including the miniatures. The foreman has put everyone on alert, and we continue to march," replied Randy.

"Then if you don't mind I am going to go have a good long cry. Call if you need me," Granda told her.

"I will do that," Randy responded then stood and gave Granda a long hug as the woman shook with fear and relief.

"Now take a rest," directed Randy.

When Pat finally reached Randy, she seemed fine. At least until the door closed and then she fell into the nearest chair and sobbed.

"Get it out of your system my dear for we have work to do. Go ahead, no one will bother you here," said Randy who held her sister as she cried.

When the storm ended, Randy excused herself, though suggesting that Pat remain where she was, and she would return.

Randy slipped out of her living area to move to Mara's and asked for admittance by the AI. Mara had directed that Randy have access to all rooms in the compound even as she and Shandra did. The Doctor moved inside and to the private room that was Mara's. Opening the door showed her that she had guessed right. Mara was weeping quietly behind Shandra.

"T, please keep Shandra asleep while I talk with mom," requested Randy.

"Mom, it is okay. Pat is taken care of, Granda I sent to bed, you took care of Shandra, and now it is your turn. Sorry, it took so long to get here. However you needed some rest and hoped you would get it while I dealt with the others," explained Randy with a smile.

"Then we did it, right? Got everyone taken care of and you in control?" asked Mara.

"Yes, Thunder is in control. You have chosen well my other self," said the T voice via Randy.

"I never wanted to test it to find out, however now that we have, some training is necessary though we will march on once I'm back on my feet. That should only be a couple of days," replied Mara after a good cry.

"You are an amazing woman Mara N-Sign, and I am so proud to be working with you," said Thunder Press speaking through Randy with her consent.

It was the first time in her memory that Mara had received such a compliment, and from Thunder Press, which surprised her.

"You are the one that makes it work. All that anyone requires of any of us is to follow orders, and I'm so proud that the family did that in all instances," Mara replied.

"Mara, if you had not asked to work with me, my story would have ended. The woman you replaced died within a week, and the story did indeed end for her. Though the book worlds are still there and under your control via Granda, we know how they end. Because of you, we can continue in this real world. It will take both of us plus the entire family to make this work and free our world of the evil that is trying to take over. Your command structure is working well, a lot of folks have productive lives, many escaped death because of you, and the story continues. Thank you," said the T voice.

"All we can do is our best. We have some amazing people in this family, and they are all loved. When I'm back on my feet, we will get back in step with the upcoming activities. We have a horse show in a day or two as I recall," commented Mara.

After giving Mara a careful hug as Thunder, Randy checked her wounds and directed her to sleep as much as she could to allow healing. She slipped out of the room, and Shandra again was guard though she never woke up while T was in the chamber.

Randy returned to her room and found Pat still there and lying on the couch.

"Are you truly okay Pat?" asked Randy.

"What? Oh, yes, I'm fine just needed to get rid of the fear and pain. Now I'm ready to get back to work. Thank you for your time and care. We nearly lost the ball when Mara went down, and then I saw Shandra signal for you. Knew we were still in business and got the first batch of felons taken care of so that we would be ready for whatever came next," said Pat.

"Pat, do you realize that we are all related? Sometimes it seems you don't fully understand that you are part of this amazing family. It is more than that for we are each a part of the whole. When one of us hurts, we all do. If one is injured, we all are. Mara will have full healing in two days, and we will get ready for whichever family event is scheduled to happen. So far, I have heard two different dates, and the events switched between them. For now, some rest is necessary for everyone. You know your sister, and if anyone is doing anything, she will want to be there so want you to order rest for two days or three nights for everyone. Then it is back to duty. Kari is taking care of the under-five group, the teachers have the older ones, and we are all, did you get that? all, going to get some rest," directed Randy sternly then she smiled at the startled look on Pat's face.

"Very well, I will order it to happen. In fact, I agree it is past time. Randy, may I have a hug then I will get the directions to one and all?" replied Pat with a smile. She was so relieved that someone knew what to do now while they were so shaken. After exchanging hugs, the two parted ways.

Randy returned to her quarters where she had her communicator on and could listen to the meeting without being present. As a doctor with a patient, no one would be expecting her.

"Okay, people here are the day's orders, in fact, for the next three days and nights. These will be break days. No one will be working. We have a couple of shows coming up and a couple of days of rest must happen first. Kari will take on the under-fives while Joy will be on call for complex area concerns. Tutors, would you be willing to oversee the rest of the kids? No classes and don't leave the compound, otherwise do as you will. Men, would you do a two-hour watch in pairs at the front door? The regular guards are also in place although this does not apply to them. No one is to fly anything. You can ride if you like only on horses, within the property, and no one moves unless in pairs at the least. Mara will rejoin us when the break is over. Merry, please keep us fed buffet style. Good time to clean out the refrigerator. You also need a break for you have a large feed coming up. Notify your group to do what they can to prepare. However, you need to either break now or immediately after the show. Are there any questions?" Pat asked.

No one moved or said a thing, including the newest members. The meeting was over, and Pat departed. This time she was going to follow her orders and go to bed. With the trauma of Mara's injury and the pain following, Pat knew she needed the rest as much as her twin. Randy had dressed the area for her and made sure she was operational before sending her to brief everyone.

Two days later, at four a.m., found everyone back on schedule. Mara and Shandra started for the stable though Randy stopped them before leaving the house. The Doctor led them to the medical suite. There she checked them both over, much to their surprise.

"Don't look so surprised. No, it is not a lack of faith. Let me show you something," said Randy.

She then put words to action.

"Shandra bear with me and remove your blouse, Mara the same."

They did as she told them to.

"Now, face one another. Do you see the bullet scar on Shan? Now turn around sis. Shan, do you see the bullet scar on Mara? Pat has the same. I have not checked Granda yet, however, would be willing to bet she has them even as I do," she then pulled off her blouse and showed them. While the scar colors varied, the same injury was in the same place on all three of them.

"My goodness, we must be more careful. I promise both of you there will be no more just my adventures. Never would I purposefully do that to any of you," said Mara with tears for she never knew that could happen.

"Yours is the most severe, though all of us will heal and all will forever have the scars. I stitched up Pat as well. It is something I thought you might like to know. The plus is if any of the Lead Group is injured, you will know it immediately. That is why all of us had to rest when you were injured," Randy advised.

"Thank you both, for taking on my injury so it would heal quicker and for taking over when I couldn't. Now we can get back on schedule. Do you see any problem with our resuming the program?" asked Mara.

"Since we have had a week of rest, you can safely return to duty. However, the calendar will show only two days off. Would you mind if I joined you, just for today?" asked Randy with a smile for she finally allowed her fear and pain to show if only to those before her.

"All those with the scars will join us for any training that is open from here on. There is some training you won't be able to join, and when that time comes, you will be advised, otherwise join us. You now need to be protected even better than we have been," said Mara with no hesitation at all.

The three walked to the door, and Granda was waiting when they got there. They worked their mounts, did the drills, fed the animals after a rubdown, and returned to the main building and showers. Shandra helped get clothes out for the kids while Mara prepared for the first music class with littles just as the school children departed for the barn. They were all back on schedule and Mara was much wiser about what could happen.

Granda began training with military trainers in hand to hand. When her expertise improved, she joined Randy, Mara, and Shandra. Soon Pat and her partner were also seen with them. In fact, training was picking up in all areas. Finally, Mara and Shandra were asked to train at the gym with those who worked out there. Not to train everyone, only those who were the trainers for the rest. A block of time was made available.

After the workout, Randy called on Granda to give her the same information; she was astonished. There would be a lot more caution used by all of them. At this rate, if one died they all did it seemed.

Randy replied that might not be true. Each person had an injury in the same place; however, the severity was different for each, and it appeared that it was in relation to their position in the lead group. Pat and Mara were the severest with the same injuries at the same time, then Shandra and Randy followed by the rest of the lead group. Randy realized that her injury was not evident until Mara was out of surgery. Then she too felt the fear and pain enter her body. Now Randy knew how to aid her mom and others who would be feeling the same thing. The Doctor spent lots of time reviewing her part in the time when Mara was injured, and her training was speeded up. She worked out whenever the leaders did for she needed the same knowledge and abilities. Orders would go to everyone that bulletproof vests and chain mail would be worn daily except for sleep. Randy worked out every morning with the lead group before their day began. In the afternoon, she had training with Mara and Shandra. Then when they could work it in, there was another training session. No one worked on Sunday, and the rule remained in force for bodies needed a day of rest. That did not change the order of armor, however.

Chapter 9

Other voices are heard

Mara called for Jo two days after their return to duty. They met in Jo's suite as Mara's had kids coming and going for one reason or other.

"Thank you, Jo, for meeting with me. How are things going? Do we need to make any changes in your area?" asked Mara to open the conversation.

"Well, there is one thing that puzzles me. The shows the Family is scheduled to do is always changing. I am not doing it. However one day it says we are riding this weekend and the next one we are making music. I thought the riding one had already happened. Either is fine only they are at different locations, and that means different preparation," commented Jo.

"Blame that one on me. My mind kept changing the schedule due to my injury. Now you can set it and leave it that way. The original intent was to have the family riding first. We need to get things started with the horse shows then our various ranch groups should be put on the schedule. My apologies," she told her events manager.

"Whew, was getting worried. Thank you. What would work best for your schedule?" Jo asked.

"I would like to hear the Family Band. Kennet and Alina have solo work to present. They have been working together as well. In fact, many in the band have been working to that end. If asked I will join them with Shandra. However, that is their choice. I would like to see a group of littles give a single presentation to get them able to perform before an audience. Plan on about three hours total. It will be at the stadium. Let's get that one done before we look at the next event."

"I'm all for that. Did you know we have top name events scheduled through April? Some more known than others yet all are good and should hold everyone's interest. If you want to, we can have horse shows morning and afternoon while the human ones are in the evenings. That way you can attend one and participate in the other if you wish. Don't want to burn anyone out, either as spectators or as participants. I would like to have the family band anytime in the next two weeks; then we must go East as I recall. The first show by others will be when we return. Not sure when that is, due to our Thunder time, though it will work that way I'm sure," replied Jo with a broad smile and a chuckle.

"Understood, let's have the riders perform on Saturday, get married on Sunday, and have the band play on Monday. That way if we are gone said performance would be as if we are in place. From there on we can have horse shows by our various ranches during the summer months, catch a few garages or estate sales, then the family can do a show with the band or as riders a couple of times a year. Might use the music for winter since it is an inside event, and the riding can be summer due to the transport of animals. Would that work for you?" asked Mara.

"Certainly. With one exception if you allow. Why not use tomorrow to record the music, do the riding on Saturday, wedding on Sunday, and all bases are covered to leave when you get back from your honeymoon," suggested Jo.

Mara agreed to the change for she knew Thunder would coordinate it.

Jo thought for a moment, and Mara waited for she knew something was on the mind of this daughter and it was best to find out what it was.

"There are times when I wonder how you keep up. Mom, the time has come for me to let you know where I stand. Sometimes I was not sure; however, my mind is made up, and you have my loyalty as your daughter, enterprise director, pilot, and any other way I can help. We could not have a better leader. It is an honor to work with and for you. You take on the hard stuff and even put yourself in the line of danger to protect the rest of us. My preference is that you do not do that again. However, it is noted and appreciated. Mom, you are loved so very much by all of us. Have you any idea how much every member of this family loves you?" asked Jo.

"Probably not, however, do any of you know how much I love you in return?" asked Mara with a smile.

"Yes, in every decision you make. It is always for others and never for yourself. Now what else can I help you with?" asked Jo.

"Keep on as you are going, and we are in good hands. If the calendar remains clear, we will depart soon for the East. We will be challenged there as well as have the craft show that will allow us to see what is available from the crafters there. I will pick up Heidi and Becky, so they don't think we have forgotten them. Also, it gives you a chance to see where they are at in their areas."

"That works for me. Have a couple of other suggestions if you don't mind? The men don't have assigned duties, other than door watching. Would you object to making them part of any cleanup we have to do that relates to felons or gaining of the product?"

"After Sunday, they will be gone for a few days, upon their return all will need to be trained as part of the Main Group. Since you are getting married on that date as well, you have an option. We can take separate honeymoons, which isn't a good idea or we can have a very private one with all of us together with different areas to enjoy. Any suggestions on that one?" asked Mara with a smile and a twinkle in her eye.

"How did you know I have never married?"

"It really wouldn't matter if you had been or not. That is not a requirement to get married, only that you are divorced, or your spouse is deceased. I have the full history of all my family. Nothing will be said unless one of you does. My records say who was married and who was not. Also, it identified those who have been married and are not present. As your mother, several suitors have petitioned for your hand in marriage. Therefore, I need to know your selection before any of them are told yes," replied Mara.

Jo stood in place with her mouth gaping open.

Mara had to laugh.

"Yes, dear one, you too," responded Mara to the open astonishment.

"Please, mom, who has asked?"

"Yes, he is on your list of possibilities. Do you want me to add your name to the list for Sunday? I can notify him if you like, or you can do it yourself."

"If you agree, please tell him, and he can talk to me about this. You certainly know how to shock a body. I'm going on sixty and never had a proposal in my life," Jo told her mom.

"Well, that has just changed. Do you mind?" asked Mara with a smile.

"To tell the truth I am tremendously honored. Not at all sure how to proceed from here, however, I am going to try my best to be a good wife if he will accept that my current family, meaning you, takes priority in this life. If he agrees we will have a partnership," she responded.

Without further comment, she got up and left.

Mara sat staring at the door for a while then she began to laugh. Some fifteen minutes later when Jo returned, Mara was again laughing, only this time it was with a red-faced Jo.

"Sorry about that mom. Guess you can see how you shocked me. I even forgot I live here," said Jo with a red face.

"Not to worry. No one will know, except me and I love it. Thought I would stay around and see how long it took you to remember," Mara replied.

"Well, I found him, said yes, and then recalled where I left you. Told him what I had done then left him laughing and returned to let you out and apologize. To me, I'm still that same broken-down individual you rescued from a life in the military. It is when I look at you and see my mom that I become the young person who has the joy of calling you that. Thank you," responded Jo.

"How about a hug then I will give you back your suite? You are much loved, and this mission could never have happened

Sharron L Ensign P.O. Box 583 Helena, MT 59624
Assassins Target Mara Bk 3
406-458-7091

without you, any of them in fact."

Jo had tears in her eyes as she rose to her feet to give a hug.

She held Mara gently then hugged her tightly and couldn't seem to let go, which is when her Mom realized the woman was crying.

"It's okay dear one. We all must take time for tears as life hands us a few curves we were not expecting. You are loved, and never will you be belittled or made to feel less. You are part of what makes this family work with such success."

"Let me sit and think back over this time with you. Soon this too will be second nature. However, it will take a little while for me to accept this change in my life. I don't recall anyone fully accepting me as who I am before. It is a strange yet wonderful feeling. Previously it seemed like there was always a push to succeed to make others appreciate me. Now I know it doesn't work that way. Learned that from watching you and Shandra. You both are much appreciated. Now I know what love I is, I can share it with others."

"Now I really must get busy. By now Shandra is looking for me no doubt. I told her I wouldn't leave the complex though, so she wouldn't be worried. See you at supper," said Mara who then departed.

The following day was Friday, on the home calendar. However, it showed as Saturday to anyone else. The band assembled, and a recording was made for when they could not be at the stadium to perform. It went extremely well, and there were even a lot of curtain calls as those in attendance seemed to enjoy the group. The actual show was filmed and would be given life by Thunder at some later time when they couldn't be present. Although the show was on a Friday, there was a full house. Ushers and the business office heard how much the performance meant to the attendees and another concert was scheduled for in the spring before the horse shows began.

Shandra and Mara received a surprise. Dan asked them after he did his first performance with Gwen if they would join them in a song, which they did. They each played an instrument, each sang a solo, and at the end, the last verse was sung by all of them even as they played instruments that allowed them to do that. The two women had already done a quartet with Kennet and Alina

Saturday again appeared the following day, for arena use, and was the day of the riding event. Mara felt they were ready. The show was to be at two in the afternoon and would take four hours. It had been advertised as a viewing of the horses during the morning until noon when the BBQ would be ready. Then the whole group, including horses, rested until thirty minutes before the show. At that time rigging was put on all of them. Mara chuckled to see the rainbow of color her family wore, including the animals that would be participating. She also noted that the guard dogs were all in a separate color as well as wearing the same as their handler.

The call to colors went out, and the spectators were on their feet as the first rider was seen entering the arena right behind the national and state flags. Mara and Shandra took the lead with the rest riding by colors though she kept the small ones close behind her. Military riders who knew how to maneuver the large flags while on horseback presented the colors.

"Hello folks, meet my family. I am mom, and we are here to show you our four-footed friends in action. Hope you enjoyed the BBQ and now it is time to give you a show," said Mara, though the greeting had been recorded to be sure all heard her voice and could not record it.

They did the normal down the center to present the colors, then a complete circle on the outer side of the arena. Then the horses were stopped, and every other mount faced outward as the littles took over the inside of the area to put on their part of the show. When the littles finished, they took their places in a ring near the double ring that held Mara.

Next were the teens, then on up the group by size and age. When it was time for the Quads the spectators were expecting something grand, and they got it. Mara and Pat moved their studs forward, and the littles took their place. Until then no one seemed to realize that there were real studs with the mares in the show. The animals were brushed to shine. Shira joined them on PI though the rider was Alina. As the Quads did the drills, they moved to support Mara and Pat in their maneuvers. Then the rest of the family began showing other skills around the outside of the leading riders. At the end of the show, everyone in the stands was standing. The riders bowed even as their rides did the one-footed horse bow. The leaders dismounted to wave and then did the rear mount as they led the run from the arena.

"Thunder, please take home those who are overtired, like the littles," requested Mara.

"You won't get any of them to leave now. Every child is feeling ten feet tall. They need to enjoy the environment as kids now. Their shirts are changed out, and they will not be recognized though there is an adult with each of them. The Regina group offered to do that as their part," Thunder replied.

"Then change everyone's clothes, though please send the horses home. We will brush them down when we get there."

"They are gone," Thunder replied.

The members drifted around in the crowd, though in pairs at the least. Mara, Shandra, Alina, Sherry, Kennet, and Granda were close to one another as they moved. Then Randy and Merry joined them. Quads were nearby yet not seen as part of the group.

The Police force was seen keeping an eye on things, and they ran into the Mayor right after the show as he wanted to give them congratulations. No one heard anyone's name as they moved.

At a sign from Mara, her group began moving to the outer edge of the event, and there they disappeared to be taken home. The youngest needed some rest, the older needed to blow off steam and brush down all the horses, the tutors said rest was in order, and Granda agreed.

Shandra stayed at Mara's side and even directed her toward her suite and the private room inside.

"Now, rest mom. You are newly healed and need to relax some. No telling what is next on the schedule. I will be here and advise you if anything requires us," said her daughter with a smile only to hear a light tap on the door.

When Shandra opened the door, she found Randy waiting.

"Hello dears, it is time to check out my patient. You were very energetic out there, and everyone did a fantastic job. I could watch all of you for hours. Hopefully, you allowed our recorder to keep a record. Thank you for allowing me to take part. Merry said she wasn't going to be left out and turned the kitchen to her back up so she could ride as well. Even Melissa and Sue were on board," even as she spoke she was checking on the wound sites on Mara. When she had noted that only thin scars remained, she smiled and continued.

"Thank you, mom. I haven't had that much fun in ages. Will we ever do this again? Even having done it once is a fantastic experience," and they could feel her excitement and elation once she let down her Doctor walls.

"Finally, daughter mine, you have found something you enjoy. Yes, we will be doing it again although it won't be until next summer. By then a new show must be developed. If you like a real challenge, try to think of a new theme for when that time comes. You can even take the lead using the name of mom so that no one would know who you are. There is a busy winter ahead first and prefer we remain close to home during that weather. If we fly out it will be for a month at a time; otherwise, we will stay put. This is an area where severe weather when walking, riding, or driving can be dangerous," said Mara with a broad smile.

"Let me think about it," replied the surprised woman though her mind was already working on ideas.

"You have a few months yet," laughed Mara and Shandra just grinned with a reminder to herself to never show that much enthusiasm for something.

"You are already too busy, so you won't be tasked with anything else unless I am also, plus you are my special guard, and no one is going to take that title from you," whispered Mara. The message was Thunder sent, so Randy was not even aware of the conversation.

"Gee Randy, you seem to be in shock," laughed Shandra.

"You could say that. You see I had ridden yet was far from

being an expert until I joined this family. Now you want me to lead the parade, so to speak," then she laughed.

"Honey, you ride like an expert, and I know that from a group of experts that travel with this family. Russell even agrees," Mara told her.

"He said that. What a shock. He was a champion Equestrian when in his twenties. Life is sure full of surprises, and I rather like it. Thank you, mom, for the family I am related to and for helping me grow in this new life," said Randy who then gave Mara a warm hug. There wasn't anything she wouldn't do for her.

"Now Sis if you are passing them out, where is mine?" smiled Shandra who immediately received the requested hug.

Randy laughed as she thought of all that had led her to this time in her life. A rejected wife who worked in a clinic as a doctor and now she was the second lead in command for the family. Randy was also Thunder's private physician and surgeon, now a champion rider. Plus, Randy was Thunder and trusted with much. Randy had traveled more since she joined Mara than she had in her life previously. Add to that the age she would be for the rest of her life, and she was in shock.

"Not really in shock, just learning and growing with the rest of us," Mara advised with a loving smile.

Mara was up at four and on the move. She looked around as she moved from place to place and discovered a lot of others moving as she did. Mara chuckled for this was the day they were going to be married. Her Pastor was coming to the stadium, which was booked for the event, to officiate. She could not think of another way to have room for those who might come.

Shandra asked for volunteers to decorate the venue and was amazed at how many offered.

Merry and her group spent the whole week making food for the event so that the team could participate and still have a meal ready for the weddings. A cleanup crew was assigned when the event was over.

The men took all vehicles, to be used by those getting married, into town and had them cleaned inside and out. They were then locked up at the stadium except for the buses that would be used to get everyone there.

The tutors removed all kids and at the same time had the clothes they would each change into for the events. Another bus would take them to the stadium yet not until just before the event. Once the kids moved to tutor coverage, the women began preparing. Keri moved from one woman to another getting them ready for their weddings. Their dresses were at the stadium to change. However, makeup and hair had to be taken care of first.

Since guards would be required, Dan, Gwen, and the group of kids that came with Regina were put in guard uniforms and were about to burst they were so proud of the honor. The home guards would be in place there during the event. There were nineteen couples to be married and what an event it was. The brides were in white while the men were all in black suits with light blue shirts and dark blue ties. The group would depart in vehicles of two persons in each. Since all were the best qualified of the entire Clan, guards would not be necessary.

One week after Mara nearly died she said her vows to her new husband Jimmy, along with the entire leadership team. For that day, she lifted her barriers as Thunder and became Mara in truth. She laughed, cried, and hugged everyone else that was married. Her mom and Eva were present and could not have been prouder. Then all the newly married couples departed for a secret location for their honeymoons. When they returned the next morning at the main ranch, the clock said they had been gone twelve hours, while all who participated knew they had been away a whole month. Now it was time to get back to work and work they did.

As usual, the trip was scheduled to begin early in the day. However, Mara felt that a day could catch her up before the departure. The plane was nearly full, of those who would participate. Joy, Dan, and Gwen were on the flight manifest and looking forward to the trip. The new husbands were also a welcome addition. Mara chuckled at the guard dogs cropping up here and there. They had to be tested to be sure they were ready for the flight; however, Shira did the testing, and those who passed met with Mara. Wider seats had harnesses and allowed the dogs to lay down. They weren't comfortable for passengers to sit in due to being so short from front to back plus having a lip to keep a sleeping animal from falling to the floor. There were kennels near the one they guarded if the animals preferred not to be in a harness. The harness had a breakaway clip that allowed the guard animal to release themselves in the case of an emergency.

The plane went by a direct flight to Nashville Tennessee. There they found Heidi and Becky waiting once the aircraft was inside their hangar.

"Hello, dear ones, glad you could come. Have some pleasant surprises for you, we hope," said Becky.

Mara smiled and nodded though she said nothing. She had requested the changes after all yet would seem surprised for the two women. The motel went to three floors and doubled in width when a property next to it became available and became a parking garage. When the businesses began having more clientele the people in the neighborhood sold to a corporation that owned those businesses. They got fair market value, and the area expanded to meet the requirement of this new enterprise. The restaurant had to double on one level to address the need of those staying at the motel, however that land was part of what they inherited, due to Becky's forethought. There was a second floor for Becky's business office and home of the monitoring equipment and AI for the establishment.

A large property became available nearby and was another Thunder purchase via Granda. It became the Craft Show of the Century site or CS of C. It was a large building that allowed show areas of twenty feet by the side. The vendor fee was twenty dollars a spot with an entry fee of five dollars for visitors. That allowed the AI to scan every person who entered to note any carrying weapons and look for trouble.

Since it put the three businesses near a freeway exit for Nashville, it was an ideal site for them. Becky spent her free time getting vendors for the location, and it was booked full, using word of mouth. Anything homemade, like maple syrup products, was welcome, even if the home was a business. There were elevators for those needing such or moving products to the upper floors. Becky had a large map made on one wall of the entry, and the AI could place the information on each business in the squares. She noted that the first one on the bottom was a jug of maple syrup and chuckled for that word had entered more than one conversation with Mara.

Becky asked if they would like their first meal of the day to be breakfast or lunch, which made no difference as it was a buffet and catered to all pallets. Granda immediately said breakfast, and thus the family moved to the restaurant when Heidi said that their rooms were reserved taking up the top floor of the motel.

Upon their return to the motel, they were advised that the third floor was for the hotel owners and would not be rented out. Each selected a room, and with an assigned guard and husband next door they settled in.

There was a conference room on that floor as well, and Mara called them all to that space.

"Okay folks, new rules. We are here on business. That means the women come and go as our duties require. You won't know where we are going or when we return. What you will know is that the current intent is to focus on this area. The craft shows, the restaurant, and the motel. If we need you the call will come, and you will be where we are. Check out each location and be prepared to give a report of anything outstanding. At the same time, I need to know if something needs repair. So far being together is working as we are all married except for those who are new to the group, and they need a year or two to catch their breath. If sixty-some of us are in a cluster, it will cause problems. Move in pairs without it being obvious. Due warning one and all, we have some very dangerous people, men, and women, looking for us. Their intel may let them know we are in the area. Do not let anyone realize where we are staying or any of our names. Where we are from and how we got here is one not to answer unless you say from here. Business meetings require Randy, Shandra, Kennet, and me. Cherry, Gretch, and Mike will be our guards. Same as home, when the information relates to you, you will be made aware of it otherwise know I am doing my best for one and all. If required Rae, Jo, and Jero will be on call. Jimmy, I would like you and your team to keep a close watch on Granda for those seeking us will kill without a thought," Mara explained.

"A question please?" asked a female voice.

"Go ahead," Mara said.

"Is there any chance we can go to the Grand Ole Opry while we are here? Some of those folks might be a grand draw at home," commented Jero who was excited at the prospect.

"If we attend a production we go as a group yet move in pairs at a minimum. Up to four together shouldn't be a problem, if we are with husbands, we are just friends on an outing. Do not get lost. If what I expect happens, we will all be very busy. Everyone will wear full armor and be armed. You have the skills if this gets nasty, remember them, use them to protect yourselves and others." Mara was not sure how good an idea bringing everyone was going to be. She had known that Jo and Jero would want to get to the Opry and had set up a show just for her group by contacting some folks that Thunder suggested.

The promoters agreed to contact performers and see if it could happen. Word came as the airplane landed, though there was a catch. Performers were willing with one proviso. Someone had heard from a friend in Texas that there was a family from Montana who made good music. When Mara admitted to knowing them, the promoter asked if she could get them to perform this one time? Mara said it would be her honor. Now she was trying not to give away the surprise too soon. She had also asked for a southern gospel show with some name talent. It was also scheduled. Mara laughed when the same person asked if that would allow a second family show.

"I will consider it," she said with a chuckle.

"Don't wear your regular clothing for they will be watching for it. Wear whatever you are comfortable in, however, if trouble comes don't be surprised to find yourself in your traditional outfits," Randy warned.

"You were each given a communicator. It will only connect you with the one above you. It will move up the chain unless you ask for any of the T numbers. That means you have spotted trouble and we need to know that. Stay where you are, and we will find you," directed Pat.

"Any other questions?" asked Mara.

"Yes, with all this going on, can we still go shopping?" asked Granda.

Everyone broke out laughing, as intended.

"Shops open at eight a.m., so we should be right on time," responded Mara with a smile.

When they reached the CS of C, they found a long line waiting to get inside. Becky appeared next to the leaders and with a whispered conversation pulled the lead group out of line and around the building where they entered a back door that she opened with a key. Once inside Mara couldn't help her shock at the interior. It looked like a fancy hotel without rental rooms. A person in a doorman's costume was waiting for them and stamped their hands for a three-day pass. They took an elevator to the top floor to begin their shopping. Becky had taken the day off, except for checking with her staff at the restaurant from time to time, for she wanted to be the tour guide for her family.

Items of the greatest value were on the top floor. Sculptures, oil paintings, books, handmade whistles, drums, blown glass items, pottery, quilts, Afghans, saddles, boots, and the list went on. There was a snack bar on each floor also. On the second floor were items of fabric or leather, like vests, coats, and dresses, intermingled were traditional craft items though the best quality matched to items of that value on various floors.

Mara placed an order for nearly everything on the top floor. Becky took her order to a back room and set them inside to be available when the group left. They were T moved to their home, and there was the same type of room on each floor.

It took the family three days to see the event by doing a floor a day, with other activities filling in, like eating, thought Mara with a smile. If they had done it the normal way, it would have taken a month.

They departed the Craft show building in time to hear a woman's voice shout.

"Grandmama, where are you?"

"They took her this way."

Mara recognized both voices. The first one was Regina and the second one was Lynn though both were shouting in a foreign language which Mara quickly understood. She looked at Randy and saw that she and Shandra also realized. They took off at a run and heard footsteps keeping pace. She did not have to look back to know it was the rest of A-Quad who also understood. Then a new sound was heard, and the women immediately changed direction for it was their mounts joining them. They mounted on the run and soon caught up with the two girls. Each was given a hand up as they continued to follow people trying to carry two people. Then Mara noted that people on horseback were coming from all directions. People she knew.

"Drop to one, moon out, grass grows," sent Mara.

Half the riders pulled in their mounts while the rest kept going.

Mara called for a book, and those ahead with their captives ran into it without realizing where they were going. One of them stumbled, and instantly a male arm was seen, and it smacked that person in the jaw. Jimmy got loose, secured the man, and joined the run until Kennet caught up with him and offered a ride.

"This is T1, I told you to call for help not get caught," Mara placed in his mind.

"They hit us with darts. Must have been knockout. G isn't awake yet. Thank goodness for the girls," Jimmy replied knowing his wife would hear.

The women dismounted once inside the book, and the horses ran after those carrying Granda. The entire clan now had their personal mounts. Mara, Randy, and Shandra waited for the captured call. Meantime they were watching the door to the book for they were sure that soon the entire group of assassins would be inside. When T advised that all were in place the book closed.

Pi was seen headed toward Mara and mounted on her back was Granda. Randy was waiting when she got there, to check her out.

Chapter 10

Show or shows to remember

"Check for drugs first. Your dad said that they shot them with darts," Mara told her daughter as she continued to watch the rest of those in the book.

The book began to shrink, and those that were inside had no choice except to move toward the center as the pages seemed to press the unwelcome ones in that direction. A corral formed and one-hundred-seven entered. Each of them were carrying weapons. Mara still watched.

As each of the assassins tried to shoot her, they found their weapons would not fire. They were in a book that only she controlled. Mara whistled loud and clear which brought her entire lead group to where she was. The horses continued to watch over those in the corral.

One man stepped to the front of those inside the fence and aimed a different weapon at Mara. She smiled and removed the same type of device from her person. He fired, and she reached out and caught the missile headed toward her and with true aim threw it back. He fell to the ground, and she froze him there. Then she released the assassins and pulled Lightning. Her family did the same, and in Thunder formation, they returned all projectiles. Mara realized that Randy was on one side of her and Shandra on the other with Kennet slightly behind. That was as far as she could see for she didn't dare take her eyes off those ahead.

Once all felons were down and immobilized, the Quads searched for weapons. Both men and women had their armament and electronics appear in a stack beside them. Photographs were taken and matched with what they had been packing. Then they were left lying on the ground.

"I call the Thunder court to order!" said a voice not often heard. It was Joy, and she looked at Dan who moved behind her as a guard.

"I stand as judge, and this is my guard. Who is a prosecutor?" she asked.

"My report is on record, and I stand as an attorney," said Regina.

Mara said not a word as she watched her kids take on the most dangerous group any of them had ever encountered. She remained fully alert for she knew this bunch probably still had some tricks to pull.

"Team Flat!" directed Dan.

The T group dropped to the ground, except Mara who was still watching though from behind a force screen with Lightning in hand.

Ten people seemed to materialize before her. Each carried a weapon and noted the scene around them. They saw her standing and ignored her, or so it seemed. None of those on the ground tried to get up.

Then in surprise, Mara felt Randy join her, then Shandra, Kennet, and Jimmy. Granda then came, complete with a few bandages administered by Randy. Soon the lead group was there in their entirety, the women stood in front, and the men moved behind them to watch their backs.

"What have you done to our people?" asked one man.

"We allowed them to rest," said Randy.

"In their underwear?" he asked.

"Would seem so. However, the weapons each of them wore and the fact that they are assassins had some bearing as well," Randy responded.

"Where are their weapons?"

"They just up and disappeared."

"Interesting. All by themselves, I'm sure."

"Won't find any of our fingerprints on any of them, if you find them," Randy replied.

"Why are you harassing them?"

"Why were they attacking our family?"

"They were following orders."

"That doesn't surprise me. Brison, when are you going to grow up?"

"How do you know my name?" the man asked with a frown.

"Overheard it you might say."

"Who are you?"

"Doesn't matter, I know who you are."

"Brison, as you said."

"In the past when anyone called you out you sent a goon to take your place. Do you plan on doing that again?" asked Randy.

"You're no assassin."

"Maybe, maybe not."

"You don't have the same taste and feel as this bunch."

"So far you have not tasted me, and no way will you feel me," she replied.

He removed his jacket, signaled his people to move back, and waited. Randy did not move.

"Changing your mind?" he asked.

"No, just waiting for you to make up yours. Remember I have seen you in action before."

He stood as if in thought and Randy waited.

"Garrison, she has something she is hiding. At a guess, I would say this is the Leader we have been seeking. I can take her unless you want to give it a go," Brison said to the air.

Another joined the group. This man came with weapons in his hands.

"Now we know what is going on," Randy commented to the air.

"Took you long enough," said Garrison.

"Maybe."

Randy whispered into her mike.

"Make us all the same and shuffle when I say."

"Are you going to talk us to death or can we get this over with?" Garrison asked.

"I'm ready when you are."

He removed his jacket and had weapons all over his body.

"T we will need to be speeded up. He is high on something and hypnotized, so we can't get any answers from him, he thinks. When he takes two steps forward, he will turn to wink at Brison, that is when to make us identical. Watch Brison, he prefers to stab people in the back. His boss wants to awe us with his armament. Keep the focus on the rest of the group. Tell mom to not trust any of them, including those on the ground." Randy said without moving her lips.

As Randy watched, she noticed that the horses were running from behind the assassin group. She chuckled for they were blocking the door out of the story. Smart, was her thought.

"Mom don't panic. I'm still in control. Trust me please," whispered Randy.

Mara didn't hesitate.

"You bet!"

Garrison took two steps forward and turned to his second. Thunder put the entire T group in black garments with hoods. When he turned back, she was waiting. She knew his style and would handle this one herself. Shandra knew to take on Brison who wasn't near as good as he thought.

Randy's group seemed to shimmer, and the battle began. The horses remained behind the team until the fight was over and the court held.

In minutes, the entire force of assassins was in immobilizers, and those with weapons lost them. The horses then pushed the prisoner group out the door to the book and found what looked like an entire law enforcement team for the state waiting.

"May we meet with your leader?" asked a woman standing by her vehicle.

"Who do you want? The head of our group or the person in charge of the event that just took place?" asked Mara.

"Since I can see the result of your labors, I will take either or both. I am Officer Jennifer Razor lead law enforcement officer in this state."

"I am Mara, and these are my daughters. Would you ask your people to take the oath? It is not something detrimental to any of you, however necessary to protect my family."

"You are who I thought you are then. Welcome. Yes, we will take your oath gladly," Jennifer responded, and at a signal, the people fell into ranks and faced Mara.

"Randy, this time you give it. You earned the loyalty of this group. They have been able to see us the whole time as if here. Only we know that we weren't." Mara advised.

Her daughter had a small smile then stood tall and gave the oath to the officers. They would discuss later, for now, that was the only acknowledgment.

"Would you mind if your people remove this bunch while we chat? Their weapons, dispositions, and list of properties are here for you, as well as their sentences. Pat, please give them the prisoners," directed Randy.

"Randy, please check on Granda and the rest of our group to be sure no one was severely injured. We will not start without you," suggested Mara who then turned off her mic for Shandra was standing nearby.

With a smile, Randy departed, though she had already checked everyone.

"I have an offer for you before Randy returns. We have a couple of engagements to attend and would like you to come along. The reason is none of the group knows about them as it is a surprise. At some future time, you might need to know some of our talents and mention an event that you attended where we were to be sure we are the right people," Mara advised the woman.

"It would be a pleasure," replied Jenn though she wondered what she would be seeing. People were not usually this open with her. However, she had received a call from a police chief she knew in Montana, and he said to watch for a group that would ask for her oath.

Mara received Jennifer's contact information as Randy returned when she heard her Mom's mic coming active again.

"Family, we have a meeting would you please return to the craft show until I call?" asked Mara. Everyone departed in pairs, and soon only the four women remained.

"Mom, just so you know, I get the calls too," said Randy with a grin.

"Should have thought of that. Just don't share what you know please," responded Mara with a matching grin.

"I have a family as well, and nothing is harder to manage than a surprise regardless of the size," Jennifer laughed.

A silence bubble formed over them, and the group sat at a table that materialized to discuss.

"May I call you Jennifer or Jenn?" Mara asked the new woman.

"I answer to both."

"Mom, a name we haven't used yet, why not use the short version in case we need the longer at another time?" suggested Shandra who had been silent to that point.

"Jenn, meet my daughters Randy and Shandra. I am Mara, mother of the clan. My twin sister Pat was the one who turned over the prisoners. My daughter Joy was the Judge at this event, and the young man who stood as the guard is my son Dan. The young man you saw standing behind the Thunder Twins was my son, Kennet, and Alina was the one that had a wolf riding with her. There are others. However, that gives you an idea."

"I'm sure you have heard this before however, you all appear to be in your early twenties, how can you be mom?" asked Jenn.

"We cannot answer that one; it's a security issue. However, what you learn will always be the truth. We have a rather large family. My husband can vouch for that," Mara chuckled for she could still see Jimmy's face when he first met the whole group at the barn raising.

"And mine," laughed Shandra and Randy together.

"Ask your questions, and we will answer what we can without compromising our clan."

"I have some information to pass on to you. Others in my position have held a meeting, and all of us mentioned that we would like to know more about the person called Thunder Press. Somehow I was elected to try to find out more. An agreement was made to serve as a point of contact if you ever came my way. The areas that have called me here in Tennessee are Texas, Oklahoma, Michigan, and Nevada. What they asked was if you will call for the head law enforcement agent in each of those locations if you do business there. Once that happens they can vouch for you without giving others information that should not be released if you agree that is," said Jenn.

"Yes, we can do that. That oath you just gave is one that must be honored up to and including your life if you break it. Once oathsworn none can give any information about any of us, which is why I had no problem naming names when you asked. Now in answer to your first question. How does one my age become a mother to this fabulous family? Some are mine who came by birth as well as by adoption. My grandmother is the head for she allowed me to learn from her. Now that I lead she has retired though she was the woman injured in this roundup. Her age is the same as mine, twenty-two. My daughters are twenty-one and quads," Mara's eyes sparkled as she waited for the woman's response.

"Finally, someone who understands what having quads means. My four have survived having a mother who is head of law enforcement in this state while we were going to school, working, and growing up. Mine were born to me, and my husband has not put in an appearance since. Some friends stepped in and helped until the kids were six and began school. Now they are teenagers, and that is another problem. However we are getting through it," said Jenn.

"I have three sets of quads. Love them all. Are there any other questions? I understand some of my family feel that it is mealtime. Would you care to join us at the buffet portion of the restaurant? It is our favorite place when in town," laughed Mara.

"Wouldn't want to intrude," replied Jenn though she had a feeling she should get to know this group.

"Okay, then let's go. Pat, we are on our way," sent Mara.

When they reached the food place, Randy led them to the back room and family.

"Why don't you remember to eat, ever?" asked Granda of her granddaughter.

"Business first my dear," laughed Mara.

"Not in my book," said Granda and everyone laughed for that had a double meaning to the family.

Soon everyone had full plates and was seated yet no one touched their food.

"If no one objects I think that Randy should bless us. Please dear," said Mara who was so very proud of her daughter.

Once the blessing was said everyone began eating except for the last four who went to fill plates. Mara picked up the bill that was waiting and paid the entry fee. She noted the reserved sign in the window of their dining room.

"Mom, did you get Pi?" asked Joy.

"Pie, who said pie," replied Kennet who got up to find if it was true.

"Yes, dear, she is out in the pasture. The others went home," Mara told Joy.

"Keri, how is Kelly doing? Does she like riding the miniatures?" asked Mara to keep the conversation going.

"She is doing her best to get dressed in the morning, so she can ride Jo-Jo. I have no idea the origin of the name. However, that is her choice. I'm amazed that a two-year-old can ride so well. She and Ruskin have become good friends," replied the beaming mother who could recall how both she and her daughter had nearly died until Randy took over.

"She told me that she would ride Jo-Jo until other horses the right size came, then she would let others ride her friend," said Dan.

The dinner conversation continued allowing Jenn some glimpses into their lives. When the meal ended, Mara nodded at Jimmy, and he left with two other men. In a short time, they were back and resumed their seats.

"We are going sightseeing. Jenn is going to join us at my request. I'm sure days off are allowed in her profession," said Mara.

"Sometimes," replied Jenn, though her mind was reeling at all she was learning, and wondering how she was to fulfill being POC, for those who were lead officers for each state had someone. Not all would be invited to join her. However, as some showed a keen interest, she would add them to her list.

"The buses are outside, and the men are driving. All aboard," directed Randy and Mara smiled. When they got outside, they found three tour buses waiting.

"Mom, you did well. I appreciate you allowing me to step in when I know you have had enough. The last thing they should have done was kidnap Granda and dad. I know how tired you must be, so sit back and let the rest of us earn our keep for now," Randy said after asking for a silence bubble.

As they departed their transportation at the Grand Ole Opry, their clothing changed to evening leisure attire. Mara stopped at the ticket booth to speak with the person waiting inside.

"We are the N-Sign Clan and believe that you are expecting us," Mara advised the young woman.

"I'm not part of the performers but would you object if I just sat and listened?" asked the eighteen-year-old who did not challenge her, ask for ID, or in any way show doubt that Mara was who she said she was.

"You are welcome. May I know your name?" Mara asked as Alina stepped up by her mom.

"I'm Baira, called Beri," the girl replied.

"Alina, would you be willing to serve as a contact for Beri?" asked Mara.

"Yes, mom. Come with me Beri our seats are waiting," replied Alina who still had a bit of a Swiss accent. She knew that her mom was asking her to serve as a guard to Beri.

"Let's find our seats. No Jero and Jo you will not rush behind the curtain. You will sit and enjoy. We will meet the performers after the shows are over," said Mara.

The men of the family sat behind the women who were their wives. The two guests were centered in the group while the rest sat in a way that put them all in the middle of the auditorium and where they could easily hear and see the performers. Then another group of people entered, and they stood to one side. One woman moved to the front of the seated group.

"May I speak to Mara please?" asked the person.

"Present," said Mara as she stood.

"Since we are on this schedule wondered if you would mind if we listened in before our turn?" asked the woman whose nametag said, Sherry.

"Have a seat," Mara told her in warm welcome.

Soon the program was going. Mara had listened to at least two dozen performers before a break came.

"Stay in your seats until your turn comes. Walk up the left-hand side of the stage, and the show will continue followed by another show you can hear. Shandra, Randy, Granda, we lead."

Soon Mara sat with a twelve-string guitar on her lap.

"Hello folks, we need those in our audience to take an oath. My daughter Randy will give it to you."

A security bubble formed over those in the auditorium and those on the stage.

"Thank you, Randy, I am Mara also called the mother of the clan. Don't get up and leave yet," she said as she saw someone on the far side stand up.

"You will be the one leaving," said the man who had not even heard the call.

"Why? We were invited and are here to meet some performers," responded Mara.

"You are here to spread your propaganda, and I'm to see you shut down!"

Thunder froze the man in place. They would stick to the schedule.

"Those of you in the audience, it looks like you may have a full day of programs. Please remain in your seats and do not participate unless a member of my family asks you to. Have faith that what you see is happening and that you must not take part."

People began filing into the auditorium until it appeared that it could not hold anymore.

"G might be best to take everyone to a book. Put our current audience in risers by the separate groups with those who have already performed in one and a stage for each group yet to make their appearance. It seems these gate crashers want next turn," said Mara in a voice of edged steel.

"Mom, I'm up again. See the man who spoke? Now look at him closely, he is Brison's twin Berryson. Garrison is their father," reported Randy.

"I'm sorry, yet agree you are the best one for the task. Let me give you something first," Mara then reached out to her daughter and whispered in her ear.

Randy backed up and looked at Mara in amazement then smiled and put on her Doctor's face again. The people in the building moved to a book where they sat in risers according to their reason for being there. Except for the last bunch who was left standing in a corral.

Mara looked around and had a small frown. There were the performers from the stage; next were the Southern Gospel Group, the bunch in the corral, then four more sets of tiered seats appeared behind the women. Four women walked over to Jenn and spoke. She nodded, and the women departed to join the law enforcement group now occupying the last four sections.

"That was the women who asked to meet you, and the groups are their support group from each of their states. I note we are all behind you and none will participate."

Jenn advised Mara quietly then spoke louder.

"All oaths show as given. Please proceed," said Jenn in a firm voice that carried.

"Hello, Berry, what made you think the party couldn't go on without you? I ask you as I did your brother, when will you ever grow up?" Randy asked.

"My dad and brother are missing, and they were to capture some folks at a craft show in town. Care to explain?" he asked.

"No, no reason to do that. Why did you come?" Randy again asked.

"We are here to eliminate some people who think they can run the world. They will be put out of business before we leave here," he said in a nasty loud voice.

"That's your call though not sure I would recommend it," Randy advised for her last warning.

He didn't even reply to her, yet weapons were seen throughout his group as he spoke to them.

Randy continued to wait though she noted that now her position was in the rest of the force taking vacant positions. She saw four flashes all aimed at her and pulled Lightning to return the fire. Like a well-drilled group, her family of women did the same. The men were holding guns and stood behind the lead group to be sure no one blindsided them.

When the corral group, was laying on the ground, the Thunder women raised their swords, and the men moved to the corral group and placed immobilizers on each prisoner. Mara explained that those captured were very dangerous and though she had Thunder freeze them, she felt that the immobilizers needed installed as well and sent Jimmy and his team to do the duty.

The Thunder Court would follow, and Cherry stepped up as judge and called the court to order. Followed by Gwen? As prosecutor? Mara had worked every position since becoming Thunder. Now she could supervise her group and let them learn as she did.

"As a lawyer for the state, you will answer my questions or face contempt of court charges. None of you will speak until your turn comes. Who oversees this group?" asked Gwen and there was no smile to be seen.

"I have the honor," said a woman from the back of the group. She moved to the front when released from the immobilizer.

"Name, address, assets, and a list of all crimes you have directed, led and participated in any place. You see I am a lawyer with licenses throughout this world and a few others. Now speak!" Gwen said firmly.

When everyone had spoken, the testimonies were signed, and the photos and all arms were identified by the person who wore them.

"Officer Jenn please notify your force of pickup at the Opry. Any vehicles near the event that belongs to this bunch will go to your local cop shop for teardown. Those units will be replaced with new and put on car haulers, and I will take care of them," Mara advised.

"They are waiting," Jenn responded.

"Pat, please open the door," directed Randy.

Those waiting entered and moved the prisoners as well as all else that was the result of a Thunder Court. The ones injured were charged with attempted murder though their histories showed that they had many accusations of murder against each. All of them went on buses to be chained to the seats and wearing cuffs. No shoes, belts, ties, hats, coats, jewelry, or glasses were allowed. None of the prisoners spoke only followed directions given by the person in charge of that line.

When the felons and law were gone, Mara stepped onto the stage.

"I made a promise that my family didn't hear, yet. A family group is going to perform for you at this location to avoid any other interruptions. There may be two separate performances. The first one is the one we started before the interruption. It is musical in nature, and we will see what happens after that. Then we will hear some Southern Gospel and see what else is on the agenda," said Mara while Randy grinned a face-splitting grin.

Mara turned to the piano and began the drill. Randy followed then Shandra and Granda. By the time everyone had played every instrument the audience in all tiers were standing which resulted in a few curtain calls.

"Mom, may I call the Gospel groups?" asked Randy.

"Go ahead; you might even know a few of them," responded her mom with her smile evident.

"When all commitments are taken care of, the performers, other than family, are to meet with Jo and Jero who are taking bookings for an auditorium in Montana. It gives me the greatest of pleasures to welcome the singers of the Southern Gospel groups. Who leads?" asked Randy.

"That would be me. How can we follow the Opry, the Thunder Court, the Family, and do it justice?" asked a woman.

"Remember who you serve, as do we all. The schedule was agreed to before we knew you were available, or your performance would have been first and Family last. The stage is yours," said Randy with a smile. It had just dawned on her that none of them would know her for she was ten or fifteen years younger than they expected.

"Ran, do you allow an old friend to say hello? I'm not sure it is you although would greatly regret not being able to speak with you," said a person nearby.

"Gloria, how did you know?"

"One never forgets some people and age has no bearing," the woman responded.

"Stick around, and we will talk after the meetings are over," Randy told her for this was a woman who held a door open for her at a time in her life when there seemed no way out.

"I would like that and thank you."

"Ran, I hope you changed that name," said another with a bite to her voice.

"I am Randy and a doctor," she responded.

"Then you made it. This group put on a couple of fantastic shows here," spoke another woman in a pleasant tone.

"It is what we do," Randy told her.

"Appreciate being allowed to see it all."

"Which group are you with Betsy?" Randy asked the rude woman.

"I'm part of Texas law."

"We will be meeting with your group once the program is complete."

"I will tell them."

"Not to worry."

"Thank you, Thunder. I always wondered if they remembered though my life has begun anew and each of us has worked our way to the top in our fields. Gloria, I will talk to you, and that is all other than what mom directs. Betsy can forget she knew me once upon a time. I am home with my family, and that is all that matters," Randy told T.

"I'm glad for we wouldn't allow you to leave," said Mara as she and Jimmy were seen standing nearby.

"No worries mother and dad. I'm here for the long haul," replied Randy who then gave each of them a hug.

The first performance began, and everyone sat back to enjoy the rest of the program. When the last person left the stage, Mara again stepped up.

"Originally I said performance for performance. If we can hold you for another short period, we will fulfill our bargain. Will take just a moment to call for our support team," Mara advised and called for the mounts for her whole group and included the children in the call.

Soon everyone was mounted on their personal mounts. Kelly was babbling at her mount and waving her hand around as if explaining something to her mount. An arena replaced the corral and the seating moved to both sides where all could see. Alina called for Shira and took her place in line on Pi. First, she asked Jenn if she would play host to Beri until the program was over at which time she would return with Alina.

Pat and Mara led the group with Randy and Shandra behind them. Next came the littles and then by age as the group rode in. It was identical to the ride they made at home to be used at the arena if they had to miss a performance.

When the day ended, they had spent seven days meeting commitments, just with the performances. People were thanked and allowed to depart in the same order they appeared. All performers were enjoying the day and the presentations. Smiles were seen on most faces, and no one seemed bothered by the time frame.

Shandra was asked to brief the top female officers of each state. However Randy pulled her aside first, and they had a private conversation. The woman called Betsy never recalled having seen them in action. She did not meet any of the T groups or attend any training. Her place in law enforcement was no longer open to her, she forgot the oath and was removed from the area. Betsy never again wore a law enforcement uniform or carried a weapon.

Chapter 11

The family grows

Another became the lead law enforcement officer in Texas. The one who was thinking about applying was leaving her spot in Oklahoma due to family concerns and moving to Texas, where she hoped to be offered the position the other woman had held.

"Hello ladies, thank you for joining us. We will be doing business in each of your states soon. Now you have seen how we operate it will make it easier for you to know the procedure when you get a call. Also, the oaths help. Officers, thank you for taking the oath. Have you any questions before you are released?"

The entire field of people was frozen in place and a bubble of silence was placed over Amber and Mara for this woman would need protection Thunder advised her host.

"Not a question, a comment. I doubt this is a program usually presented to outsiders. Thank you, for allowing us to attend. It is an honor not only to meet you but to learn a bit about your amazing talents. Though we cannot share what we have seen, we can honestly recommend Thunder to any of our co-workers as a part of law enforcement," said a tall, beautiful woman.

"Thank you for being willing to meet with us. We are not a threat to any of you. Our intent is to make your task a bit easier as we take on some that might otherwise fall through the cracks. We have a few tools that are not available to everyone," Mara replied.

"A few? How understated that is. You people have done so much that we consider impossible and make it look like something to strive to accomplish. If the opportunity ever comes up again, I will enjoy sharing some time with you," Amber replied with a smile.

"It will happen. Any other comments or questions?" responded Mara then she became Thunder and released the whole group to repeat her question.

"Any other comments or questions?" she asked.

No one moved or spoke, so the meeting with Shandra ended and the law enforcement personnel, minus Jenn and Amber who were asked to remain, departed the area.

They joined Randy who sat before the Gospel singers talking with them.

"I get the idea that you have questions you would like to have answers to. Things like why we asked you to come, who we are, who the other people are, and why you? I can answer if you like or will ask the leader of the group to answer them. What is your choice?" asked Randy who spotted a few former friends in the group waiting and listening. She had no desire to blow her cover and continued to listen to the conversations around her.

"Mom, I think a few of these folks may have some questions they are not willing to ask me," laughed Randy.

"She's your mom?" asked one in astonishment and a few nodded their heads in agreement though it was uncertain if because they were shocked or because they believed it to be true.

"Yes, and proud to be so. I have around seventy in my lead family from age two to age fifty-two. After that are some grandkids, great-grandkids, and let me see, no great-greats are here yet, for me at least," Mara explained to the person asking.

"What you ladies have seen today is my family in action. We train constantly to maintain our expertise in all areas. It is not a case of showing off, but rather proving we can do what is required. Like with you ladies, some days are very long. However, it is necessary if we are to survive. We work hard and play just as hard. Backgrounds are done on all allowed to join us. Everyone is oath-bound to keep our secrets. Thank you for allowing us to hear you folks perform. Our schedules make it almost impossible for us to attend shows until a stadium opened in my hometown. Now we might get to see you folks from time to time. Hope so," said Mara.

"Mom, the gospel singers are curious and wondered why we invited them to perform?" opened Randy.

"We enjoy a lot of music as you noticed by what we play. However, at the top of our list is Praise and Worship to the creator of all. You are the best in your fields of expertise even as we are in ours. I hope you don't feel this is a wasted day as there were so few to hear you perform. We will try to balance our part of this as we go."

"Who are the 'we' you refer to?"

"Well, that requires a few different answers. When we play instruments, I am the mom and the instructor for my family. When we ride, there are many trainers involved, yet I'm still the mom of the group. At the time of a court, I become a representative for Law Enforcement for I have a license to operate anyplace that has a side representing legalities in place. It does not matter the nation or planet if the law is being broken. We are Thunder Press."

"Who are the other attendees that were here? Why were they looking for us?"

"That was a group of Assassins sent to put us out of business, or so they said. They have tried to find our home base, threatened my family, and committed many illegal actions against society. This group is now in the hands of the local authorities with their sworn confessions presented to the Judge that will carry out sentencing."

"First off, we are honored to be able to see you folks in action and that you feel we will keep the oaths, which we will. Meeting you, a person or group only a few of us ever heard of sparked our interest and before long we had to turn some away for lack of space. I am Sherry and for now, the leader," the poised woman who stood in the place spoke.

"Thank you for taking time out of your busy lives to accommodate some space of peace and joy in our lives. None will forget the performances you gave and what a talented group of professionals you are. Hopefully, we will see you all in Montana in the not-too-distant future." Mara closed out her part for she was getting shaky and passed the meeting back to Randy.

"I have something to share then we must leave for other duties wait. When you meet someone, which opens a door for you, have faith that they will be a friend, not an enemy. If a voice says to do something, test its strength. Is it a friend or foe? Always give your best. Do not hold back or you may lose the battle. Follow the voice, and it could lead you to a better life. Honor those over you, trust those who earn that confidence, and make sure you are trustworthy as well. In the end, we are all part of the same family if we are confident and obey," Randy told them.

"Preach on sister," said a woman.

"I carry many titles, and that is one I cherish. My duties vary, and each of us has a variety of skills. Now I'm sorry. However, we must depart. God be with each of you until we meet again," Randy finished. As she spoke with the performers it allowed any wishing to sign up for a gig in Montana to meet with Jo and Jero and get their names on the list.

The Gospel singing group departed leaving only the N-Sign Clan and their guests, including the girl from the ticket window.

"You are amazing, daughter mine," said Mara as she gave Randy a hug. Mara was so thankful that her daughter stepped up and took over leadership duties when her mom was so tired she could not function.

"So are you, mother mine," Randy replied for she had not been certain that Mara would allow her to take over, even for a short time, yet there was no conflict between them for which she was thankful.

"Would you three have time to meet us at the motel tomorrow? Tonight, we need to get some rest. No business will be discussed tomorrow, just a day to relax and enjoy. Go to the motel next door and ask for the manager. Her name is Heidi. Tell her you have an appointment with Mara, and she will personally bring you to an area with hot pools, waterfalls, and us. Goodnight friends and thank you for coming. Jenn, you too are to join us tomorrow as I know you have teenagers to keep tabs on. Amber, that means you as well for we will be taking you home when we go. Your room is waiting at the motel, and you are booked as part of this family," Mara advised for she was still in control even when exhausted.

The woman blinked her eyes at the comment. Amber was shocked that she was going to join the family, even if for only a day or so. What an amazing group she found them to be.

Mara made sure that Amber had a room as did Beri and both would spend the night there. Food was catered to the leaders for Mara finally admitted she was not moving for a while. Merry was with them and would make sure that everyone had food. Mara asked that they have no visitors that evening, for she needed a break, which meant her entire family needed one.

When the team reached the hotel floor that was theirs, Randy led Mara to her room, and there she received a double shot of vitamins to get some energy in her body. Then her mom was tucked in bed, and she called for Shandra to stay with her after the guard also received a shot.

The lead group awakened the following morning feeling rested, so they knew that it was a Thunder night. Mara called a meeting when she was sure folks were up.

"Okay, here is what we are going to do today. Breakfast is in the foyer downstairs as it comes with the rooms which won't apply to us. Merry will pick up an assortment for up here so that you can eat whatever you wish. Our guests will need to be brought up here. I neglected to give them time so Alina would you get them? Their rooms are two-zero-seven and two-zero-nine. Bring them up here please."

Mara looked at the sideboard in the room and there was everything that would also be found in the foyer downstairs. Since the service was throwaway items, no one had to do dishes. It was nice when you owned a place to stay and could say what you wanted when, without it costing any extra, she chuckled.

When the two women followed Alina into the conference room Amber was first to spot the breakfast and asked if it was for them.

"If you notice we waited for you, now everyone takes a seat, and let's bless it before we begin," said Randy for she spotted something others had not. Mara was still exhausted and this would indeed be a rest day for everyone.

"Mom, I would like some time with you, and if you want to

speak to Amber that might be the time to do so," said Randy.

"Yes, I know. Let's eat first then Alina can entertain Beri while we chat," responded Mara without any challenge.

As normal at breakfast the family chatted about things in general, however, no business was discussed, including the previous day's performances. When Mara finished her breakfast, Randy met her mom and they departed with Amber to Mara's suite.

"Have a seat Amber. I think for our conversation we need a bubble of silence if you don't mind. We believe this area is fully secure and an AI oversees the area, however, it seems to me like you were asking for a private conversation, and you shall have one. You are going to be given a bit more information. I'm not sure why you wished to spend some time with us, however, my understanding is that you want to be part of this family. Did I understand correctly?" asked Mara.

"Yes, may I explain?"

"Certainly, if you wish, though you do not have to," replied Mara with her beautiful smile.

"Thank you, Mara. You don't even know me, yet you put me on the schedule right away. I know how exhausted you were yesterday and appreciate your welcome. Yes, we need to have a conversation and it might take a while. I would rather work with and for you than anyone else. The reason for leaving Oklahoma is there is a contract out on me. It is time to disappear or hire backup. When Jenn was asked to try to locate you and make sure I got a chance to meet you, it was to explain this situation. She knows there is a problem, only not what. We busted a drug cartel, and I was leading the strike. Someone informed on me and gave my ID to the Lord. One saving grace is I always wear gloves that are not seen and do not leave fingerprints. Usually, one of my talents is the ability to disappear in a crowd. This time it wasn't as easy. Someone totaled my vehicle the day I was to depart for Tennessee, so I changed my persona and came as you see me. This is not my normal style. I work as a model in my off-duty hours. Being a model and good at disguises helps. Being a UCA also helps. Never is it my intent to bring you problems. Just aim me in a direction and I will get out of your location before this blows up if you would rather not have the problem that I am. The night's rest was much needed. I have not slept in a week. Nor have you, as I understand it. I'm asking for sanctuary if you allow it. I will do anything you tell me to if you allow me to remain. At the same time, I will not beg, nor will I intentionally bring danger to you and your family," Amber tried to explain.

"Randy, will you please explain to this 'former' UCA what is required? She falls under me. Meet your newest sister. Amber, your name is a giveaway, here we allow you to choose the first name, however, the last name is mine and you get lost in the mix."

"You mean it? You are offering to adopt me, even knowing I'm under deathwatch by assassins? Mara, I accept most wholeheartedly. You would even adopt me and give me a new identity?" Amber asked in shock. She had worked hard to become who she was and didn't hesitate a minute to give it all up for a chance to join this amazing family.

"Amber, welcome to our family. Mom, please lay down over there on your bed, we are going to have a chat. We knew of your coming and to get you secure. That is why we had to have you with us when we took on the one hundred assassins. None of those we spent three days with will ever recall seeing you in any form. I am the family surgeon, among other duties. Do you have any tattoos, scars, or disfigurements that will need to be removed or changed?" Randy said.

"I can only say it again, I know this is not a setup. I feel you folks are one hundred percent the most awesome people anyone could even meet, let alone be allowed to join their family. Let me show you something," Amber responded. Then she reached up and from her throat she began to pull upward, and a full-face mask was removed.

The features under it were clear except for a jagged scar that ran from one ear to the opposite shoulder.

"My dad tried to kill me. Nearly succeeded too. He is no longer living. They put me in the witness program. The governor of Oklahoma was under orders to not give out any of my birth information. Someone got to him. He was the one that put me in charge of that bust. We did what we were sent to do and captured the entire bunch. All of them are in prison. Wish I had your group to take them to a T court and find out what really happened. I am good at what I do, however, it is time to change me. Will you help me do that?"

"Yes, I will do that. You are looking at many hours of careful surgery. You will wear a mask while you heal. It will be a gauze one. You can trust me fully. No one except mom, her guard Shandra, and I will know what transpires. She will remain with you during the surgery and the clinic is in our home. You will remain in an assigned suite not far from mom's suite because she has kids to watch over, among other things. That will put your suite next to Alina who already knows who you are, and no one will learn it from her. I ask that you wear a true mask when outside the house for when we move you will need to as well. The rest of the time you can remain in your room without bandages if you like. The air is purified, and I will change your dressings daily. We have finished the work we came here to do. It is time to return home," Randy explained.

"My turn?" asked Mara.

"Yes, Mom, if you will remain lying down," her family surgeon told her.

"Amber, I am Thunder Press. Do you know who that person is?"

"I thought it was a myth. You mean that is your real name?"

"While you gather your thoughts, let me tell you a bit about me. I will only give you the truth unless someone else is involved and they maybe aren't given the information, so I must be evasive at that time. It will be explained later though not at the time. Does that work for you? Yes, it is my legal name, however, I also have others. I was born Mara Jacobson. You have seen us in Thunder court. Those you saw lined up before the felons are my daughters who are also Thunders. We carry swords called Lightning. Now comes the touchy part. A recent event might explain it the best. We had to move some folks by air and found out some had infiltrated the flight. I became the pilot of the plane they were on, at the same time I was giving a brief to the person who made us aware of the infiltration, while still being seen on my original ship, and then we turned in the infiltrators to the American Government which means I became four of me. You see what you thought of as a day's activity yesterday, was not. It took us a full week by the time we heard the two concerts, captured Assassins, and then did our riding drill and concert. What you apparently did not know is that the two thousand picked up later were those you captured, and they too were judged in Thunder court. My daughter is correct, I am not rested, however you were invited, and it is my desire to get to know you as all my children are known. Randy knows I will follow whatever directions she gives for I owe her my life. Trust her for she knows her skill and does it well," Mara explained.

"You must be beyond exhausted! And you got them all here? Lady, you are amazing!"

"I'm not the one that is amazing, my family is, and they keep me operational. You are correct, I'm exhausted. It will take me a week or so to get my feet back under me and that is why we will not move from here until I am ready. Once that happens we will fly home. That is why Randy is in charge."

"I think I picked up a conversation where someone said you are the mother of this clan, and your age is not what you seem. Not that it matters for you know your people and look out for everyone," commented Amber.

"I graduated HS at fifteen, University was finished at sixteen, and by seventeen my family began. You will be told the whole story little by little," Mara told her latest addition.

"I wondered why you seemed to fully trust me even before you knew my story. When I said, you are beyond belief I meant what I said. It appears to me that you live on faith. You say it and it happens. This is all very new to me and is glad to see that you do life outside the box."

"Yes, it is so. You see we welcome you and our way of showing you we intend to keep you is for you to receive full disclosure and never again worry that anyone will give you away. It is not done, and I will personally take care of anyone who tried to do so," Mara advised Amber.

"We have a few Assassins of our own and mom is not lying. In truth, I doubt she knows how, unless it is to save the life of one of her kids. Relax and if you give Alina the keys to your room she will see that all evidence of anyone having been there is removed. Your belongings will be in your suite at home when we get there. That way there is no way to find out where you went. Kari is an amazing makeup artist and will give you a new look. She may also have the materials with her to do a full makeover. We always carry our normal wear in various sizes in case of need. You will be put in boots, jeans, a hat, and a jacket. No one will notice that you are any different from the rest of us. Your last name is now N-Sign. What would you prefer for the first name?"

"If I'm to be your daughter, why don't you choose a name for me then? I will be happy with whatever you choose I assure you."

"I like your name as it is. At the same time, it is necessary we change it. You have sisters Randy, Joy, and two sets of quads that are adults. There is also a set of two boys and two girls that is a quad. Shandra is also your sister and my personal guard. There are others, however, let's let you learn them a few at a time. Randy, if you will, her clothing is in the closet in your room," directed Mara as she thought about a name.

When Randy returned, the name was ready.

"Your birth sibs are Kennet, Joy, and Alina. Then there is Jo, Cherry, Shandra, Mike, Gretch, Spicer, Chris, and Rae. That is in the lead group. There are others. I name you Kara Lea or KL if in a hurry. Welcome daughter to the fold," Mara told her.

"May I have a hug to seal the bargain?" asked Kara Lea.

"If my doctor will let me stand up for a hug," replied Mara with a chuckle.

"Okay," said Randy with a grin.

In the process, Randy also got a hug.

"This is what will happen. I told you we would be at a special place with hot pools, waterfalls, and us for a relaxing time. We are going there once I finish a second interview. I will lay down and if I fall asleep, just let me be and in time I will rejoin you," said Mara.

"Randy, I will remain here if you show Kara where she can stay until we leave. Wait until we get home to let her pick out a suite. For now, I think we need her to serve as a backup if I'm to be down until we leave. For now, will you please send in Beri?"

A tap on the door and Kara Lea immediately went to answer it. It was Alina and Beri waiting at the door.

"Now, if you three will have a seat in my front room, I will have a chat with Beri and then we can change locations," Mara advised.

The young woman Beri sat in the chair that Mara designated and waited to see what was required.

"Beri, you didn't hesitate at all when I said come. Why is that?" asked the Monarch, Mara.

"I had a dream that you would claim me. I was told to finish high school and to get a job at the Opry, even if it was a volunteer position. You let me listen to the beautiful program for free. When you said to stay with Alina she told me that it was a forever gig. Please let me stay. I'll do whatever you tell me to, if I know-how, and will ask training if it is an unknown task," replied the girl.

"Tell me a bit about your background. Where is your family, what has your life been to this point, why do you wish to go with us, and anything else you think I should know?" Mara replied.

"I am a street kid. Didn't have a home. Couldn't stay where I started as it was dangerous. Different people allowed me to sleep in a garage or an extra bedroom for a few days as I attended school. Found an older lady who agreed to be my grandmother to get my class grades and such. I graduated three months ago. All I own is what I'm wearing and my diploma of graduation," explained the girl.

"You now have a forever home, if you want one. That includes training in the skills we use daily. We are a branch of law enforcement that works worldwide. Sometimes we even seem to go further. An oath was given by you that you would keep our secrets as we keep yours. Beri, you are keeping something from me that is important. Please explain," the Monarch directed softly.

"If they find me, I'm dead. I'm tired of running. I refused to work in some professions. Then their groups were busted as soon as I refused. They thought I informed others about them. That would have been stupid. I'm one kid, not an army and even armies would have a problem with some of those groups," responded Beri.

"You are the second person to join me in the last month or two with similar problems. What town are you from?"

"I grew up in Pleasant Valley Iowa. Hitched a ride to Nashville and got the job you found me at for I knew it was time," Beri did not hesitate in answering all questions, except to be sure her responses were as complete as she could make them.

"Okay, as soon as Randy returns she will see that you have clothing for the remainder of our trip home. We will be here for a few days while everyone gets some rest. Duties await each of us upon our return. You will be given training. Would you ask Alina to get Shandra and Randy for me please?" said Mara as she remained on the bed. Something was not resonating right with her, and it had her apprehensive, which she usually wasn't. Was it the girl or something she would be involved in that would affect Mara's family?

The girl departed on her errand and soon Mara's daughters were in her room.

"Shut the door and call for a bubble of silence," directed Mara without moving.

Neither of the women spoke once the bubble was in place. They could tell by their mom's voice that something was afoot.

"Something is not right. I think the girl is more than she is willing or able to explain. Not sure if she is here of her own free will or if there is someone who put her in this position. As she sits, she is a danger to us. She gave oath therefore she cannot tell anyone anything she knows about any of us. At the same time if this is a legitimate call we need to get her free. What are your thoughts?" Mara asked her girls.

"Somehow someone is feeding off your energy. You are more tired now than you were when you awakened. That is not a good thing." Randy allowed her concern to show.

"Shandra, have Pat set up communications for Kara Lea and soon. Randy, you are known to be concerned about me. I will borrow energy and we will get this done. As soon as Kara Lea has what she needs she is to get a makeover and come see me. I'm not sure how vulnerable we are. We did not allow either woman the keys to our level. That does not mean a lot to some folks, however since we use palm prints to get in, they should have been denied entry. By the way, this is the last time we stay in a motel that allows others access. I need a local property that will house up to two hundred people in our normal suites. Prefer new taxes and maintenance paid for five years while I find who to put in control of our homes. It will be up to them to pay taxes, hire maintenance, do annual things like change furnace filters, etc. I think that might be a good job for Kara Lea. Totally different from what she was doing and therefore won't make her as obvious."

"Yes, mom, I'm here. What can I do for you?" asked Kara Lea after tapping on the door and then waiting for someone to answer. She stepped inside, looked around, and nodded to Randy and Shandra before speaking.

"Silence bubble," said Randy, and all felt it form.

"Wait, Pat to twin room," sent Mara on her communicator.

Instead of coming in the door, Pat was standing with them immediately.

"Need to check my ears. They aren't working properly," said Mara who then looked around the room. Kara Lea, Shandra, Randy, and Pat were soon checking out the entire room.

Mara had explained to Kara Lea what she wanted her to do. It would require her to remain with the lead group without anyone realizing that she now controlled the events with approval from Mara's daughters.

Randy wanted to be sure of Kara Lea and used Lightning to check her out. She was good as gold.

Sharron L Ensign P.O. Box 583 Helena, MT 59624
Assassins Target Mara Bk 3
406-458-7091

"I will check my sources and see what is available. Might I suggest the building in lot forty-two? It will hold what you need and follows the main pattern," said Kara Lea.

All those present knew what she was suggesting, and it was immediately in place. The new home for them in Tennessee was a ranch located behind a hill yet within four miles of where the current motel was located. It had the required two hundred suites, an onsite AI, was fully stocked with groceries, and ready for occupancy on two hundred forty acres.

Kara Lea spoke into her communication device with a direct line to Mara.

"The papers are signed, and Jenn is waiting for you. She got here in the last few minutes. She will follow my lead. Randy, you need to check on Mara in whatever way will best secure her, though I have a suggestion. Shandra if you stay with Randy, it might be best for everyone knows you are usually Mara's guard. Let me wander around with Jenn. After all, we are both outsiders, when it is convenient," said Kara Lea.

"And?" said Mara softly for she understood what was being asked by Kara Lea and wanted to know her own part in what was going on.

"You remain with me and Jenn will join us," replied Kara Lea.

"Randy, check mom for drugs. We all ate together. It would have been easy to slip something in her drink while she was speaking with one of the family," said Kara Lea.

Randy immediately dropped a medkit from her armband and did the required test.

"Right in one," replied Randy.

"Please Kara Lea, don't be the problem, only the solution." Mara pleaded.

"On my word as Amber and Kara Lea, you have nothing to fear from me. I am in truth your unknown guard. Shandra, I'm not here to take your position. I need this haven and will serve as an unknown backup. No one other than those here present will know that. Mom, we need you out of here and now," said Kara

Lea.

The women walked out of the suite and no one realized that Mara was with them.

The women all nodded and departed. Mara was doing much better now that the counter agent was in her body.

"I need a rental car so that I can move around some. I will even pay for it if you allow."

"Not necessary. There are three vans in the parking lot. I have a set of keys with me. We will use one of those. Need to inspect the place you just purchased," responded Mara.

The keys were exchanged from Mara to Kara Lea, however in a way that no one would know there had been an exchange. Kara Lea had opened van doors as if inspecting the inside. Jenn came out of the hotel and joined them. The women acted as if putting something inside. Once Mara was inside Kara Lea shut the door and moved to the driver's side. The van moved away from the lot and took a paved road that passed near the place the family now resided.

When Mara started to speak, Kara Lea shook her head.

"Good to see you again Jenn. Did you ever have problems with hearing when you were a kid?" Kara Lea asked.

"Yes, prone to ear infections," Jenn replied.

"My sister Pat also had that problem," commented Kara Lea.

Mara asked Thunder to let Pat know to meet them at the new location for the vans were bugged.

Within minutes they were at the new location. Kara Lea had a smile on her face when she saw the place. An operating ranch with horses in the pasture, a woman waiting in the yard, and it looked wonderful and inviting.

Kara Lea departed the vehicle and spoke to the woman.

"Hello folks, I'm Iva. The stock is thoroughbred racers. Two studs on site. Metoo, come meet your new family," said the woman in a louder voice.

Sharron L Ensign P.O. Box 583 Helena, MT 59624
Assassins Target Mara Bk 3
406-458-7091

A beautiful German Shepherd came running. The dog stopped and sat down with head cocked to one side. Then it moved to Kara Lea and offered a paw. She shook the paw and waited. If the dog went to Mara they were in trouble. The dog moved to Jennifer and again offered a paw. It was accepted and shaken. The dog then sat down on its haunches and lifted both feet in the air. The women relaxed. Yes, Metoo knew that Mara was there and that it was not to be known.

"Thank you, Metoo. We are honored by your presence," said Kara Lea with a smile at the new guard dog.

Chapter 12

A needle in a haystack

A second van reached the scene and Pat stepped out of it.

"Hello sisters, how goes it? Have a couple of messages for you," said Pat.

"Iva, we would like to use the barn to have a conversation, if you don't mind," said Kara Lea.

"Not a problem. Send Metoo to get me when I am needed," the woman replied.

They walked to the barn and saw two horses waiting for them.

"You are here too? My goodness, thank you dear ones. Someone is out to get me again. This is my second guard Kara Lea or KL. She has our full trust. We are not sure what is going on. Someone put a drug in my food. What have you to share?" asked Mara of her twin.

"The vans are all bugged. I have disabled them, and they will drop off after we take the units through a car wash. Suggest you move everyone by a door. Someone is getting too close," reported Pat.

"I will not be boxed in. We will tour the building after which we will use the door to enter our planes and depart via book," Mara said firmly.

"I'm thankful to you for getting her outside the area. We must have access to my sister, for she is the one in charge. Thunder, Mara, Randy, Shandra, and I are with you a hundred percent. At present time Granda is not advised of the situation. She will be once we are in a more secure environment. A concern I do have is this girl Beri. What if someone is using her to reach us?

Would you consider putting her in a book until we are clear? That way she won't know where she is going to tell anyone else if that is the case. I would suggest that x-rays be taken of her as a requirement for employment. Kara Lea, would you allow the same? We need it for our records regardless," said Pat.

"Certainly. I do have one concern. I do not look as I did yesterday. It is my hope that Beri will feel that you accept me as if I belong and therefore I'm not the woman she met yesterday. I have a new name, a new hairdo, and different clothing. Also, you gave me free rein to come and go. It makes it appear that I am part of the leaders not part of the staff. Will that work for you folks?" Kara Lea asked.

"We will make sure to address you as a member of the family with duties you are trusted to do if you agree. The next challenge is to get Mara home. To do that we need to also free up Randy and Shandra. Any suggestions?" Pat asked.

"Yes. Jenn, you said you would do whatever I asked without question. Does that still apply even if you find yourself in another state?" asked Kara Lea.

"Yes, in this case, it does. I have notified my family that I'm on assignment and a relative will step in with the kids. The office knows that I'm on a mission to train with Thunder. No more needed to be said. Tell me what is required," said Jennifer.

"Jenn, you just became my guard for the moment. You and I will board my ship direct and meet everyone else there. It will still put me where I can be found by my family, however, my number of guards is growing. Or I can rest in one of the pilot's rooms during the flight and not make it known by any except my guards that I'm even aboard. Two of my stallions have also shown up here. Will put them on the flight for return," Mara suggested.

"It might be best to send them home direct for once we depart this location there may be an attempt to strike at the home base if they know where it is located," said Kara for she had asked Mara if she would allow a copy of the memories needed to do the task she had volunteered to handle.

"Yes, they know where we live, however, we have a full army

ready to meet them if they enter that area. What concerns me is leaving Heidi and Becky holding the bag after our disappearance. It could make them very vulnerable," Mara said for those who were adoptees to her as well. Since she knew that KL already had those memories all Mara had to do was activate them in the woman.

"Iva suggested that you take Metoo for training in your organization. Iva and her three sons will remain on duty here to be sure no one bothers the place. She is well qualified to care for the horses and is an excellent marksman with any weapon. I hired her when Thunder and I bought the place. That allows you a bit more flexibility for when you must be elsewhere in a flash. Is there some way you could leave a group here to keep an eye on your two employees? By that, I mean Heidi and Becky, is it?" Kara commented.

Randy was amazed at how much the woman knew about the family, then she saw the slight nod from Mara and knew it was all happening as it should.

"I hate to leave first string here for I need them from time to time. Just a minute," said Mara as she contacted Shandra.

"Daughter, we are discussing. Thank you for keeping us all working together. We are going to have to depart soon, which will leave H and B on their own. Yes, they have the training, however, there are only two of them and we have just put many people in prison by our actions. They need some support in case anyone connects us with them. I'm open to suggestions. Would MB offer any possibilities?" asked Mara.

"R says it is time to have my former injury checked. Be back with you in a few," replied Shandra.

"They are headed to the clinic and will do the research and get back to us in a few minutes," Mara told her staff.

KL chuckled but made no comment.

"Nice to have you aboard Karlea. You fit right in. Jenn and I will go directly to the ship and wait for everyone there. I am going to leave Beri in your care, indirectly. If she is guilty we need to remove her and all memories of us, if she isn't then we need to get her to safety. Normally I handle my own problems, however until my body cooperates better will sit back and watch you pros at work. Jennifer, you will be paid for your time and inconvenience as you serve as a guard for me. Karlea you know your place in the scheme of things and once you take your test your income can be computed. For now, trust you will be paid."

"Mom, we agree. I have some information for you. How many are on the top level? Can have a full company in place within a few minutes. Would you object to their staying at the ranch to cut down on costs? They can eat at the buffet and have Becky put it on the account. They will watch over Becky and Heidi until things settle for us. Then we can send a plane to bring them home again," Shandra reported via her direction communication device.

"Okay, then two studs and two women are departing. Oh yes, and a dog named Metoo. Shira and Pi are aboard and know we are coming. I hope you left a few meals aboard for times like this," laughed Mara.

"Go you one better, will have Becky fix up your favorites and deliver them myself," said Randy with laughter via her communicator.

"Hope the door works for you," said Mara though she was trying to keep a light mood on the group.

"Granda guarantees it," replied the Doc with her matching smile.

"What would we do without you?" asked Mara in truth.

"Let's not try to find out."

"Agreed," replied all voices.

"Metoo, go get Iva, please. If you don't mind we are going to take you with us for some training. Then if you want to return here it will be done. I am Mara and head of this Clan. Thank you for not making my presence known for we know someone is trying to locate me. They think I'm at the hotel yet aren't sure. Yes, I will wait while you get Iva," Mara told the dog.

Soon the woman and dog joined them.

"Metoo says I need to hurry and come see you because you

are invisible," laughed the woman Iva.

"Iva, my daughter says she hired you to keep watch over this property. Is that correct? What is your requested salary and how much does it cover? We may show up for a month at a time, however, the rest of the time the property is in your control. The ranch is owned by a corporation and under a number. You will be paid by number so that no one can give you problems by connecting you and my family. My banker will be in contact with you. Her name is Rae. Oh, KL, how about getting Iva's oath," said Mara who then looked for a place to sit down.

Each time KarLea was asked to do something she smiled and did as directed. Mara noted how the shine in her eyes seemed to get brighter each time she was trusted to do something for the clan.

Jenn quickly pulled a chair out of the tac room and placed it on a firm surface for Mara.

A vibration in the air had them all alert. Out of a stall came Randy and, in her hand, was an x-ray machine. KL chuckled again and moved to the stall for her internal picture to be taken.

She fit in well as a cowgirl from Montana, even as she had fit in as a model from Oklahoma or a top law enforcement officer in Texas. Now she had new duties and would fit the role of whatever was required. She saw Mara's smile and knew they were communicating.

"I get the impression you can read my mind," said KL.

"If you believe it, then it is so," replied Mara for she needed to teach her newest member to trust in all cases.

"I am honored, and relieved," KarLea told her mom.

"Well Randy, we now know the door will open for you. What other tricks do you have up your sleeve?" asked Mara.

"Never know until I must use one of them," her daughter responded.

"Iva, my understanding is that you agreed to be hired by me, yet no salary was discussed. Give me an idea what it will cost to have you and your sons work the ranch for us," Mara directed.

Sharron L Ensign P.O. Box 583 Helena, MT 59624
Assassins Target Mara Bk 3
406-458-7091

"We used to own this ranch and our dream was to be able to work for whoever purchased it since two of the sons are leaving and the one who will remain wants to stay with the horses. With two incomes leaving the bank, we can no longer afford to keep it. Your purchase will free up some funds for us to live on and then the bills become yours. Now I can keep books for you if you wish. I'm a certified veterinarian, and horse and dog trainer. To my friends the ranch is still mine, however anytime you come, you are family and welcome. Your schedule will take precedence and you move into the mansion. I live in a ranch house outback. Mansion was just too big for me to maintain," responded the woman.

"So, what you are saying is you will need to hire a housekeeper every time we are in town?" asked Mara who chuckled for their housekeeper might be moving when they did.

"Well, that might work best," laughed Iva.

"Let's let things remain as they are for now. When we get home, I will be in touch and advise you as to what needs to be done. A building crew will be one of the items that need to be handled. They will come and certify the buildings on the property plus make a few additions that are required if my family is to live here, even for a short time. There needs to be a file on every animal on the property. Lineage, breed, offspring, etc. If any of the animals have been shown, are qualified racers, or some such status it needs to be noted. I will try to get the team to you by the first of the month. We are headed into winter and need this property weather secure before then," Mara advised.

"Just for your information, you purchased two sections of land. Samson is putting his property on the market as of tomorrow and wants the same deal I have. Between the pair of us, we have four sections. He has a place to live while his life is productive yet not at the expense of maintaining it all. His property is adjacent to this one. We might even get married and run the two spreads as one, if you agree," Iva was watching to see what kind of a response Mara would return.

"KL, your issue, you started this," laughed Mara as she put her daughter to work.

"Okay, if it is my issue, you have both sold your property,

and will be getting married to live on his half of the ranch while maintaining both properties and when we come we will live here in the mansion so there is room for all of us. If you elect to take the horses with you to his place, that is fine as we often bring horses with us. Depends on what requirements face us when we get here. We will put both ranches under one corporation so that it is easier to keep it all together. Yes, to your keeping the books, we are a bit far away to do that, though they will be monitored. Send us an update monthly so we can keep up. We have a couple of other ranches to oversee," KL looked over at Mara and they both began to laugh.

"Okay, so we have about fifty. I didn't know the count," said KL.

"Now if all parties are satisfied, KL you need to take care of the paperwork. Jennifer, you need to go with Metoo and me, too," said Mara for she was very weary.

"Sorry mom should have gotten this done quicker," apologized KL for suddenly she realized that Mara was very exhausted.

"Come on mom, I'll hold the door," said Randy, and the three women and a dog entered the stall to find they were on a large ship in the first-class section.

"Okay, Mom, to bed with you. I put two meals in the warmer for when you got here. Jenn, please be sure she eats. Don't let her wander around on her own as she gets dizzy when this tired. I will check in when a chance comes that my absence is not notable," Randy told Jenn then gave Mara a heartfelt hug and departed.

"Finally, now I can get to know you and how you fit in the story of my life," said Mara with a sigh.

"Not a lot to know. I have a set of quads which you know. All are good students and seem to enjoy learning. Given an opportunity, I would like them to spend some time on a ranch and learn the responsibility required there. I can't afford one, however. The kids still need to get some college degrees and then they can move on with their lives if that is their desire," Jennifer explained.

"Have a suggestion. First some questions. What age is your

group? How good are they in school? What year are they? Would you consider turning them over to me for a year? Will give them some training and make a few suggestions that might help them on their road in life. If they find they like our lifestyle, then you can join them. If they do not want to remain at the end of a year they will return to you here," Mara offered.

"You are kidding I'm sure," said Jennifer.

"Why not wait with the response until you have spent a little time with us at home? You know our name, yet do not know us or the family you hear often referred to. While you are with us, trust that what I say will happen, does. Shall we find the kitchen in this place and see what there is to eat? I'm hungry, so must be feeling some better," Mara said.

"I'll take the stairs and you move ahead of me. That way if you stagger I can catch you," said Jennifer with a chuckle. She found that she liked this non-conformist woman. It would be great to work with her for a while, if not a lifetime. Somehow that thought did not give her the jolt that it once might have.

"Here is my normal place. Let's set up the table and eat. No business at meal though anything else is fair game. Don't be surprised if Randy and Shandra show up now and again. They are the ones in the line below me. They prefer I know what is going on. In truth that is also my preference. Now, where are we going? You will be going to an operating ranch. Between the Thoroughbreds, Miniatures, Arabians, Racers, and Saddlebreds, to name a few, we have about fifty to a hundred ranches. You saw us perform at the arena yesterday. We own an arena where shows are held to showcase the various breeds. Also, the family rides once or twice a year to show off our skills. It is also a way to find the people we need to hire for openings we have in our staff. As my group grows a larger staff is required and I have found that restaurants and performances are a good way to do that. By the way, you didn't get a chance to bring anything with you. As of this moment you are a cowgirl on vacation. Here on the next seat is your new clothing. We don't have a shower on here, however, will let you soak in a hot tub once we get home," Mara advised.

"I have never been on a ship this size. Would you explain about it and why you have such a large one?"

"This one was used on a rescue mission for some family members. Now they are safe, yet we find we still need this size of a unit. In fact, we have more than one. Each time we go someplace we pick up those who ask to join us if they can pass the background check and we have the need. We also have a few other types of ships available. How would you like to fly one?"

"Who me? Fly a plane? Suppose I could if the need was there. Never really gave it much thought. Know that I don't usually fly due to cost," Jennifer responded.

"Well, I think that is about to change. First, you were hired by me as the most qualified law enforcement officer in this state. Next, you became my POC for any captures in that state. Then you became my guard, which also gives you a salary. While you are in Montana you could go to the university and pretest a few courses if you like. Means you would speak a few languages and have a few more skills. Your choice. Now I hate to cut this short, however, if I'm not to tip over and fall out of this chair, I am going back to bed. Please aid me in the climb then we can both take a nap," advised Mara.

Jennifer rose immediately and took the woman up the stairs to the bedrooms, each of which had two beds. Once Mara was settled Jenn returned to the first-class section and cleaned up their lunch leftovers for they might have to eat another meal later if one wasn't delivered as these were.

Mara was sound asleep when Jenn returned.

Jenn lay on her bed and thought about the amazing week. Her mind traveled back to meeting Mara and the family. How she had been welcomed and allowed to be part of what was going on. Never did she ever expect to meet Thunder Press, let alone become an employee of that dynamic personality. If this was how she appeared when exhausted, what must she be like when fully charged? Then her mind switched gears. This woman wanted Jenn to learn to fly and speak languages. Why? She had also mentioned the possibility of taking on the quad for a year. It would give her a little wiggle room to get some things done that hadn't been since they were born. She loved her kids, could she send them away for a year? That would have to be discussed with them first. As her mind ran through the information she had learned, she fell asleep and dreamed she was reading a book that she entered. It was Thunder catching her up on Mara's beginning for Jenn would be an important part of their life for the rest of hers.

"Hello, Jennifer, are you hungry?" asked another voice.

"We just ate, I think," replied the woman though she was instantly alert.

"That was many hours ago. Our group is preparing to board the flight and didn't want them to surprise you. Mom will remain here, and you guards can switch off as we fly. That way you can meet some of those who travel with us. The lead group is in first class and has no problem answering questions. Our current schedule shows we will arrive home at about four in the morning. If the airport crew is not there we will sleep on the plane until later and call them. Four a.m. is our usual time to start the day for leaders. The others sleep in until about six then the day's classes begin. Now that you have had a little time to get some rest, have you any questions of me before the influx begins?" asked Randy with a smile.

"Randy, I have been offered some amazing things. I dreamed of a world that is connected by entering a book. Somehow it seems to be very important to this family and my interaction with you all. I fully trust those of this family that I've been introduced to. It is nice to be in that kind of environment, even for a short time. I am in awe of your mom. She is a woman I would like to be like. Not once has anything been said in refusal of what was asked of her. Like playing when tired, holding court when exhausted, and then riding in a display of horsemanship that was amazing. Now she is still in control even when sleeping. What would it take to be like her?" asked Jenn.

"Asking," said another voice, and Mara sat up in bed.

"Just asking? Then I ask," replied Jenn in complete surprise.

"Training will begin the day after tomorrow. For one day we rest, eat, and relax. It was what was on the schedule for Nashville, however, didn't quite work out. Jenn, thank you," Mara said in total sincerity.

"For what? Mara, I am now your pupil and anything else you

will allow me to be. Yes, you will get my kids for a year. Yes, I will train with your trainers. The University courses will be tested. I'm not sure why, however, know it is to be done. How are you feeling?" asked Jenn.

"Randy is here to give me a shot to balance my system. You see there is a cost to my being four people at once. My internal being uses up more of some vitamins than others. Thus, we must restock me to get me back in balance. Go ahead Randy, I can talk while you poke holes in my hide," laughed Mara.

"I took my shots at home, for by being here I am timing it which means the whole family is and balance needs to be restored. Thus everyone, except the pilots, will sleep on the way home. There will be a watch on board in case of emergencies, but that is all."

"Would you do me a favor? Our other passenger Metoo needs to know how to use the inside potty. She doesn't even know where it is let alone how it operates," Mara advised her daughter.

"I think I can handle that task. Metoo, come along, going to teach you something new," said Randy and the pair departed.

"Well Jenn, have you any questions of me? I think I might be able to answer a few now. I'm doing better. Thank you for watching my back. Don't worry about not hearing Randy. She is cleared to enter any space any of us are in without anyone else knowing. She always has full access to me. Let me show you something that shows I am not just talking. This is where the assassin's bullet struck and nearly killed me. It endangered the entire leadership team because none of us knew that to strike one of us is to strike all in the family lead. Every one of us was injured with the same injury in the same place. Pat and I had to have stitches I know for a bullet was removed from my body by our surgeon Randy. Not sure about the rest but do know they were injured. On doctor's orders, all of us had to rest while drawing energy from the whole family to get us up and running again. Now we know what it is like to be shot and nearly killed. It changed our training. I am never allowed to leave a group meeting, even to guard the back of one of my troops. All that is left for me is to make sure someone else takes on the challenge. They tell me I'm not expendable, I disagree, however, do understand their reasoning. Tomorrow morning, we will walk the rounds to let everyone know I'm alive and on my feet. You will get to see others as they train. I won't be doing that for a few days yet. It generally takes three days for me to get my strength back. Now, I will hush and listen, what would you like to know?" Mara asked.

"You have told me more than I knew to ask. As you heard me say I want to learn to have the poise, talents, and courage you have. It no doubt has a huge price tag, however, that is my desire. Now I understand what your UCA meant when she said that. We met although she never gave her name until you gave it at the barn. KL you called her I think," Jenn replied.

"Her name is Kara Lea, and she is my daughter. It becomes Karlee when I'm in a hurry, so it became KayL in public. As with all my kids, we have a close bond. You will meet the little ones when I give them breakfast, which normally I fix if Merry is busy. I'm sure that Randy will not allow me to be in their vicinity until my energy level is back. It would never do for me to fall on my face in front of my kids. Do you play any musical instruments?"

"Not for years. Had a few beginning lessons, however, money, time, and interest ended about the same time. I played piano, harp, and trumpet. That was four kids and a lifetime ago. Do you play? Oh, it just dawned on me who you are. Goodness of course you do. That was you with the family band. You are the mom of that group. Amazing performers that are so well trained regardless of age. Another to put on my bucket list, be a mom like you. You seem so young to have such a family that trusts you in all things. How do you do it?" asked Jenn for her first question.

"Are you ready for another shock?"

"Yes."

"My physical age was seventeen in June. My life age is twenty-two as I recall. I am six months older than any of my children and thus will always be that much older than any of my kids, grandkids, or any other one down the line. None will ever pass me in age, though each will age through their years until they reach twenty-one. At that time, they will remain that age the rest of their lives," Mara explained.

"I believe you, but still am amazed, or should I say, more amazed at you and this family. Nothing will be shared that you tell me and while I see the task as insurmountable I have also seen one who has accomplished it and must try. Do you have time is the only question? I can only stay for a month then must return home. Will it be time to make a start in my training?" asked Jenn.

"We will have the time needed," said Mara with a smile. Never in her wildest dreams would she have believed that the top law enforcement officer in one state would ask to join her family and now to have two of them was a real shock. Then there was the waitress who made the same request. Everyone had different skills, yet they all worked as a family and team. Whatever she needed would materialize if not already in the collection.

Mara got up and moved to a water closet across the hall, with Jenn at her elbow in case of need. Since Jenn was also looking for such a place, she waited until Mara was done and then escorted her back to bed before using the facility herself.

"What is my schedule when we land?" asked Jennifer upon her return.

"Remain with me and be my guard. Shandra is normal, however now she is helping Randy get everyone in line to go home. Oh, it seems everyone will be sleeping, us included. When we get home, the schedule will be adjusted to allow our flight crew time to rest as well. I planned our trip to Tennessee, and you see how it was changed. On the other hand, some must be dealt with as they come up. Just go with the flow until we see what must be caught up from our absence. The leadership team will go into town for breakfast if Randy has time. If she doesn't then none of us go for she must remain with me until I'm on stable ground again. The team is seeing her as being me, so they do not become alarmed by my absence. Just relax and go with whatever happens. Our pilots will check in with me in a minute or two. Shandra will be with that group. She is not only my guard, but also the lead pilot, and when we fly that is where she pulls duty. We have many backup pilots in case of need. Sherry is with us and will fill in for her this time due to the necessary duties Shandra took on to keep me secure. The double quad is all pilots, however, needed more as guards and other duties.

When a fleet is on the move they all pull duty."

Suddenly Mara quit speaking. She sat and listened while Jenn waited.

"A group is trying to enter the hangar. It is time to stop this. I will not run. Randy, we need to meet them where we are. I will join the line. Put the plane in a book with everyone aboard except the lead team," Mara directed and rose to her full height then began to loosen her joints for the sword drill.

"You do not operate without us watching your backs," said a male voice over her communicator.

"Wouldn't dream of it," replied Mara with a smile for it was her husband Jimmy.

Jenn and Mara departed the plane and saw the lead team waiting. Shira, Pi, Gigot, and Metoo were standing in place ready for whatever came. The plane vanished. Mara smiled when she saw that KL was with the lead group.

"Jenn, you cannot help this time. I am now Thunder. Stand back and watch yet keep your back covered. All the women look like me and all the men look like my husband Jimmy. Now we go to work," said Mara as she stood relaxed and ready. What she did not add was that neither she nor Jimmy looked the way they normally did for they now were characters in a book.

Jenn immediately noted the change. She also noticed that KL was now standing as a guard for her while Shandra had moved to guard Mara.

"Jenn you do not participate, you need to hold this position. I will guard you. You have on chainmail and armor. Keep your focus on the felons before us. Now the dance begins," said KL as she stood relaxed and waiting.

She did not mention that one of the items being done while Jenn guarded Mara, was to learn the sword drill where Shandra and her sisters were the trainers. At the same time, she did not know about the training Jenn received while asleep.

The door to the hangar opened and the group stepped outside as if just leaving a plane. Outside stood a group of people and a shout was heard when the door opened.

"May I help you?" asked Randy for she would not let Mara overextend herself.

"We have a bone to pick with this Thunder person you people claim to be. Where is he?" asked one of those waiting.

"I'm right here, what do you require?" asked Randy.

"Your head on a platter. You upset the wrong people this time. Once you are out of the way we will release those you have hidden away, or so you thought. We have rights and you have violated them in every instance," said a woman at the front of the group.

"Hello Betsy, what brings you here today?" asked Randy.

"I just told you, but you never listen. We want our friends free. It's your life and their freedom," said the woman who did not acknowledge Randy as ever having known her.

"Beri, why are you with this bunch?" asked Randy.

"You labeled me traitor and oathbreaker, where did you expect me to go?" asked the eighteen-year-old.

"I did not label you anything. We had a family member who was ill and some of us have been aiding her," replied the Doctor.

Metoo moved out of line after first an inquiring look at Mara.

"Yes, you may," replied Mara. "Thank you for asking."

The dog moved toward the group waiting. When she reached Beri she sat before her and waited.

"Why me? They said you labeled me, and I had to leave. Now you defend me? Why?"

Metoo lifted a paw to the girl who reached out for it.

"Don't touch her, she is dangerous. That dog is trained to kill. While you are focused on her, the rest will kill all of us," said Betsy.

"Beri, come to me," said Mara.

Sharron L Ensign P.O. Box 583 Helena, MT 59624
Assassins Target Mara Bk 3
406-458-7091

The girl took the dog's collar and was led behind the Thunder line.

Sharron L Ensign P.O. Box 583 Helena, MT 59624
Assassins Target Mara Bk 3
406-458-7091

Chapter 13

Fulfilling promises

"You had to do it the hard way, as usual, didn't you Betsy? You will come with me," said Randy who moved forward and led the woman to a side door that appeared to lead into the hangar. Instead, it led to a book that was waiting for a story. Once Betsy entered, Randy walked back to her group.

"Now you will each face Thunder Court. It was your choice to follow the directions given to you by that woman. Yes, I once knew her. Never did I do her harm. She made some choices that put her on the wrong side of the law, and you will not find me there," said Randy before the entire front line of Thunder moved and no one other than the lead group knew anyone's identity.

In the center of the front line was KL and guarding her were Jenn and Shandra.

At the first shot, all swords were out of their scabbards and work began. None of the lead group looked back only straight ahead as they dealt with the felons before them. Blades flashed as bullets were returned to the sender.

"Stay where you are, I call this Thunder Court to order, Judge Thunder presiding. Who is the prosecutor?"

"Since our two are not done with that training, I suggest that Shandra take the role," said Randy.

It didn't take her long to figure out that both Jenn and KL were using Lightening and the only way they could have done that was if Thunder activated the blades. To her, that meant that they were now both trained for that duty. That did not mean they had the lawyers and judge degrees required to enforce the law.

At the end of the trials, Randy returned for Becky and put her in the front to be judged by her own voice.

"I hated you and that name. No matter where I go someone mentions Ran and there you are again. Go away whoever you are," shouted the woman before Randy stepped up and put an immobilizer on her.

"Because I once knew her I am disqualifying myself from this trial. However, for safety's sake I will remain as a guard, though silent," said Randy via Thunder who did not let anyone figure out who was speaking.

When the trials were over, Jenn was asked to call for backup to pick up the felons and the resulting testimonies. She quickly did so and Pat walked by her side to give her the clues needed to do what was required. Once all were gone except for the Thunder group, the plane was returned, and everyone ordered aboard.

"KL, note the time on the ship clock," said Mara.

"Yes, it is seven p.m. Is that Tennessee time or home time?" she asked.

"We will be home tonight although no one will be awake. When we do get up, everyone will be fully rested. I want to commend you and Jenn both for the marvelous job you did during the capture. I could stand back and watch to not use up any of my limited energies. Thank you both for that gift. Now it is time for some food and sleep," directed Mara.

Merry walked into the room with a tray of food for each of them. She and the stewardess had things ready in a hurry so that folks could get some sleep. All were very tired; however, food was a must when one used up as much energy as they had.

Then walls were raised in the first-class section and as they did not have a full ship, every other seat in the regular class dropped into a hole in the floor allowing walls to come up around the passenger occupying the remaining seat. Soon all were settled and before the flight left the ground the passengers were asleep. With a few exceptions for Randy, Mara, the two new additions, and Beri had a meeting in the conference room at the back of first-class.

"Beri, sometimes it takes a long road to get where we want to go. You took that way. At the same time, you are oathsworn to me. What that means is I am also oathsworn to you. When we were occupied didn't mean we had forgotten you. Now you will begin the training that all new members take. Not as punishment, but to give you the skills you need to operate in the places you must go. You will see what is required in a couple of days. Now, we will be taking a few days off. Have you any questions of me?" asked Mara.

"I thought you booted me as everyone else has. I try to do what they want yet it never seems to work out. So, I am the one that found the crazy lady who was giving you such problems?"

"Yes, that is what you did. Thank you. Now you need some rest. When we get home, everyone will have duties. Just follow us when we reach our home airport and on to our home. We will assign you a room in the first section of our home. As soon as I can you will be put in training. Others will also be starting I'm sure. Now rest you well youngling. I will see you tomorrow," said Mara who got up and gave the child a hug before she departed.

"What must her life have been like that she trusts us to do whatever we say. She even left the group that made ridiculous promises they had no intention of fulfilling if she would deliver me to them. A lot of promise in that one, if she continues to believe," Mara said.

"The confusion served a purpose. Now if only she doesn't get a swelled head due to bringing in the crazy person, we might have a candidate for the clan," replied Randy.

"Don't tease, Randy, she really wants to belong and always has. I have some ideas on how to use her talents, however, will have to wait until I'm fully up to speed," said Mara for she would have to handle this one herself.

"Now let's have a chat with Jenn and Karlea. It is obvious that you are now both trained for Thunder missions. You have a few things yet to learn although the basics are there. You both did an amazing job in controlling the felons, especially as first-time trainees. Do either of you have questions for me?" asked Mara.

"No, in faith I will do as you direct and know that I am being trained like all the rest. Thank you for the opportunity to allow me to be a part. Mom, we continue to learn," Kara Lea told the Monarch.

"Truth, we do continue to learn. When we stop, we die. We will spend time together in a few days. For now, everyone needs some rest. You know which seats yours are. Get comfortable for a few hours and sleep. See you later," said Mara.

The newest members departed for their sleep seats.

"Randy, you have rescued me again. Thank you, darling daughter. I am very grateful. Shandra and the two who just left need the shots you gave me. They are new and more of their energy was used. The drug that took my energy came from the kitchen so apparently, your former acquaintance found a way to reach us. Your seat is ready and right in front of mine. God Bless," said Mara, and everyone moved to their claimed seats.

"Hello, Shandra. No, I have not, nor will I ever, forget you. Thank you for taking on so much while I was out of commission. The two new ones really stepped up. You trained them well. We can talk more when we get home. Rest you well daughter mine," directed Mara.

"Love you mom, take care of yourself. Was a bit scary putting an untried stranger as your guard, yet like you say they both came through well. Now goodnight, see you tomorrow, or whenever we happen to wake up," Shandra chuckled.

With a smile, the two women got comfortable, and the ship was silent. Usually, Shandra flew home. This time Sherry had the duty, and all slept well. Shandra had spent the time training KL and Jenn, with help from Randy, so that everyone would be ready for whatever was ahead. As a result, her energy level was low as well.

When Mara awakened, she glanced over at Shandra to see if she was waking yet.

"Yes, I'm awake. Nice rest we had. Wonder how long it took to get us back?" commented Shandra.

"I am thinking three days. Haven't felt this well in a while. Another batch of shots and we should be ready to go back to work. I know I'm hungry," Mara laughed.

"That makes two of us, so imagine we have missed a few meals," Shandra chuckled.

"Thank you dear one for getting our two-gals ready for front-line duty. That was one fast transition. Have you any ideas as to what we will do with Beri?"

"Why not put her under the Seeker and see what happens?" asked Shandra.

"My thought exactly but wanted your take on it."

"You don't have time to do it, so that would be my suggestion."

"And I third the suggestion," said a voice at their door.

"Come on in Randy. Welcome," Mara said as she made sure the door was unlocked.

"I thought that these rooms were fully secure," Shandra said with a smile from the room she shared with Mara on the flight.

"They are unless Randy is in the mix," laughed Mara.

"Oh, we never worry about her. Never do I want her out of my life," Shandra replied.

"How are you doing Randy?" asked her mom.

"It is six a.m. on Friday, I think. The flight took two hours, and the rest of the time we have been asleep. We all needed it to be sure. Now let's get those shots you mentioned done for all of us and get ready for the day," Randy said with a smile as she pulled a shot Pac from her garment to get them taken care of.

"Didn't realize how tired everyone was until I awakened aboard the plane. Really needed that time of rest. Yes, I have your shots, all of you. Let's get that done, then we can see who, besides us, is up and go for some fresh air," Randy commented.

As they moved from the first-class section to the public section they used their handprints to allow their moving. Those in First Class were still sleeping. The main floor found everyone asleep there as well.

"Oops, hold on a moment, I forgot Metoo," said Mara as she turned to reopen the upper access. The dog was sitting at the bottom of the steps waiting.

"Yes, I forgot, sorry about that. Thank you for reminding me. Now we are going to pick up all the guard dogs and go for a walk before everyone else is up and moving," Mara advised.

Metoo took off on a quiet run and soon had all guard dogs waiting at the exit from the plane. Mara laughed and thanked the dog for the help. They moved outside into the new dawn just beginning.

Mara began to chuckle for she knew that Kara Lea and Jenn were right behind them. Everyone limbered up for a short run and took off down the trail with them following Mara as she had been the one with the greatest loss of energy and they didn't want her overdoing. When she turned back, so did the whole group. As they ran to the plane they saw buses entering the flight area. Soon faces were seen looking out the windows and a line formed to wait on luggage before entering the buses waiting.

Mara called for the leadership team to join her after the buses were loaded. Most knew to wait for they always had a meal out when they returned from a trip of any kind. It allowed Mara, or Randy, to pick up new people if directed by Thunder to do so.

Beri was sent on the bus as she was put in the care of Seeker to begin her education. The rest boarded a van and made a quick run home for showers then took two vehicles to go to town.

Those who had children departed for home as soon as they could. This was their first time away for any length of time and all wanted to see their youngsters. Mara made a note to have a hidden stairway in each of the leader's suites, so they could reach the basement without entering the halls of their home.

Before anyone could say anything, Mara did.

"Welcome home again, dear ones. It is good to be back," she told them for she knew that if KL said anything it might give away that this was her first time to see the ranch.

"Be it ever so humble no place like home. How much time do

we have to get ready?" asked KL with a chuckle for she had received her mom's thoughts.

"Showers take ten minutes, five if in a hurry, which I'm not. Then meet in the basement where we will grab a van and head to eat. If we try to eat here and it is not a training day, we won't get to relax and eat. Now go, before everyone finds out we are back," directed Mara and all ran to their rooms.

"KL and Jenn, you are in the back hall, Beri is in the front one. Metoo, you stay with me while you are here. Cut through my place you two. Alina is settling Beri before going to her own suite. Her room is next to yours," Mara advised.

Soon the new people were settled, and Mara could head for a shower of her own. As soon as she was dressed she took off on the run for the basement. The littles were around someplace and while she loved them, she needed this day to regroup. Looking back, she saw KL and Jenn tiptoeing behind her. When she opened the basement door to the garage she saw that the others were waiting. Her mind was quickly accessing, and ideas flashed as she moved. If she had a secret stair to the basement, why not have the vehicles that her group used in a hidden area as well. That way they could drop and be gone without running into someone on an errand that wanted to go also. As she requested the new area was designed according to her thoughts.

Shandra drove one van and Cherry the second one. Jo took on the third unit which was empty, in case they needed more transportation. There were buses available in town if needed. The new people needed to see some of the Prescot and begin to get their bearings as to how to find things.

Mara often laughed at what new people found of interest. This time she was going to take them to the craft village, so they had an idea of what was available there as well.

"Mom does Metoo go into the restaurant with us?" asked KL who was thoroughly enjoying the area she found herself in. The towns were spread out and much smaller than the big cities she had lived in before. She continued to smile at the relaxed environment and peace.

"Yes, because Shira will watch over her until she learns the new rules. It is allowed because Metoo is so well behaved. Would you object if she worked as your guard? Since she needs to be trained she can watch over you and take directions from Shira who watches over me," Mara advised.

"That would be great. She is so beautiful and well-mannered. Metoo do you mind being my guard dog?" asked KL.

A sharp short bark was the reply which made KL, and others, laugh.

"Just so you know, that is yes, and a growl is no," Mara advised.

Shira and Metoo wore harnesses showing they were working animals and were therefore allowed into the restaurant.

"Okay, Kara Lea and Jenn, we are going to eat and meet any destined to join our group. Conversation at meals is general. No questions, they will be answered when we get home. Be aware of the space around you and remember a Thunder call means we all have work to do. Stay slightly behind anyone with Lightening. We are now in an area where we are known. Use caution," Mara advised for she knew the van was clean. It just came out of their secure garage, and it had been checked by Pat.

Kennet asked if they could go to the pie house. A nod at the driver and the van changed direction.

When they reached the restaurant, they noted that there were a lot of cars in the lot. More than usual. That put the lead group on alert. The Thunder Clan this time was only those in leadership positions.

They walked into the restaurant and went directly to the large room on the left of the entry. Each of the women claimed a seat then two got up and moved. Jenn and Kara Lea were told to go sit where the two had moved from.

The two women chuckled and moved. That put Kara next to Mara and Shandra while Jenn was located by Randy and Jo.

"Hello, this is the only space we have for larger groups. Do you mind sitting here separate from everyone else?" asked a waitress with a smile.

"No, we don't mind. Thank you. Have you seen Merry of late?"

asked Mara for she knew she was being warned.

"She went to school and that was the last we heard of her," responded the woman though she met Mara's eyes then looked at Merry.

Mara looked out the window and saw three more vans pull up and park next to their three. An equal number of men got out and entered the restaurant.

"Waitress, have you a corner where we can sit and not interfere with your regular customers?" asked the man in charge.

She looked at Mara and with a nod, she told the men she would see if another group that just agreed to sit in the back room would mind if the men joined them. Patty went in and spoke with Randy though they knew she was aware of who Mara was for she was oathsworn to her.

"Ma'am we have a full house. Would you mind if a group of men shared this room with you? The man in charge said they would not interfere with your meal," Patty told her.

"Not a problem. We just want to relax and enjoy breakfast we don't have to cook for a change," replied Randy.

"Mom, would it be alright if Jenn and I visited the gift shop? I see they are just opening it." Kara Lea asked.

"Please KL, may I join you? I haven't come to town very often because of how busy everyone is. I would like to look around too if you don't mind," said Alina.

"Sounds good to me," said KL and they got up after ordering their meal so they could shop while they waited.

"We have now divided the force. Let's see if that makes any changes to what is about to happen," commented Mara over her comm device.

"I see we guessed right," said Jimmy.

"Looks like it to me. Not sure what is going on though," replied Mara.

"Mom, it isn't us they are after; however, it looks like trouble.

Two women are hiding under the counter in the gift shop," KL reported softly in her communicator.

"Can you get them out?" asked Mara.

"Yes, however, what do we do with them then? One of the women said that they will destroy this restaurant if the women get away."

"I heard the directions. Won't break orders, however, can you tell me? Do you come here often?" asked Kara Lea.

"Now and then, why do you ask?" Mara replied and quickly looked around.

"Metoo seems to feel we are missing something," the woman replied.

"Okay, let's be on alert and enjoy our meal. Thank you," responded Mara.

"Metoo, come speak with me please," she asked mentally.

The dog did as directed and explained what she saw.

When Mara checked her weapons, the whole group knew something was about to happen.

A group of young people was seen getting out of their vehicles outside. As the women watched them, they seemed to be shoving one another around, though a couple of the group were treated rougher than the rest.

They entered the restaurant and were loud.

"Remember you two, you are paying for all of us. You will do as you are told, or your life is over," said one loudmouth.

Mara checked with Metoo and found that yes, this was the trouble. She also said that the two, needed help and more were coming.

"Give me a couple of minutes," said Kara Lea who was walking toward the bathroom. Metoo walked at her side and though neither looked back, both were very cognizant of what was going on around them.

When they were inside the restroom two women entered after KL made the request.

"Will you trust me? We need to get you out of here for the moment. I am a law enforcement officer and understand some trouble is headed your way," KL advised.

"Please, get us out of this restaurant," said one of the women who explained what was going on, as far as she knew.

"I want you to walk through that door there and when you are fully clear the door will close but don't worry for we will come to get you once things are settled. No one will bother you for the only ones who can join you are my mother and me," KL told them.

They did as directed without hesitation. If they remained they knew they would be dead.

"Looks like breakfast will be later. Guess it is time for me to enter the game," Mara said as she rose from her seat.

When Mara stood so did Jimmy and soon the entire Thunder group was on their feet. The waitress said something to the cook and waited. KL left Jenn with Alina then moved to meet Mara and fell in at her side. Shandra placed her hand on her sword as they moved through the restaurant. As a person was cleared as having no criminal intent they were told to move to the gift shop.

Jimmy and his group were standing in the door to the shop and only allowed in those that Mara and her group okayed. The shop was an open area including a hall and the only door out was the one that patrons entered the front by. The men became a human wall like a door to the store.

Kennet moved to the pie case as if to see what was available.

Granda continued to sit and watch, with Dan and Gwen at her side.

As the troublemakers were identified they froze where they were. The two who had been shoved around and threatened were directed to depart by the back door of the facility. They too were now in a book and advised that nothing would bother them there. When the sorting was done, Thunder One directed that the problems be moved outside for a T-Court.

Randy gathered up those in hiding and told them where to stand. She cautioned them to not get in front of the swords of the leaders, then she took her place in the formation.

One of the young people moved to Kennet and whispered.

"Please tell whoever needs to know that this is a setup, not only for us but for you folks as well. Watch the road," she cautioned.

Kennet asked the AI to relay the conversation to his mom.

Mara held a mental conversation with Shira who moved to watch the area around them. Then the lead Thunder saw movement. A security bubble formed over those outside the eating establishment.

"M, they are behind the building as well as coming in the drive. I saw movement by looking through the building," said Jimmy.

"Thank you," she responded while keeping her concentration on the front.

"Granda, we need local backup. Tell them to begin moving in from two blocks out and not to miss anyone headed this way," directed Mara.

The area where the Thunder group stood enlarged as people were pushed inside. The entry was in the car lot while the felons were now in an open book to allow protection for those in the restaurant. Only Granda could see what was going on. The rest of the patrons were now sitting at their chosen places inside to eat their meals and were told to remain there until released, by the waitress.

Mara watched as the group coming continued to grow and wondered what was going on. Suddenly she called for Thunder to stop the influx. Something was wrong. She directed that the gathering be put in the lot behind the police station with a security bubble over it and that the Thunder lead team go there. Everyone still aimed their way was to be frozen where they stood, as was the whole area. They would try the ones they had and see if they were felons or wannabees.

That was when she saw four people step together and aim at the leaders. Once the shots were fired all the Clan returned fire. Once all felons were down, the court was called.

The court was called to order with Mara in charge. Her prosecutor was Randy. Shandra and KL became guards for them with Shira and Metoo also in their places.

"This Thunder Court is now in session," T1 ordered.

"Don't think so," said the mouthy young man who had threatened those he ordered to pay the bill for all those entering the restaurant in a group.

"Contempt, first charge," replied Mara.

"What we do is our business, and you have no control over us. You infringe on our rights, and we will sue you until you are dead and maybe even after," he replied.

"They are all wired. Would you Thunder strip them or we will be here all day and night," commented Ken to his mom softly.

Mara immediately turned Thunder loose. Wires, weapons, glasses, belts, shoes, rings, and any other jewelry fell to the ground where Jimmy made sure all was recorded once his wife gave the go-ahead. Bags were used to hold each person's belongings and their name was placed on that bag with the date and time. The men to be incarcerated stood in their shorts in an open formation where the Thunder women were watching their every move although each wore immobilizers.

"S, need the women also prepared," directed M as she continued to watch the group that had all weapons, wires, and other miscellaneous items removed and labeled as directed. The women about to join the men in prison also stood in underclothing. The one thing everyone had in common was the immobilizers each wore.

"We are divided," whispered Randy to her Mom.

"Yes dear, however, it is the only way to get them all taken care of at the same time. We have about two thousand prisoners. Hopefully, this clears things up while we get some other duties taken care of," responded Mara/Thunder in a mental conversation with her double as well as Randy and her double. They could split again if needed to meet the requirements although Randy asked her not to due to her recent recovery.

KL offered a suggestion that they change their way of doing business and even suggested how best to do what they had to in processing the felons.

As each person was called forward to answer questions, it led others to be called to do the same.

"Okay young man, your turn. What makes you think we will let you slide as you abuse others, bully, bad mouth, and lie? Since you set up this charade, you now will give us all the information required about who you are, your misdeeds, what you own, and why you have targeted us," directed Judge Thunder who called halt to the line movement when she saw the first troublemaker present himself.

"They paid me well and even trained me to do what was directed. You can't win. As soon as you boot me to the curb others will follow and each time it will be people who are ready to deal with you. Fresh crews are waiting in a continuous stream. As I said, you cannot win," said the smart mouth.

"Thunder!" said Mara firmly and the area erupted with everyone in her group taking on that persona. With military precision, the felons gave their testimony, were placed in formation, and frozen as the next group was dealt with. The sun did not go down as Mara's group watched the felons follow the directions given to the first interviewed. The wires, weapons, and all were removed and identified, the same questions were asked, different responses were given, then that person moved to the formation and fell into the next open slot until people quit coming.

Mara and Randy looked at their watches even as Shandra and KL looked at theirs. Small smiles were seen.

"P, call in," directed the Judge.

The felons were marched to concrete pads at the back of the property by the police station. By the time they got there the steel cages were anchored into the concrete and a large tent overall. When all were in place the immobilizers were returned to the Thunder group and yells were heard from the buildings.

"Hey, you can't do this to us. Tiny room, no privacy, no bathroom, military cot, no TV, no phone, and pink clothes. We have rights!" shouted smart mouth.

"Best get used to it, you will no longer have a voice, and the only people you will see in the rest of your rather short lifetime, are those who hose out your lodging, issue you clean cloths, and see that you get two meals a day if you behave," replied Mara in a firm voice and though she spoke softly, all heard her message.

"How do we know that it is over?" asked KL.

"We outlasted them, this time. We have found that they very seldom, if ever, repeat the scenario when they lose. By putting them on rotation they had to answer all questions and follow orders. Even had to strip themselves, instead of us doing it," advised Randy.

"What happens with the women that were attacked?" asked KL for she needed to learn if she was going to be as useful as she wanted to be.

"The two found in the gift shop saw the group coming and hid. Neither of them had any idea how the incoming group knew where they could be found," commented KL.

"Randy, need you to do an x-ray of all new hires. Add that to our SOP from here on please," directed Mara before she continued.

"The last two that were being shoved around may have some broken bones. Those will have to be set. They were the ones who alerted me as to more coming. Found out afterward that their kids were hostage by this bunch at the time, so had them T removed," Mara advised in a direct send to KL and Randy though Pat and Granda could always listen in with Ken.

"I thought that might be the case. Glad to hear you took care of the issues. Sorry to ask here, however very concerned about what I was told when they were hidden. All those women were in bad shape. Thank you for the info. No more questions until we are home," replied KL.

"Once we get them home they get to decide if we keep them or not though they have taken the oaths. Seeing families safe may help them make wise decisions. Now it is time for everyone to have a meal," said Mara and the entire team was once again at the restaurant where they went inside to resume their places and eat the meal that the waitress served as soon as she saw they were ready.

"How many need to order?" asked the waitress.

"All the men and a few women for sure. Might be some kids in the mix also. KL would you take care of that since you know the women better than I do?" commented Mara with a smile.

"Glad to mom," replied the woman for she found so much new knowledge in her mind she was having to catalog it quickly and store it until she could truly study the material.

Chapter 14

Starting over in life

Metoo looked up at KL as if to say, "Can I come too?"

"Of course, you come along. Help me find any kids that may have joined the women we just rescued," replied KL before moving to where she saw a couple of women sitting to one side and they were the ones from the gift shop.

"Are we safe or has this just begun?" asked a young woman when she saw KL and recognized her as one of those in the group with swords.

"It is our belief that you are safe. If you chose to remain with us, you will be trained to defend yourself and others plus a forever family, if that is your desire," KL advised in a very soft voice though she asked for a silence bubble over the four women and some kids sitting with a couple of them.

"Thank you. Our husbands were in the group the court charged. Please, don't send any of us back, Please? We will be dead if you do," said one.

"No one is sending you anyplace. Where we go you will as well for it is our home. There you will have all your questions answered. This is too public a place to give away any of our secrets. My orders are to see that all of you order some food. When it is time to leave, you will go with us. Relax and trust all is well," advised Karlea.

Rather than have the women feel isolated, KL sat down with them and spoke of the area, what it had to offer, the University, and what is required, then went on to speak of the hospital and clinic and how fortunate the residents were to have such a pair of facilities. She explained that this was ranch country and there were many in the surrounding area. Before anyone realized it, all had finished eating, including dessert. Mara looked over the group, made a mental calculation as to what the bill would be, and called KL to her side where she was given the funds to cover what was due. Once the bill was paid and the waitress given her gratuity, the group departed to load on the vehicles waiting. Instead of the vans, they came with there were now buses waiting.

KL continued to watch over the four new women until the buses reached the ranch. Once the vehicles were unloaded the drivers put them in the basement garage and departed. The next time they needed to use the vans, they would be in place with the buses back in the holding garage in town.

After rooms were assigned to the new people, Mara asked KL to meet with each of the new ones and find out what they wanted to do now. Stay and be trained or be taken to someplace they felt safer.

"Mom, they want to remain. The kids asked to stay if their moms left though the moms too want to be part of us. I can well understand their reasoning. Now that they are settled in and will be staying, we can shop for them tomorrow as they came with only the clothing they were wearing," KL advised.

"They will need clothing to dress as we do. Yes, a shopping trip is advised. We also must find out how many of the Clan do not have the gear necessary to live with us and do their jobs. That includes you and Jenn," Mara advised.

"You gave each of us a set of clothing, however, would be nice to have more than one change of clothes," laughed KL.

"I get the point, however, all of you need enough clothes to have clean clothes daily since we sometimes have to change more than once that day, depending on what our duties are. For instance, we might ride horses for training. Shower for music training and eat. Then what happens if we are called to a book world? We change clothes after a shower and go. The shower is because we do not know when we will again have that opportunity. When we return guess what? We get to shower so we can eat or do whatever the next tasks are. Yes, you need more than one change of clothes," Mara laughed.

"I'm learning. Not fast enough though I'm working on it," her daughter responded.

"You are doing fine. Now you said you wanted to have a question time. Do you want to include Jenn, or should I have Pat brief her and I brief you?" asked Mara.

"I have no objections to a brief by Pat. My only thought there is if I'm to be your hidden guard, it seems to me that you are the one who should train me, with Shandra of course," replied KL.

"Yes, there is that. Shandra, please come to my suite conference room for a Q and A session. You and me plus one." Mara sent.

"Randy, I know that Pat is busy. Would you have time to train Jenn just for today? I will begin working with the new ones in a couple of days if you allow," Mara advised her third in command.

"On my way, if you will tell me where you are hiding."

"I'm with Shandra, who is also looking for me, KL, who has found me, and now you. We are in the conference room in my suite. We can begin there if you like then would you be willing to show Jenn around while I answer questions for KL? The questions one asks versus the other might require different security, or so KL feels," Mara responded.

"Agreed."

When Jenn and Karlea were situated Randy and Mara waited for questions though the first one did not come from either.

"Why is this particular group assembled?" asked Shandra.

"They said they had some questions," Mara replied with a smile.

"No doubt, though so do I. Please explain to the three of us how you managed to disappear yet didn't at the Nashville location," Shandra began.

"You know how that happened. KL rescued me with Jenn, and we went to the new housing ranch there. When Randy showed up to get x-rays of them both she was right behind Pat who found the vehicles bugged. We met Metoo and checked out the new location. Since I was a bit wobbly Randy sent me to the plane with Jenn so that KL could get the required training from you to do new duties we did not have time to train for. Okay so far?" asked the Monarch.

"I got that. Randy did well, although she isn't you. Our sleight of hand seems to have worked. They didn't find you, whoever 'they' happens to be. Question number two from me. Are both women now trained to fill in for us, or to just be part of the Clan and guards?"

"They are to fill in and to guard. The ones they guard are me and Randy unless you are available for that duty. Pat has six people that trade-off to guard her and all are fully qualified. Granda has assigned guards as well. The rest have learned to guard one another. Unless something happens that they end up guarding you. And before you ask our bird dog Beri is in the care of Seeker until I am back up to speed. Does that answer your questions Shandra?" asked Mara again with a smile.

"Mostly, how long is Jenn staying and since both are family why aren't they both staying here for the rest of their lives?" asked Shandra with a matching smile.

"KL is staying. Jenn must go back to claim her kids and move. Should have them here by Christmas or before, if Jenn is agreeable. If not then they will be here next summer," Mara advised.

"I disagree. Bring the kids here by Thunder, give them some time to look around, then deliver Jenn's notice of a new job and they can get with the program. Mom, we really don't have the time, nor do the women, to be scattered all over the nation. Let's do it right. Get everyone together and get with the program," added Randy.

"Which is what we are doing. Jenn your turn."

"I agreed to stay a month then go back and get my kids out of school, quit my job, and pack up to move here. That is still what I plan on doing. The way you are talking it is you blink, and I am no longer employed, my retirement is here with my kids and I'm a Montana resident. Did I miss something?" Jenn asked.

"No, you did rather well for your first tour of duty with us." Mara was watching their facial expressions as they were trying to believe yet not fully sure yet. Time to bring out the big guns.

"Jenn, would you please open that door and allow some air in here?" directed Mara.

The new woman got up and did as she was told. Standing on the other side of the door was her quad of kids. Each had a carry sack with what they wanted to keep, otherwise, they were dressed as the rest of Mara's group was.

"Hi mom, we did as you said. Picked up what we wanted to keep. Had Jeana get us out of class and tell them we were moving. Then went to your boss and told him that T had hired you and we were moving. Didn't take care of moving but was told it would all be here when we got here for this is our new home. Did we do it right?" asked one of the kids.

"Yes, you did fine. Keep your faith kids. You will need it with this bunch. Okay, Randy if you would like, my questions are answered, and it is time for you to do what you must with my kids and me. They need shots, x-rays, records, and to know who you are in the mix," directed Jenn with a smile. Finally, they could settle down and be a family again.

Randy laughed and stood up. Mara did the same and received hugs from Jenn and her quad. Jenn introduced both women then departed with the quad and Randy.

"Okay, that covers Jenn. She is fully here now and ready to go to work. Her mind has been racing as she tried to figure out how to get this all done. Now it is, and she can relax. As she said, Randy needs to make up records on her group. Tomorrow those five can join the training that I will not be participating in until Randy gives the okay. That means she must take some blood tests to be sure I've whipped the poison and my levels are as they should be," Mara explained.

"Okay KarLea, what are your questions?" asked Shandra.

"I would like to know what you found out about the drug cartel that I put in prison. What was going on and did I do it right?" asked KL.

"Yes, you did it right. The Governor tried to release them; however, Thunder was on-site and added him to the group that was sent to us for sentencing. Now all of them have been given sentences. All will be carried out once the justice system makes its decisions. Oh, it seems that the drug lord and Governor are both no longer an issue nor is the drug retail that was being set up in Oklahoma. Next?" Mara said.

"Did you know that I somehow was given memories from you that aided me in doing my job while in Nashville? I would not want to have them without your permission," said Kara Lea and both Mara and Shandra knew she was being fully honest.

"Trust me and let that one sit for a day or two please, then you will have your answers," commented Shandra.

"Okay, I can do that. I like your town and my new duties. Love the family and my new guard dog Metoo. Never did I expect to find myself going from being hunted by assassins to being where I now find myself," Kara Lea replied.

"We are still being hunted by Assassins only now we are an army and ready for them. Everyone trains to be the best they can be and fill the duties required. You have already met those people and helped put them in prison. Most of them have been put on death row and some may have already gone on. However, there are always more, ready to take their places. The questions you have will be answered, though not in the way you are probably expecting. Give us a week or two and if you still have them we will meet again and address the issues," Mara told her.

"Then my only question is: Please give me an idea of what my duties are starting tomorrow," KL asked her new mom.

The following morning found everyone up at the usual time. Jenn and Karlea were ready for whatever the day held. It was apparent that the newest quad was also ready. Kennet had taken them under his wing and given them the schedule for the first two hours. After breakfast, they would see what happened next.

The two new guards were directed to follow Dan and he would get them where they needed to be when. In two days, they would be training under Mara.

Today Mara's only requirement allowed was a ride to the U with the new people. This was their day to be tested. She had to chuckle at the various ways of riding. Some could barely hang on, others were sliding off, while there were a few who wanted to race their horses and the animals refused.

Once the horses were stripped of their saddles, Shira stood to watch until time for the testing. Each of the group of riders moved into the test hall with the case of a musical instrument in hand.

"KL, watch and follow me, the rest won't even know I'm here," said Mara.

"Sir, we are the test group from the N-Sign Clan. My instructions are to see that all of us are tested for our proficiency," KL immediately stated their reason for being before the man.

"I'm always amazed at you folks. Okay. Each of you has a stack of tests. Put them at your desk or table and start at the top. As you finish an exam, bring it to me to be checked while you return to take the next one in your stack. Equestrian and music will be just before lunch then you may finish the rest of what you need to after eating." Mizer was always amazed that this group meant what they said when asking to be tested as Masters in each field of endeavor.

Mara and Shandra sat to one side and watched the group. Suddenly they realized that there were exams sitting by them. Just for fun, they decided to take them while they waited. As the others had done, they took their finished work to the instructor before returning to do the next test.

When everyone was done, the group mounted to return home. Most were very quiet.

"Mom, did we really do what I think we did? Took forty exams and passed them all as Masters? I do not recall having any knowledge in most of those areas, yet the answers seemed to be in my head," said Kara Lea with a puzzled look on her face.

"Yes, you are now as qualified as the rest of the lead group. There is a catch, however. If you ever decide to leave, the knowledge will leave also except for what you came with. You won't recall any of us or those under my jurisdiction," Mara explained.

"I don't see that happening. Thank you for all this new

knowledge. Someday would you mind enlightening me as to what exams I took?" Kara Lea asked.

"You will know when we reach home for your diplomas will be waiting in your suite. Since you asked to be as well educated as I am, to take the place of any of us that are injured or classified as at risk, you will need to know most of what I know. You now have that information."

"I don't mean to be dense but… there were questions there about real estate, flying a plane, riding a horse properly to include trick riding, music, legal, and the list goes on. I have never, to my knowledge, had training in any of those, yet I answered every question," Kara replied.

"You have now taken them and can function as a Master in any of those fields. When you need it, the information will be available from your mind. No one can fill in for me, for example, unless they have the qualifications that I do. Yours was given a little early due to my being out of commission. You have been using them since Nashville and doing it well I must say. Didn't you once say you wanted to learn to be like me? Well, now you might say you are a copy of me. How does it feel?" asked Mara with a chuckle.

"More than a bit overwhelming," responded Kara though she smiled.

"Not really, you just must learn to use the new knowledge as any tool that is issued to you. I had to take a few today as well since we have new people with us and therefore it means new knowledge. Now all of us in the lead group have it. Have you looked at the languages yet? Listen to Seeker giving instructions to one of the new women. The woman's native language is not what we normally use. Listen and see what you learn," directed Mara.

"Amazing! And we speak other languages as well? How many?" Kara asked.

"Around fifty I seem to recall. Never know what country we might have to visit due to Thunder's inheritance. Then there are folks in this country that do not speak our language and might need aid from time to time. Have already found a use for many of the tongues. Seeker speaks them all, Lynn had five when she came and now speaks them all. My husband Jimmy says he just opens his mouth to see what will come out next. We use different languages each day just to keep our fluency," Mara explained. Though they were riding along, direct communication was established between the two women while the others were relaxing on the ride and glad to have the exam over.

Suddenly Mara felt the studs stiffen.

"Hang on, emergency," she shouted, and the mounts took off for home.

They saw the entire clan mounted and facing the main highway.

"Jimmy to me," called Mara and the man rode to where she waited.

"What is going on?" she asked.

"A bad wreck on the highway and we have been asked to assist as being the closest. M, I'm not sure if this is true or not. Please can you check it out before we leave this property?" her husband asked.

Shandra immediately had her hand on her sword. She was watching Randy and Pat who were doing the same. Heads were shaken.

"No, it is not true, however, there are some folks in trouble and they need our aid. Our best maneuverability is on horseback. It seems that something is stopping them from moving any farther. None of their vehicles will start for one thing," M explained.

"Form formation Q. Watch for people in distress and use a great deal of caution. We have troops covering all of us," Mara advised for she had designed the drill and filled her people in privately.

The riders moved their mounts into position to guard the first three leaders, though they saw Randy as their doc, not as a leader. Only Mara and Granda knew that Randy was third in line in leadership and in a conflict calling for that formation, therefore Kara Lea would become Randy's guard or lead. The call was left to Mara if she was part of it and to Randy if Mara could not be there.

It was becoming harder and harder to cover all bases, so Mara directed that the lead group needed trainers that were not the lead group. Yes, they would work out with those trained but would not be their teachers. The time was needed for other duties.

The riders moved toward the Hiway, and Mara checked the time to give the AI a starting point.

They had barely reached the fence line of their property when they were challenged by mounted riders.

"Stallion, please have the horses dump them all," directed Mara and the bucking began. Soon all horses were standing on the ranch side of the fence.

Mara and her group sat quietly on their mounts and watched the rodeo.

The distance to the ranch headquarters was three miles. As she looked in that direction she saw another stallion directing a herd of horses to her location. She told him to bring in the felons and put them in the corral.

Each time one of the riders entered the gate to get his or her horse, the stallion had them in a group of other horses and soon the entire group was inside. Her riders would help once the group of felons was inside the fence. Everyone spread out and pushed the walkers toward the stable area and the corral.

"Yes, we do this all the time," replied Mara to Kara Lea's silent question.

Her daughter smiled and nodded her head at receipt of the comment.

"Randy, it has been suggested that I lead this court to show the new people how this should be done. Do you see a problem with my doing so?" asked her mom.

"I knew you were close to that point. Go ahead, unless I tell you to stop," responded Randy.

"That works," Mara told her daughter.

Mara moved to the head of the group with Shandra by her side. Everyone was ready when the first weapons were seen. That was when she felt Kara Lea on the other side, and she could sense Ken right behind the three of them. Everyone else had formed a second line behind the four. Once the felons were all down, the court could begin.

"Who has prosecuting duty?" asked Mara.

"I do, however, have no problem with being guard either," replied Kara Lea.

"Mom, could I take the duty?" Alina offered for no one had offered to give her a turn before.

"Your call Karlea," Mara told her guard.

"Let her go, I will do it next time," Kara Lea said for she knew that that meant that Mara would not be the Judge for the next go around and it was time for double guard felt Kara Lea to which Randy agreed.

"You realize if she runs into trouble you have to pick up the slack?" Mara wanted to know.

"Of course," was the chuckling response.

"This court is called to order. Judge T presiding. Prosecutor are you ready?"

"I am your Honor," Alina quickly told her.

It didn't take Mara long to realize that Alina must have done a lot of studying for she was well versed in the duties she volunteered for. No one would fault her. Her questions were obviously researched. Her accent was gone, and none would know she was of Swiss descent.

"Who is in control of this group?"

"I am."

"Then step to the front where you can be seen," the prosecutor directed.

One person shuffled to the front. Between Thunder and the

immobilizer, one could not deny orders or refuse questions.

"Need your names, addresses, family, everything you own, and a full list of all illegal activities you have taken part in since you were born," began Alina.

"That would take a while. Let's just say I've been busy."

"Contempt of court, one offense," responded the Lawyer.

"Now answer the question. If you really want to stir up a hornet's nest think about who I am. Not only am I a duly assigned law enforcement officer. I also happen to be of the family Thunder. Now, do you want to argue this point? It will get you a quicker sentence, though probably one with which you will not be happy," Alina advised.

He felt the edge of her Thunder voice and only answered the questions asked. No one could ever pay him enough to try to get this bunch ever again. This was his first try and no one ever got to do it a second time.

"Now tell me all about all groups that have been sent to target us. Add in all groups being prepared to target us. How many, the names, locations, reasons, the cost to those hiring and who they are."

As he had warned he had been busy. Once he was silenced Thunder took control and the man answered all questions though the men had to help him get rid of a lot of wires, and other devices he should not have had in a court of law. Everything was identified and tagged with his name and case number. All offenses that were mentioned showed all who precipitated not just the man in court. By the time the session was over, there was three times the number of people for there was only one-third of the mounts that would be required for that bunch to ride away. The horses would not be leaving the ranch unless as mounts for the Thunder Clan.

Merry was given the duty to call the Sheriff's office for pick up. They were given the numbers to be gathered and six buses arrived at the location. The riders would be a bit cramped, however with three persons in every double seat, all were accommodated. There was an armed officer in each unit and all prisoners wore leg irons as well as were locked into their seats and wore cuffs.

KL looked at her timepiece and found it was the same time as the group departed for the University. She looked up and saw Mara was watching her with a smile on her face.

"Okay folks, you have now seen a Thunder court in action. Remember it for I may not be the one holding them as often. The younger ones will do duty while the senior leadership group will observe. Don't mess up. Alina, you did a great job. Now everyone brushes down their mount, there is grain in each stall. Next, we go to our suites and get showers with fresh clothing. I have asked Merry for an afternoon snack," the mother of the clan directed.

Everyone hurried to do her bidding.

When Mara and Shandra reached Mara's suite they found Alina waiting. She was told to join them in the conference room.

"What can we do for you, Alina?"

"I acted before I thought. Sorry, my apologies to you both. It was bad timing to ask to be a prosecutor at that time. Should have asked you in private first," said the young woman.

"No, you should not have. You are my daughter and have most of the training that everyone else has. The ones we inherited lately are training at their own pace, even as you were. No one will be pushed to do something they really are not interested in. If you felt a nudge to do something, then do it. It might be the key for us to do something different, or that we are becoming predictable. All your suggestions have been good ones and have been used. To me, it seems like you are getting bored due to a lack of challenges. Am I correct?" asked Mara with a smile.

"Okay, I'll accept that diagnosis," replied Alina with a grin matching her mom's.

"What do you most want to be or do?"

"I love to ride, be Thunder, teach others, and be part of this amazing family. The problem is you are all busy constantly while I do something for a couple of hours and am done. Am I doing something wrong? It seems to me like something is being missed by me. Should I be using my business degree or helping Pat with electronics? Maybe I should train a guard dog, horse, or horse. Mom, I'm not complaining, it just seems to me like I'm not doing my part. I needed to talk with you however you have been ill, tired, and didn't pick a good time to grump. Again, I apologize. Please tell me what to do and I will give it my best," said the girl.

"Just a moment please and you will get your wish. What do you think of Kaylee? Have you worked with her much?" An idea was forming in Mara's mind.

"She is as busy as you are, almost. I'm not sure but it seems to me like she wants to be doing something that benefits the Clan too."

"Kara Lea and Jenn, my conference room, please. This is Mara."

"Yes, mom. We're here," replied a pair of UCA who had just run from the stable to the house to answer the summons.

"I'm looking for some women to run classes for me and take on some new challenges. Since neither of you is aware of the days here or what is available I am going to fill you in. I have some new dogs that need training as guard dogs. There are a few businesses that need overseers. You three need to take one of the jets and a certified pilot to get more comfortable flying. There is a ranch of miniatures behind this one. It needs to be looked at and suggestions made on how to best get them ready for winter. That includes stables that are currently behind the big horse stables. We have small kids who ride those horses, and they must be available. Both kids and horses need training. That could necessitate an underground, maybe using the pit where the animals now live though that is a long walk for our small ones who ride them. There is a bank in full operation. We go to garage sales to find things that people in our group might need at a decent price. Due to inheritances, we have a backlog of antiques that need researching, so they can be liquidated at the best prices. There are websites set up to post them on and we work in cooperation with a full network of folks who do the same. If someone buys on the net whoever is holding the requested item gets the price asked and the store page that is listed, gets a finder's fee. Rae will be your trainer for the last group mentioned from the bank onward of this list. We have a technology school that buys up parts and makes computers, and other devices, that are needed for use of our rather large family. A family that numbers over ten thousand as I recall. We need to know about businesses that are liquidating, bulk buys that keep down the cost. There are the artists coming to appear in our stadium and arena areas. We have a hotel to house them in, however, they only come once or twice a month. One floor is set aside for the performers and their team. Then there is a business in Switzerland that Alina needs to learn to run. When I can, help will be given however my doctor wants me to rest up this time until my batteries are fully charged. Where and what of those options interest you? Also, remember to keep up on your music and riding lessons for we have events again in the spring," began Mara and watched the women as they sat in shocked silence.

Shandra began to laugh, and Mara joined her.

"Believe it or not I am totally serious. All those tasks need doing. We cannot be everyplace. There are a hundred ranches out there that need someone to tell them how to prepare for a horse show, riding show, and set up sales. Peter is taking on most of that. There are mines that produce gold ore, and we must find ways to make use of that product. There is a wonderful leather craftsman who makes products that are beyond belief. The next time you see Ken on his horse ask him to let you look at his saddle. That man made it. He trains others to do the same. We own a few vehicle dealerships. As a result, our units are changed out every two years for by then they are well worn. Also, it allows us to change what is required due to our growing population. We have corporations of many different kinds. There are ranches, hospitals, clinics, restaurants, garage sales, auctions, estates, flying schools, tech schools, and the list goes on. Each of you asked to be more like me. Sue and Merry asked the same. There are others. Now talk to me," said Mara.

"You have been at this how long?" asked Jenn in shock.

"Yes, I asked however, you are the only superhuman I know of, well with Randy, Shandra, Rea, and Pat. Please teach me," responded Kara Lea.

"Mom, all I did was ask to be the prosecutor for the day, so you would know I listened to what you were teaching," added Alina as she realized her comment started all this.

"Okay, answers: I graduated High School at fifteen, and intended to do University at sixteen however things changed when I entered a book. Took the Master's Testing and will have my twenty-second birthday next month, to keep my old birthdate would make me traceable, though I skipped from seventeen to twenty-two. I began this job in May of this year. With T aid, it was doable for I received help as it was needed. You need to use the training you have been given. An exercise that my husband and I do is use a different language each day when conversing with each other. I have been thinking about posting that day's language on a board and having you all use that language for one day at a time. That way we don't forget," Mara told them.

"Please stop a moment," said Kara Lea.

Mara nodded at her to speak.

Chapter 15

Where to go from here

"Would you allow us some time to check out the list you just gave us? We will find out how we can help and get others to help too. Everyone needs to be involved so you don't get so much dumped on you. You have done wonderful, however, now you have a few health issues so let us see what we can do. If you allow me, I will serve as the coordinator for what we are doing. You will receive reports as often as you want them. We all have the same skills though each of us has different backgrounds which give us different results," KL advised.

"Here are my suggestions. Each of you needs a guard dog though Karlea has Metoo who is already trained. Get Metoo to help you learn how to train. Then take Metoo to the miniatures and ask her to help you train there. Once you have an idea of how to do what you want, do a report to let me know what you feel needs addressed the soonest. With that report tell me who is interested in that area and has the talents to get the job done. You are only overseers for now. I will give you guidance until you get a handle on things. That will take care of today. Let me know how it works out, then I'll send you to another area. Will that work as a start?"

"Please keep in mind, your primary jobs. They must come first. If felons show up here, then we need you as Thunder. When trips to town are called for, you need to be ready and willing to go. Same for flights out of town. There are a lot of territories that need to be checked out before we ran out of time. Jo does those tasks; however, you need to know what is required and how to do the same. Alina, you have one duty that only you can do, and I will explain in a couple of days. For now, you each have a direction and some time to see what you can learn that is not taught by your Masters' Degrees. Do not miss your music and riding training or the marksmanship and hand-to-hand stuff. Merry is our Chef and gets one day a week off, though she too keeps up with all training plus gives some herself. She has a full staff, and they make sure she gets the time, as does each of her groups. Ken is a baker trained by her, for instance. This is all ranch home duties, so you are not running all over an area you are unfamiliar with. When we have a duty someplace, we will take you with us, so you learn more of what is going on. There is quite a difference between knowing and having hands-on. Any questions of me?" asked Shandra.

"We know you guard mom; however, I feel a power from you that tells me you are much more," said Kara Lea.

"Shandra is a retired Four-Star General who oversees all guards and coordinates the work crews for our corporations. I am a Five-Star General if that helps you understand. Those are items not to be discussed outside this room. It has to do with security," Mara explained.

"On Nov 11, you will see all the military in full dress uniforms, including the two of us. Only the leadership team and those in uniforms will realize what we are wearing or the meaning. Now that we have you fully confused, go see what you can learn, and we will chat with you later. Good luck." Shandra advised.

After the three women departed to see what they could find, the two who remained had a conversation.

"You will learn a lot from them when they give the reports. You have Alina's interest peaked with information only she will have access to. Kara Lea is wondering how Metoo can help her train dogs and miniatures. You notice she did not ask, however. Jenn is trying to understand how you and I made General when you admitted to being twenty-two. After all, they did ask to be like you. We shall see if they can handle the knowing," Shandra told her mom.

"There is that. Since they are oathsworn and few have the information they were just given, it is well protected. At the same time, I fully trust them, or it would not have been offered. Due to their backgrounds am expecting great things out of them when they get a report to show us."

"Mom, you must delegate and there hasn't been time to do so when you are learning as you go. Since two of those you just sent out are UCA it will be interesting to see what they see that your older group, like me, might have missed. We need organized and trusted people in charge of each area. Oh, before I forget, we have a flight scheduled to take care of the ranches not done when we did Texas. It will be a training mission, for those who go for it will be the new team, to handle that kind of business. These three will also be on that flight with us in the lead group. Then there is a performance at the Stadium on October twenty-eighth, so we have time to do the training first. Another is set for the middle of November and one in December unless you want to do two and bring in Gospel Singers for the Christmas season. Have one person that I personally would like to hear. She would be a plus to my way of thinking. Costs a lot to get her, but well worth the time. What are you going to offer for lodging for the performers? Do you plan on setting it up like the places in England and Canada did or are you going to use the Hilton just for those who come to perform?" Shandra knew she was to ask to clarify what was going on.

"Hmmm, see you have a few questions too. Good, it shows we are on the same page. We have two events in Dec. One will be Gospel and the other, if available, will be the person you want to hear. Try to do them the first week with one person or group each weekend. Need to confirm and get advertising out to have a full house at that time."

"Why don't you ask Thunder for a secure line to those two performance groups and see if they are willing. We can take a plane to get them though I know the last one has their own fleet, or at least that they did. Might get her to do two nights with one being Praise and Worship then one for the hits she has made famous. If she can't come until spring, then we will have to hold to one night as her schedule is full at that time," Shan advised.

"I'm looking forward to being snowed in this winter. Will give our systems a chance to regroup and get ready for the summer."

"You will have cabin fever within a week," laughed Shan.

"Some truth to that I'm sure," said Mara as she joined in the laughter.

Sharron L Ensign P.O. Box 583 Helena, MT 59624
Assassins Target Mara Bk 3
406-458-7091

They departed the unit and moved to a hidden exercise area where the two of them worked on their Assassin Drills to remain proficient. Both chuckled when Randy asked if she could join them. The three spent three hours there. They returned to their suites for yet another shower then it was time to get some music training done for the three. Each of them was having a good time with kids gone, new people occupied, the house quiet and no emergencies.